Longriding Lawman

Center Point
Large Print

Also by Peter Dawson and available from Center Point Large Print:

Willow Basin
Showdown at Anchor
Rider on the Buckskin

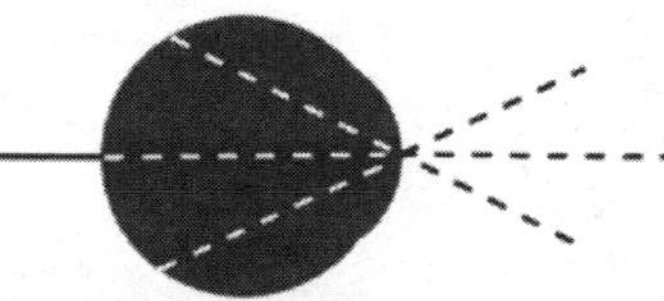

This Large Print Book carries the Seal of Approval of N.A.V.H.

Longriding Lawman

A WESTERN SEXTET

Peter Dawson

CENTER POINT LARGE PRINT
THORNDIKE, MAINE

This Center Point Large Print edition
is published in the year 2017 in conjunction with
Golden West Literary Agency.

The text of this Large Print edition is unabridged.
In other aspects, this book may vary
from the original edition.
Printed in the United States of America
on permanent paper.
Set in 16-point Times New Roman type.

ISBN: 978-1-68324-287-1 (hardcover)
ISBN: 978-1-68324-291-8 (paperback)

Library of Congress Cataloging-in-Publication Data

Names: Dawson, Peter, 1907–1957, author.
Title: Longriding lawman : a western sextet / Peter Dawson.
Description: Center Point Large Print edition. | Thorndike, Maine :
Center Point Large Print, 2017.
Identifiers: LCCN 2016048757| ISBN 9781683242871
(hardcover : alk. paper) | ISBN 9781683242918 (pbk. : alk. paper)
Subjects: LCSH: Large type books. | Western stories.
Classification: LCC PS3507.A848 A6 2017 | DDC 813/.52—dc23
LC record available at https://lccn.loc.gov/2016048757

CONTENTS

BACK-TRAIL BONDAGE

Jon Glidden's title for this story was "Back-Trail Bondage". It was submitted by his agent to *Best Western* on August 17, 1939 and bought on October 19, 1939. The author was paid $37.12. Upon publication in the issue dated (2/40) the title was changed to "Hellion, Fan That Hammer!" For its appearance here, the title has been changed back to what the author wanted.

When the three shots racketed down between the false-fronted buildings along the street, Red Sutrow was handling a piece of white-hot iron with a pair of tongs at his forge. He dropped the tongs and wheeled at the sound, and, as he hurried toward the door of his blacksmith shop, he wiped the sweat from his forehead along his thick-muscled forearm. Going out the door onto the walk, he unlaced his leather apron and tossed it on a workbench.

The first man he saw hurrying toward him was Sheriff Bill Todd and, two doors farther down the street and opposite, half a dozen others scattered from the Melodian's swing doors as two more shots echoed out, muted hollowly and coming from inside the saloon.

"What's up, Sheriff?" Red called as Todd came abreast of him.

The lawman stopped, faced across the street, and growled: "Two hardcases are across there, takin' the joint apart."

Hard on the heel of his words, the sound of breaking glass came from the saloon, and he added dryly: "That'll be the bar mirror. The damn' fools! Someone'll get hurt!"

"Going across and put a stop to it?" Red asked.

His square and homely face was wearing a shadowy smile at the sight of Hardrock's sheriff so obviously stripped of his habitual cloak of smug confidence.

Still glancing across the street, Todd said curtly: "No. I'll let 'em work off their vinegar and clear out."

"Suppose they get careless and blow a hole through someone, Todd?"

The lawman frowned worriedly. "I'll make 'em wish they hadn't!"

"Think you're fast enough, Sheriff?"

Todd didn't answer.

Red had a sudden thought that changed the good-natured set of his face to one of seriousness. "Todd," he said, "remember telling me it was a pity for a man to be so handy with guns and use 'em the wrong way, like I did mine before they sent me to Yuma? Remember how I asked you to give me the chance of carrying 'em again to prove I could be some good? You turned me down. All right, I'm asking you again. Give me an iron and I'll go across there and take that pair."

Todd looked down and his glance seemed to measure the length of Red's stocky, well-muscled frame. "You're a persistent devil, ain't you?" he drawled. "Nothin's happened yet."

"But it might."

"Sure. But I reckon, when it does, I won't ask you to break your parole."

Thus reminded of something he had long tried to forget, Red flared: "You're an unforgiving cuss, Todd. It's been three years, hasn't it? I've toed the line, haven't I? You can't keep a man down. . . ."

The Melodian's front window sprayed outward in a shower of falling glass to cut in on his words. An arm fisting a gun poked through the opening and the gun exploded in five fast-timed shots that fanned bullets in a wide arc along the street. Men scattered back from the edge of the walk near Red's blacksmith shop, diving for the shelter of nearby doorways. One bullet, ricocheting in a high whine from the tie rail directly beyond the walk, sent the sheriff running into the open maw of Red's doorway.

Red sauntered in beside Todd, drawling: "Just this once, Sheriff. Trust me this time and . . ."

"Go away," Todd said sharply, edging out to peer across at the saloon where all was ominously quiet now. "I don't draw my pay to trust a paroled member of Utah Bates's gang."

Red, all at once afraid of his flaring anger at this blunt reminder of not being accepted for anything but what he was, a self-professed, reformed outlaw, went out onto the walk and down along it toward the town's second saloon, the Silver Dollar. Half a dozen men were gathered on the near side of the saloon's doorway. Red approached one, a mustached oldster better than twice his age, and said: "Jim, lend me your iron and I'll go across there and save someone from getting hurt."

Jim's rheumy old eyes widened in surprise a moment, then he shook his head. "Sorry, Red," was all he said.

Red glanced at another man. "How about you, Ray?"

"And git jailed for helpin' you break parole?"

Red's face colored in a hot flush of anger; yet the lesson he'd learned the last three years since leaving Yuma laid a rein on his temper and he shouldered in through the batwing doors, finding the Silver Dollar's bar deserted but for the apron and one customer, who stood facing the rear.

Striding to the bar, Red called: "Rye, George. Make it a double."

At the sound of Red's voice, the lone customer turned slowly. Red found himself facing Utah Bates, the same Utah of years back, outfitted immaculately in white shirt and broadcloth, his flat-crowned black Stetson cocked down over one eye in a way that heightened the touch of sure arrogance on the long lean face. That face broke into a slow smile as the gray eyes regarded Red, and Utah drawled: "Long time no see, *compadre.*"

Warned by the horn handles of the twin guns showing beneath the tail of Utah's coat, Red merely nodded and waited until the apron had set bottle and glass handy to him on the counter and moved out of hearing. Then, pouring his drink, he said in a low voice: "So it's your bunch that's hurrahing the Melodian."

Utah nodded. "Slim and Curly. Drunk."

"You getting careless, Utah?"

The outlaw shrugged his square shoulders. "We came down here to do a job. If Curly and Slim take on more trouble than they can handle, that saves me having to split with 'em. They've about run their string anyway."

Utah was the same, Red understood then, the same as he'd been eight years ago before Red had the poor luck to tangle with the wrong law officer and get sent to Yuma. Utah was no respecter of a man who couldn't take care of himself, and now, blandly, he voiced that quality. If his men got into trouble, it was up to them to get out of it, just the same as it had been up to Red to get out of his trouble years back.

"You're still the same, Utah," he drawled.

"Mostly." Utah edged a little closer. "Heard you were down here, Red. Thought maybe we could shake Curly and Slim and take care of this ourselves."

"Take care of what?" Red asked warily.

"There's a stage due through here in a couple hours, right after dark."

"Sure. It comes through every day."

"Only today it's taking a winter payroll up to that mining outfit in the Smokies. They do that every year about this time, take in enough gold to meet their payroll over the winter. The roads close up in those hills when the first blizzard hits."

Utah was smiling in that thin, inscrutable way so familiar to Red. Red asked: "How much?"

"Twenty thousand. We'd split it even."

Red saw that he hadn't touched his drink. He nodded down to it, asked—"Have one with me?"—and, when Utah shook his head, tossed off the whiskey. Then, taking a full and deep breath, he drawled: "If you ride out of here right sudden, Utah, I'll keep quiet about your being here."

Faint surprise showed in Utah's gray eyes that so evenly met the level regard of Red's blue eyes. "Say that again," he said flatly, in a way that had warned many men of a sudden and violent death before his superhuman fast draw.

Red shook his head. "I'm not giving you away and you're not taking that payroll, Utah." He was remembering something that lay unsettled between him and Utah, a question that had intrigued any number of men who had known them in those outlaw years, a question as to which of them was fastest on the draw and surest of the target that stopped his bullets. "And get this. I've gone straight for three years now. I've got my own business, and, if these damned pious people will ever forget where I came from, I'll be able to hold up my head one day. I'm not wiping all that out for some easy money. Not now or ever, Utah."

"Gone soft on a woman, Red?"

Red had, but she didn't know it, and he said: "Maybe."

Utah had long ago learned the use of patience, and he used it now. "Think, Red," he drawled, "this is only the beginning. Just you and me, working the easy jobs from here all the way north to the Tetons. We'd make a pair they couldn't match. A year would see us well-heeled and we could hightail to a new country. We'd collect a hundred thousand apiece, maybe more. Name your own figure."

"My own figure's about eighty a month, straining my guts swinging a four-pound hammer and breathing the dust of hoof filings. That's the way I want it, Utah. That's the way . . ."

His words broke off as the concussions of two sharp explosions beat the still hot air out on the street. A man's high-pitched scream sounded in the direction of the Melodian. Utah drawled: "Now they've done it." And Red was wheeling away from the bar toward the doors. As Red went out onto the walk, he was only vaguely aware of Utah's boot tread sounding behind him.

He looked up the street. There, stumbling down off the walk in a lurching and broken stagger, was a man bent double at the waist and holding both hands over his stomach. He stumbled into a pony tied at the hitch rail. The pony shied, kicked out with rear hoofs, and knocked the man aside. He caught his balance momentarily, took three more steps in which his boots dragged the dust. Then, slowly, he tottered sideways and fell so that he turned and laid on his back, his arms spreading out as his body jerked convulsively once, and then lay still.

Red, like every onlooker along the street, stood transfixed in horror for a brief moment. Then he was running up the walk and into the door of the blacksmith shop, where he sighted Bill Todd's high shape in the shadows beside his workbench. He stopped squarely in front of the lawman, boots spread apart in a belligerent stance, and held out his right hand: "All right, Todd. Hand me an iron. I'm going over there."

Todd looked down at him and caught the hard and angry light in his eyes.

Red went on, aware that there were other men standing nearby listening: "You gutless old fool. That's Ben Wright lying out there dead. You killed him. I'll whip the living hell out of you unless you send me across there."

Someone behind Red said: "He's right, Todd. This can't go on. If he's loco enough to want to go after that pair, give him your gun and let him."

The nut-brown coloring had left Todd's face and now it was a sickly yellow, reflecting a look of mixed anger and fear. All at once he reached down and lifted the heavy .45 Colt from the holster at his thigh. "Here," he said, thrusting it out. "Go ahead."

"If I take it, I keep it for good, Todd. I've lived three years without a gun, taking talk no man with a spine would take from these mealy-mouthed loafers around here."

Todd motioned him to silence, saying on the heel of another shot from across the street: "Anything, Red, but, for the love of God, get across there."

Red turned, rocking open the loading gate of the sheriff's weapon and spinning the cylinder to make sure it was loaded. Then, thrusting it through the waistband of his trousers, he crossed the walk and stepped into the street, ducking under a tie rail and cutting obliquely across toward the Melodian. He cast a look to either side, wanting to make sure the walks were clear, and in that swift glance he saw Utah Bates's tall frame, striding slowly past the door to the blacksmith shop and toward a place opposite the saloon.

Utah must have caught the look Red gave him, for he called softly: "Make it stick, Red."

Then Red forgot everything but concentrating his gaze on the broken window and the swing doors of the Melodian. He increased his pace now against the threat of a hidden gun targeting him from inside the saloon. He ran the last six strides, dodging from side to side, and laughed mockingly when a gun in there stabbed redly at him, the bullet kicking up the dust at his heels. He stopped finally, well beyond the farther hitch rail and now shielded by two saddle horses he had placed between him and the direct line of the saloon's doors and windows.

He called loudly, tauntingly: "Curly! Slim! How're your guts? It's two against one! Step out and make your try!"

There was a moment's silence before a whiskey-thickened voice, one Red recognized instantly as Curly's, called back: "Damned if it ain't that brick-top banty!" There followed a measured string of obscene oaths, then a brief silence. Finally: "We got enough guts to take on ten like you! But how do we know you ain't got friends, Red?"

Red called back: "You've got my word I'm alone!" He turned and spoke so that his voice carried nicely along the street, clear and ringing: "The first gent that buys into this chooses me when it's over! Hear that, Curly?"

It was a gamble, thinking that his word would carry with Curly and Slim. Both of them had always resented his cockiness, the fact that he was so sure of his guns. But they knew him, knew he'd never backed down on his word, and he was counting on that now.

Shortly Curly answered: "I always did say your hide was yellow down the middle of your back, Red! I'm comin' out to prove it!"

"Then get started and lay off the big wind!"

After that, Red waited with every muscle in his

short body cocked to a time-hardened wariness. It had been years since he'd felt the weight of a gun dragging at his waist. He didn't once think of having lost the smooth timing of hand and eye to gun, didn't once doubt that he could beat either Curly or Slim, or both of them, when it came to the draw.

The seconds dragged out and nothing happened. Red felt rather than saw the attention of all the townsmen, hiding in doorways and peering from the store windows across the street. All at once Curly called: "I wouldn't trust my own mother right now! Step up onto the walk and in behind them jugheads so your friends can't see so good! Me and Slim are comin' out the door when you're set! Call out!"

Red sauntered in between two fly-worried ponies at the hitch rail. He stooped and went under the rail, and then up onto the walk, facing squarely down its deserted length and finally saying: "Any time, Curly!"

He was standing midway the length of a vacant lot, squinting into the sun's glare that shone brightly down on him along this stretch of walk uncovered by any awning. He was glad he'd taken the trouble of wearing his Stetson so that it could shade his eyes. Directly flanking the vacant lot and ahead rose the saloon's weathered and gray board side, windowless along its entire length and therefore offering him no threat. He was wondering why Slim hadn't put in his word, for Slim had a loose tongue and bore the old grudge of once having received a thorough beating from Red after insulting a woman. But at a time like this Slim might be overly cautious. Red didn't much care.

All at once the Melodian's swing doors burst outward. Curly came out in a lunge that carried him to the walk's outer edge. He whirled around, facing Red, his chunky body cocked and hands clawed over the pair of guns at his thighs. When he saw Red standing there, hands at his sides, he straightened and some of the tenseness went out of him. His thick lips curved down in a sneering smile.

"I'm goin' to like this," he drawled. "Open up any time you feel like it."

Red said flatly: "Where's Slim?"

The sound of his voice hadn't yet died out along the street when he caught a hint of movement from above, from the saloon's roof. His glance whipped up there as his right hand was already instinctively snaking up to his gun. There, standing, spraddle-legged, near the trough at the edge of the saloon's roof stood Slim. He was staring down over the sights of a .45 and his thumb was drawing back the hammer.

In one split second Red was aware of two things. He didn't have a chance of throwing a bullet before Slim shot him. And, if by some small chance he managed to beat Slim, he saw that Curly's two hands had come alive and were streaking toward his twin .45s. His palm slapped hard against the handle of his Colt, lifted the weapon out. Suddenly, from across the street, an explosion ripped away the utter silence. Slim's hand wavered, his gun beat a hollow explosion hard on the heel of that first shot, and then he was bending double and jackknifing from the roof's edge in a broken downward fall.

Red's .45 rocked down. He instantly forgot Slim and arced the gun around on Curly. He caught Curly's expression of mute bewilderment and saw the hurried upswing of the outlaw's guns. Then his own weapon slammed back solidly against his wrist. He heard the thud of Slim's body sound on the heel of his gun's blast. Through the drifting cloud of powder smoke he saw Curly lurch and fall to his knees. Curly made one last vain effort to raise his hand and steady it. Failing, he squeezed the trigger and his bullet knocked a splinter from the walk planking almost directly at the spot where he fell face downward, dead.

Red turned slowly and looked across the street. Utah stood there, calmly punching the empty from his smoking gun. He raised a hand and silently saluted Red. Men broke from the shelter of store doorways and ran into the street. Two of them carried away the man Curly had shot before the fight started. Others came on, and the first one to stoop alongside Curly turned him over, and then looked quickly across at Red and said hoarsely to the next man to join him: "Goddlemighty. Smack through the throat."

For the next ten minutes Red couldn't believe much of what happened. Men crowded around him, slapped him on the back, and dragged him up the walk and past Curly's body and in through the Melodian's doors to the long pine bar. Bill Todd was one of these, and it was he who called: "Drinks are on me!"

Bottles slid down along the polished counter backed by the broken mirror. A dozen hands filled the row of shot glasses. Then Bill Todd raised an arm in a gesture that commanded silence. When the room was quiet, he lifted his glass and, one arm about Red's shoulders, said: "Here's to a gent with guts. More guts than I had." He looked into the circle of faces around him, spotted Utah's, and added: "And to this stranger that kept Red's guts all in one piece."

He cuffed off the whiskey, then looked from Utah back to Red, an unuttered question in his eyes. Red understood immediately what the lawman was thinking.

He nodded to indicate Utah and drawled: "Friend of mine, Sheriff. Meet Bill Ringo. Runs an outfit up on Powder River."

Utah was ringed by a group of men who shook his hand, who professed a liking for any friend of

Red's. Sheriff Todd left the group and was gone a bare quarter minute. When he came back, he was carrying two heavy shell belts and a pair of holsters sheathing walnut-handled guns. He held them out to Red.

"Here, Red! I got 'em off that stiff layin' out there on the walk. They're yours from now on, providin' you can answer me one question. You called those two hardcases by name. How come?"

A settling silence ran through the room. Red was caught, and knew it. The sheriff was a shrewd man and was sure to tie in this sudden appearance of a stranger from Powder River, a friend of Red's with the presence of Curly and Slim.

"How come, Red?" Todd asked levelly, and now the genial look had faded from his steady brown eyes to be replaced by one of suspicion.

Red laughed easily. "Take a look at those two horses at the tie rail, Todd. I happened to know the brand. Curly and Slim and me traveled together for a stretch years back . . . before I began riding herd on those rocks over at Yuma. I saw those brands and knew who I was going up against."

The sheriff's look changed, all the suspicion leaving it. He nodded and breathed—"I'm damned."—and stepped to the bar, calling for another drink.

Red left soon afterward, alone, and went across to his place and tied on the leather apron again.

From his doorway he watched the men who picked up Slim's body and carried it across to the undertaker's, idly wondering if he'd seen the last of Utah. The sun was low toward the horizon now, reminding him that he had a job to finish before dark, also that the stage would be along in less than two hours.

He was working at the back of the shed and had fired up the forge again and was turning to pick up the long pair of tongs when he looked toward the workbench along the front wall and saw Utah leaning indolently back against it. The outlaw's long face was smiling, his arms were folded on his flat chest, and a light of genuine amusement was in his glance.

"Eighty a month," Utah mused aloud. "Providing you saved every damned nickel of it, it'd take better than ten years to gather what an hour's work'll net you tonight. Use your head, Red."

"I am using it." Red eyed the outlaw directly for a long moment. "Thanks for saving my hide back there, Utah," he said sincerely, knowing that he'd be dead now but for Utah's help. "But that squares us. You owed me that for leaving me to rot in that tank-town jail and then not lifting a hand when they shipped me to Yuma."

Utah laughed softly. "All right. But you were swinging your weight around a little too much to suit me. I never let an understrapper get ideas on taking over my job. As you say, this about evens things. Except for a little matter of our holding up that train outside Cody that time. Remember?"

Red said warily: "What about it?"

"Nothing, only that postal clerk died from the bullet he caught in his guts that night. The federal marshals are still out to nail up the hide of the man that shot him."

"Which means you."

Utah, smiling, shook his head. "You're wrong, Red. It means you." Red couldn't move or think for long seconds. Utah took that interval to add: "You're coming in with me, friend, whether you want it or not. Either that, or the sheriff gets a letter in the mail telling him about the reward he can collect on you for that Cody job. It's my word against yours, and you've served time."

Slowly, feeling a cold fury mount up in him, Red untied and threw aside the leather apron, conscious mostly of the weight of the guns sagging at his thighs. Utah saw what was in his mind, and shoved lazily out from the bench, lowering his hands to his sides.

"Or we can settle it this way," he said blandly. "The man's never been born that can beat me at this game."

Red drawled—"Here's one that can."—not quite sure of himself now. He was faced with the knowledge that Utah was no braggart, that his statement a moment ago had been one of fact, or perhaps a well-intended warning. He was remembering Utah's reputation of taking on any and all bounty hunters, remembering, too, that Utah had killed more than one famous gunman, Sid Driscoll, Jake the Runt, and Barney Deshay. For the first time in his life Red's confidence deserted him.

"Make your play," Utah said, and let that statement sink in on Red before he added: "All you'll get out of it is a place alongside Curly and Slim. And I'll take the whole twenty thousand."

Slowly Red relaxed. He grinned disarmingly: "You win, Utah. When do we travel?"

Utah regarded him a moment in suspicion. But at length his look changed to one of relief. "That's better," he drawled. "I've got it pretty well thought out. About four miles east of here there's some broken country where the trail swings in close under a ledge that'll be about even with the stage roof. It's an uphill grade and the driver will be walking his teams. I'll leave town now. After dark, you come out and meet me there. We'll stop the stage and be across the state line before sunup."

Red had no choice now. He was inwardly blaming himself for lacking the nerve to go against Utah, nerve he wouldn't have lacked had he been carrying guns these past years. He was sure that Utah would cold-bloodedly carry out his threat of hanging the Cody killing on him if he failed to join in holding up the stage. Today he had gained the respect of Sheriff Todd and the townspeople, gained the right to wear his guns and prove that they stood for law and order, and here was the end of his good intentions, whether he wanted it or not. He'd have to go with Utah, raid the stage, and after that begin the old life along the dark trails.

"Better get going, then," he said in as even a voice as he could command, all at once wanting to be alone to try and think this out.

Utah eyed him intently once more. Gradually a smile came to his face. "You wouldn't try a double-cross, would you, Red?" Instead of waiting for an answer, he added as though voicing an inward thought: "I'll have to be careful of that. See you in an hour or so." He stepped sideward out to the walk, and Red stood there, listening to his light boot tread fading down the planks.

Red picked up the tongs and for the next half hour his anvil rang with the lusty strokes of the hammer. He worked until, through sheer bodily exhaustion, the torment in his mind settled to something resembling coherent thought. When he closed his shop and went along the walk to the feed barn to get his gelding, he had made a decision, the one he should have made when he faced Utah there before his forge.

He rode out of Hardrock in the settling dusk, not bothering to hide his going. Out of sight of the town, he came down out of the saddle and took

Curly's pair of guns from their holsters and closely inspected them, testing the action. Then, dropping them back into leather, he made half a dozen practice draws, timing his moves to a slowness that irritated him. He made an interesting discovery, namely that his hands were much stronger now than in the old days when he'd thumbed the hammers of a Colt. Blacksmithing had done that. He tried a dozen more draws, putting speed to the motion of his hands. They were sure, surer than they'd been before, and a small excitement rose up in him at the knowledge.

Before the light had completely failed him, he rummaged in the pouch of his saddle and finally found a smeared piece of wrapping paper and the stub of a pencil. Using the saddle skirt, he laid the paper on it and laboriously printed out three penciled lines. Finished, he read what he'd written, and then folded the paper and thrust it into a shirt pocket.

Half an hour later, in the light of the quarter moon edging the flat horizon to the east, he boldly rode in on the ledge that closely flanked the trail halfway through a strip of broken country. He reined in, glanced at the line of the ledge that was almost level with his eyes, and called: "Utah!"

A figure rose up off the ledge, Utah's. Red could see that the outlaw was no longer wearing his coat. His white shirt outlined his vest and the two horn-handled guns drew pale gray lines along the black smear of his trousers. Utah was peeled down to fighting trim. He said: "I tied my jughead in them trees across there. You better do the same."

Red wheeled his gelding off the far side of the trail, rode a hundred yards down a slope, and came out of the saddle alongside Utah's buckskin that was tied behind a clump of low-growing cedar. He tied the gelding, and then climbed back up the slope and in three minutes was pulling himself up onto the ledge beside Utah.

As soon as Red had straightened up alongside him, Utah caught his expression and a frown gathered on his face. He backed away a step, saying with startling intuition: "You've got something in your craw. What is it?"

"I've done some thinking, Utah."

"That's better. I knew you'd see it my way."

"And what's your way? Maybe I ought to know."

"That three square meals a day, a soft bed to sleep in, and going to church on Sundays is about as poor a way of living as a hog has getting fat and waiting for the slaughterhouse. That a man's got everything coming to him he can take with his two hands and hold with his guns. That if the end's coming, I don't want it to come when a beard is weighing down my chin."

"You want it sudden, eh?" Red drawled.

"That's the way it'll come to me."

"You're right, Utah. That's the way you'll get it. And it's coming at you now."

Red took a backward step that matched Utah's. There was ten feet between them now, and the moonlight was strong enough so that each could catch the slightest change of expression on the other's face. Utah caught Red's slow smile and it startled him more than Red's words.

"What's eating you, Red?" he asked, his gray eyes taking on a flinty yet half-amused expression.

"This afternoon was the first time I ever backed down to a man. I aim to make good on it now."

Utah stiffened perceptibly, and now his hands hung within finger spread of his guns. He swore solemnly without rancor and said: "You're backing out?"

Red nodded and let it go at that.

"With ten thousand staring you in the face? Lord, Red, I was only trying to rid you of that damned pious streak of yours. There's no hard feelings."

"You'd have turned me in, framed me with a murder if I hadn't come in with you."

"Sure. What of it? You were going to seed back in that town."

Red shook his head. "No, Utah. I was building myself into something decent, something you . . ." The futility of trying to explain suddenly crowded in on Red. He said in a harsher voice: "I'm going to kill you, Utah, maybe collect a reward if there's one out for you."

Utah's shell of hardness settled around him. His eyes were predatory, surface-glinted, and a smile that wasn't a smile came to his face. "You asked for it," he drawled. "Start your play any time you feel like it. That stage is about due and I aim to collect that payroll."

"You open the ball, Utah," Red said flatly, his eyes falling to steady on Utah's wrists, where he knew he would catch the first sign of the outlaw's draw.

His voice was still trailing off on the last word when he caught the motion down along Utah's right arm; it wasn't open movement but the barest perceptible stirring of the muscles along the wrist of Utah's long-fingered hand.

A split second later his own hand moved up in a smooth and fast-timed ripple of speed, his glance still holding to Utah's hand that was now a mere pale blur. Quick as thought he palmed up the heavy Colt and rocked it into line, seeing Utah's weapon settle into place. He let his thumb slip from the hammer, and his palm took up the gun's solid slam.

He saw Utah's gun jerked suddenly sideways, stab flame to punctuate the prolonged explosion of sound. Then, miraculously, Utah's gun was spinning from his hand to fall with a sharp thud to the rocky edge. And the outlaw was reaching around to clamp his left hand about his wrist. Red knew that his bullet had hit the gun and not

Utah's arm. Utah remembered something then, and his left hand started to travel down toward the holster at his thigh. But the click of the hammer catch on Red's gun stopped that gesture and once again Utah clutched at his numbed wrist.

"Not bad, eh?" Red drawled. "I'd always wondered if I could do it, shoot an iron out of a man's hand. First time I ever tried. How does it feel, Utah?"

"There's no feel to it," Utah said calmly. "It's numb." The pallor of his face was the only thing that betrayed the live fear in him over what had never happened before, being shaded on the draw.

"I had a reason for not killing you, Utah," Red said. "Maybe two. The first is because you saved my life today."

"What's the second?"

"I've got a paper here for you to sign, as soon as you've dropped your belts."

"What paper?"

"Shed the hardware and you'll see."

Deliberately, keeping his good hand in sight, Utah unbuckled his two belts and tossed them aside. Only then did Red drop his gun back into leather and take the folded piece of wrapping paper and the stubby pencil from his pocket. He handed them across to Utah and took a match from the band of his Stetson. He flicked it alight with his thumbnail, drawling: "Read what it says." He held the match over the paper so that Utah could see. "And after you read, take that pencil and sign it."

Utah read, and his face took on a drawn, tight look. For what he was reading was a confession of his having killed the postal clerk at Cody. Suddenly his right hand, the numbness gone now, closed on the paper, crumpling it. He smiled thinly. "You go to hell."

Red reached down and unbuckled his belts, swinging his holsters aside, and dropped them near Utah's. He unbuttoned the cuffs of his shirt and started rolling up one sleeve. "I'm surer of this even than I was of the other," he said. "The only thing I've got to watch out for is not to hit you so hard it'll kill you." He took one step in toward Utah.

The outlaw backed away, and the workings of his mind were plain on his face. He was a cool-headed man and would have faced any odds with his guns. But, like most men who live by their guns, his one fear was taking a physical beating.

Utah held up a hand. "Let's talk this over," he said quickly.

Red shook his head. "We're through talking." He lashed out suddenly and his fist caught Utah in the face and the outlaw's knees buckled, and he went down. He lay there on one elbow, one arm crooked before his face, and said: "Hold on, Red. You turning me in?"

"Not unless you drift back here and make me,

or unless something happens to me. Get onto your feet."

Utah sat up and took the crumpled paper from his clenched left hand and reached over to get the pencil he'd dropped a moment ago. He smoothed out the paper and said gruffly: "Give me some light."

Then, as Red held a lighted match for him, Utah signed the confession. Red took it, folded it, and put it in his pocket, and then nodded toward Utah's guns. "You won't need those," he said. He turned away then, hearing the distant rumble of the stage coming up the grade. "Better light out, Utah," he drawled. "Those shotgun guards they carry are proddy as hell. Seeing us up here might give 'em ideas."

He watched Utah climb down off the ledge and run across the trail and disappear into the obscurity of the night's half light down the slope toward the cedars. He followed slowly, barely out of sight as the stage went by.

Later, as the stage was rolling out of Hardrock, taking the trail in toward the hills, Red walked into the sheriff's office. He was wearing Curly's guns and carried another pair looped over his shoulder, a pair with horn handles.

Bill Todd was sitting at his desk reading a Santa Fe paper that had come in on the stage. He looked up as Red tossed a sealed white envelope onto his desk. He glanced first at Red, then at the envelope. “What’s this?” he asked.

“I want you to put that away in your safe, Bill.”

“What for?”

“In case I ever need it.”

Todd shrugged and turned to swing open the door to a small safe alongside his desk. He put the envelope in the safe’s top drawer and then closed the door again, swiveling around in his chair once more.

He saw the guns and belts slung from Red’s shoulder for the first time and looked surprised. Then he grinned. “What’s the matter, ain’t two guns enough for you, Red? Where’d you get them others?”

“From that friend of mine you met today. He gave ’em to me as a sort of going away present.”

“The hell he did. Now that was right nice of him.”

DEATH RIDES OUT OF YUMA

This story was submitted under this title to Street and Smith on January 8, 1938, about the time that Frank Blackwell, who had edited *Western Story Magazine* virtually from its beginning, was forced to leave the company as the result of a power struggle. Ronald Oliphant, who edited *Wild West Weekly* for Street and Smith, briefly took on editing *Western Story Magazine* as well, and he bought this story on May 21, 1938. The author was paid $168.75. It was billed as a "complete novel" under the title "Owlhoot Reckoning" in the same issue of *Western Story Magazine* (8/20/38) in which appeared the first installment of the serial, "Death Rides Tornado Basin", by Luke Short, the pen name used by Frederick Glidden, Jon Glidden's younger brother.

I

The hell that is Fort Yuma can break a man in a year's time. It hadn't broken Trent Stone in fifteen. He was changed, as could be expected; at forty-three his hair was thin and white and a face that had been strong and aquiline was now stronger for a broken nose and a long shiny scar on the right cheek. The scar dated back eight years, to the day of the Whistler's riot. So did the limp in Stone's right leg and the slight stoop to his overly square shoulders. The torment of a half-broken body had changed the look in his greenish hazel eyes, made them colder, almost gray in color. And he rarely spoke these days, almost never smiled his crooked smile.

When they turned him loose, they gave him his old outfit—his guns and the Stetson with the silver *conchas* on the wide leather band—and $64. The money bought him an old roan gelding and a worn-out McClellan saddle.

Within three days' riding, at the ugly treeless towns that flanked the trail Stone took to the east, he had won enough at cards to buy a younger horse, a black, and a good, used Anderson saddle. He bought a new outfit of Levi's, shirt, vest, and short coat. The horn-handled guns and the Stetson he kept.

It was at Shale, in the Antelope Bar, that he found Kurt Locheim. It was unexpected, that meeting, and Trent Stone could scarcely believe his luck, for Kurt Locheim was the one man above all others he had hoped to see again.

He had had no warning. Standing there at the bar, downing a drink of under-aged bourbon, he felt a touch on his arm. Turning, he found himself looking down into Locheim's surprised face.

The man's shifty black eyes were wide in puzzlement as he breathed, almost with awe: "I'll be damned if it ain't!"

Trent's face might have been blocked in granite. "You'll be damned if it ain't what, stranger?"

Locheim stepped away a little, and his glance narrowed in indecision as he regarded Trent. "There's the guns, and the holsters are the same," he muttered. "And I'd pick that hatband out among a thousand." He abruptly thrust out his hand. "Hell, Trent, don't be so standoffish. Shake with an old friend."

Trent chuckled softly, let his features relax, and, ignoring the outstretched hand, drawled: "I didn't think you'd know me, Kurt."

Locheim's manner was effusively cordial. He stepped in alongside Trent, called to the apron—"Bring us a bottle!"—and then looked at Stone again and admitted: "No one would know you . . . no one who didn't know those *conchas* and those guns. Yuma did plenty to you, friend."

Trent didn't bother to answer, and neither man spoke again until Kurt had poured two drinks and downed his. Then he said in a low voice: "I'm headed over into your country. Maybe you'd like to hear about it."

Kurt hadn't changed much in fifteen years, Stone thought. There was that same measure of cunning in those black eyes, the same sly manner. Trent decided that what he had planned so carefully for years could wait.

"Maybe I would," he answered easily. "You're playing the same game?"

Kurt's black eyes flashed wickedly. "Why should I change? My luck's been up and down, mostly up. Just now it's down. I aim to change it. I can change yours, too."

"You said that once before." Trent's voice was bleak, reminiscent.

Kurt cocked his head and his expression went abruptly serious. "Remember Jake Troy?"

"Would I forget him? He made the arrest."

Locheim chuckled softly, went on: "Jake's sheriff now, not deputy. He runs Picket. The rest are too busy fighting."

"How come?"

Kurt lifted his thick shoulders in a shrug. "That's what I aim to find out. From what I hear, Picket's been a nice layout for undertakers these last few months." He dipped a hand into his pocket and brought out a dog-eared letter, unfolding it and laying it on the counter before Trent. "Read that."

Trent Stone read:

> Kurt:
>
> I need a new deputy, one that can keep his lip buttoned and work with me. Get down here as soon as you can. The job will pay more than fighting wages. If you have a partner you can trust, bring him along.
>
> Jake

A time-schooled wariness made Trent say non-committally: "It listens good so far."

"You're in with me?"

"Until something better turns up."

"Then we'll ride," was Locheim's brief answer.

They rode twenty miles to the east that afternoon. And as he lessened the distance between him and the far range of blue mountains beyond which lay Picket, all the thinking of fifteen long years settled in order in Trent Stone's mind. The thing Kurt Locheim proposed, but hadn't explained, was tempting, yet Trent knew a thing or two about Kurt that outweighed Jake Troy's promise of easy money. He knew Jake Troy, too.

Making camp that night, at the foot of a treeless, high *barranca*, Trent asked a question he had so far kept at the back of his mind. "How about that boy of mine, Kurt?"

Locheim was busy at the fire, holding a pan of bacon in the coals, so he couldn't turn and catch the expression on Trent's shadowed face. "He's still there, running your old brand. They say he isn't over-proud of his old man."

Trent Stone laughed dryly. "He wouldn't be. Is he mixed up in what's bringing us down there?"

"Sure. Everyone's got an iron in that fire. There's been rustling, a few stage hold-ups, and one big powder burning right in town. It's still the old war between Bill Hillis and the two-cow outfits."

"We started that war. What's kept it going?"

"Me, for one. I stayed down there for three years after they shipped you to Yuma. We had it nice for a while, until Hillis signed on a bunch of hardcases and ran us out of the country. But the thing was started by then. It's never died out. Lately I hear it's started up again. Maybe Jake has something to do with that."

Here was as much news as Trent needed. Old Bill Hillis was still busy fighting a war that would never have started but for Trent and one or two others siding the outlawed Kurt Locheim. There had been a reason for that war, but a small one. Four sections of free range, which Bill Hillis had newly leased, were used by Trent and those others. They could have pulled off that range, left it to the man who had a legal right to it, only that Kurt had proposed a fight that would in the end, he said, net them all a nice stake. But before things were well started, Trent had been framed—framed with the killing of young Frank Hillis, the old man's son.

For fifteen years that frame-up, and what lay behind it, had galled Trent Stone. Kurt Locheim was logically the man who knew more about it than anyone else, and now was the time to get him to tell what he knew.

Trent was trying to frame a question—one that would answer many in his own mind—when Kurt all at once spoke: "They say Hillis has a special reason for wanting to skin that cub of yours, Trent. That daughter of his . . . Barb, they call her . . . seems to have got it in her head that your Jim is the only critter that walks on two legs."

"Barbara Hillis in love with my boy?" Trent was incredulous, now remembering Bill Hillis's daughter who had been in the first grade of school at the time he left for Yuma. "Who told you about it?"

"Walt Peters."

The answer slipped out before Kurt could think. The frying pan he was holding slipped from his hand and into the fire, and he straightened suddenly and faced around.

"Walt Peters?" Trent echoed, a coldness settling along his nerves. The pattern of the brain-wearying puzzle he had spent these years trying to put together was all at once plain. He grinned, and the ugliness of his scarred face was more ominous than it had seemed before. "So Peters didn't ride down into Mexico, after all."

"Now listen, Trent"—Kurt's expression showed his rising fear—"Walt's been gone for years. I saw him last week and gave him a gun whipping he'll never forget. It was too late to help you."

Trent waited for more; it didn't come. He let the silence drag out, watching Kurt's hands, seeing that they settled closer to his guns. At length he spoke: "That's a good story, Kurt, but not good enough. You paid Peters to ride out of Picket that night. If he'd been there, he could have proved I was with him. Frank Hillis was dry-gulched. But you had to hang it on someone, and I was the goat. Peters is still your man. Isn't that the truth?"

"Trent, I swear . . ."

"I want to know . . . before I kill you."

For an instant all the tension went out of Kurt Locheim's thick-set frame. He even forced a smile, one that was intended to put Trent off his guard. Suddenly, seeing that his gesture hadn't carried, his two hands clawed and swiveled up the butts of his guns.

Trent moved instinctively, his muscles throwing his right hand true in a sure, lightning-fast draw. His Colt .45 leaped up and swung into line before the sightless muzzles of Kurt's guns had cleared leather. Trent thumbed back the hammer and let it fall. The ripping explosion of his single shot welled out across the night's distance. And as the powder smoke curled upward from the snout of Trent's rock-steady weapon, Kurt Locheim went suddenly rigid and fell back into the fire with a force that spread the hot coals three feet to either side.

For a long quarter minute, Trent Stone didn't move. His glance was fixed on the blue hole that centered Kurt's forehead, and he took a grim satisfaction in realizing that one thing about him remained unchanged—the smooth-timed working of brain and hand that had given him this deadliness with guns.

In that interval he saw his small revenge as an empty one. It had been too easy. He had made a mistake in siding this outlaw years ago, and had paid for it many times over. The happenings of three action-crowded seconds couldn't wipe out the bitterness and hate that fifteen years had ingrained in him.

In the next half hour Trent performed a task that definitely closed one chapter of his past. He slung Kurt Locheim's body across his shoulders and carried it high up the *barranca*. In the dim half light of the starry night he picked the spot where he would bury the man, beneath an overhanging cutbank on the margins of a deeply hewn arroyo.

Kurt had said: *No one would know you . . . no one who didn't know those* conchas *and those guns*. There was his stoop, the slight limp, and his face wasn't the same. So Trent unbuckled the belts about Kurt's waist, and strapped his own twin Colts in their place. He took the *concha* band off his Stetson, trading it for the plain black band of leather on the dead outlaw's hat. As an afterthought he searched Kurt's pockets until he found Jake Troy's letter. Only then did he climb far up along the overhanging slope and kick loose a lip of sandy gravel that supported the overhang.

He scrambled quickly back out of the way, as tons of falling earth thundered into space. When he looked again, through the fog of settling dust, Kurt Locheim's body was buried beneath twenty feet of loose gravel and rock.

He rode on that night, after erasing all signs around the fire. He took Kurt's dun gelding on a lead rope and led him far to the south of the trail, until at sunup he turned him loose.

All the next day he sat in the saddle, riding always east. He took off his Stetson and let the blaze of the early spring sun burn the pallor from his skin. That night he slept long and well. The next day, and for three more days, he rode toward the mountains.

II

The familiar length of Picket's main street lay before Trent Stone late one afternoon, and his glance sought out the changes of the past fifteen years. There was a new white-painted courthouse, with a graceful spire rising above the cottonwoods in the square. The old Prairie House was the same, its porch sagging and half the pickets missing from its fence. The Nugget Saloon was newly plastered with adobe, and a two-story brick bank stood at the four corners in place of the old frame one.

Half hungrily Trent Stone was looking for a familiar face, when he saw Jake Troy standing in front of a store. Jake had taken on weight, and his hair was graying about the temples; his face had become full and jowled, and he wore his soiled clothes with the same carelessness of years ago.

Trent reined in at the hitch rail alongside the awning post where Jake leaned. "Can a man find a job around here, Sheriff?" he asked casually.

Jake looked up at this stranger, and no trace of recognition showed in his glance. He was full of his own importance as he hung his thumbs from the arm holes of his vest and tilted back on his heels. "That depends. What kind of a job?"

"Anything," Trent answered, leaning a little closer with an elbow on the saddle horn and his off foot out of the stirrup. He wanted to be sure about this, sure that nothing reminded Jake of the man he had sent to Yuma fifteen years ago.

Jake took the chewed butt of a cigar from his mouth and spat deliberately into the dust of the street. Then he smiled, a meaningful smile, and drawled: "They say the Box H is hirin' gun hands. Only don't let on I mentioned it."

"Where'll I find this Box H?"

Jake frowned. "You're from out of the country?"

"North Colorado."

"And you didn't ride in here to draw fightin' wages?"

Trent shook his head, smiled. "I didn't. But it listens good."

"The Box H lays twelve miles south. You'll ask for Bill Hillis. And remember, brother, I didn't send you."

Trent thanked him, and wheeled his roan out into the street once more. He turned right at the four corners and put the town behind him, wondering why Sheriff Jake Troy took such pains to steer a strange rider into the way of a fighting job with Bill Hillis.

Two hours after sundown Trent Stone rode into the barren stretch of yard surrounding Bill Hillis's sprawling adobe house. Lights showed in the windows before the hitch rail of the near wing, and farther down Trent made out the bunkhouse with a light shining in its single window. He sat the saddle a moment, taking in the familiar look of the place. There was no change here, beyond a run-down look to barn and outbuildings.

He had lifted his right boot from the stirrup and was about to swing down from the saddle, when a voice spoke out of the darkness at the corner of the house.

"Sing out, stranger. Who are you?"

"The handle's Quinn, Fred Quinn." Trent settled back into the saddle and waited.

A moment later a man moved into sight from around the corner of the wall. He stepped out a half dozen paces, and Trent saw a Winchester resting across his arm. Abruptly Trent recognized Bill Hillis.

The rancher kept his distance. "What do you want?" he said tersely.

"A job."

There was a short silence, and in that interval Trent saw that Hillis had lost a little of his bigness, his arrogance through these years. He didn't stand as straight as Trent remembered, and in the pale glow of light that came from the window at his side Trent could see that a measure of the old stubbornness had gone from Hillis's blunt-jawed face.

All at once the rancher shot a gruff question at Trent. "Have you ever killed a man?"

Trent smiled, somehow unsurprised. "And if I had, would I be telling you about it?"

"I'll pay you one hundred dollars in gold, for one night's ride, stranger. Take it or leave it."

Hillis's bluntness, a smoldering anger that lay behind his crisp words, was as mysterious as the offer itself. Trent had a sudden desire to know what lay behind all this, and made his answer accordingly.

"I'll take it."

"Ride down past the corral and wait for me," Hillis ordered. And with that he unceremoniously turned and walked out of sight around the end of the house.

Trent had a three-minute wait beyond the corral in back of the barn. Then in the darkness he made out the approaching outline of a rider.

It was Hillis again. He reined in ten feet away and seemed to be considering the bargain he had made as he sat there.

Trent himself broke the silence. "I rode out here to see Bill Hillis," he drawled.

"I'm Hillis. You were after a job and you've got one. Come along."

Hillis wheeled away and past Trent, and for the next twenty minutes Trent had all he could do to make his tired roan hold the pace the other set. They rode north into a low line of hills Trent remembered well—a natural boundary between Hillis's Box H and the smaller ranches beyond.

Hillis pulled his horse in to a fast trot as they entered the beginning of a high-walled, brush-choked gulch between two climbing slopes. A hundred yards farther on, he drew rein and swung to the ground.

"We'll walk," he announced tersely.

As Trent climbed down, he saw that Hillis had reached out to lift his Winchester from its scabbard. Hillis didn't go on the way they had been riding; instead, he headed up along the slope of gravel and rock that lay off to the right. The older man was breathing hard, yet his stride was choppy and quick. And Trent, with his bad leg, had a hard time keeping him in sight.

The slope ended abruptly at the crest of the hill. Looking ahead, Trent could see for thirty yards down the far side. Hillis swung to the left, to the north again, and they walked for nearly a quarter of a mile along the ridge that skirted the gulch where they had left the horses.

At length Hillis slowed his pace, let Trent come alongside, and said briefly: "We'll be quiet from here on. In another minute we'll see a cabin off to the right. It'll be below us. There's some rock above. We'll hide up there." He held out the rifle. "You'll take this."

He walked on before Trent could question him. This time he progressed more slowly and carefully. Once he turned and let out a muttered oath as Trent stumbled over a loose rock. But his anger burned out quickly and he went on again.

Trent, looking down the far slope, soon made out the faint rectangular outline of a shake roof ringed by a growth of low cedar below. When he looked ahead again, Hillis was walking in a crouch, approaching a flat ledge of rock that jutted out directly above the cabin.

Hillis crawled the last few feet on hands and knees, and finally lay belly down on the rock ledge. When Trent stretched alongside the rancher, he said dryly: "Maybe I ought to know more about this."

"You'll know soon enough. Quiet, now."

For the next few minutes Trent looked below, and gradually his eyes made out the outlines of the cabin and the small, open yard in front ringed by the cedars. Abruptly he remembered the place; it was one of the Box H line camps, for below it, on a small bench, stood a pole corral and a lean-to. Inspecting the corral more closely, he saw a pony tied by the reins to one of the poles.

He had little time to consider Hillis's reasons for bringing him here, or whose pony it was that was tied down there, for suddenly both men heard the hoof thuds of a trotting horse.

Hillis reached out and clamped a hand on Trent's arm, the one that held the rifle. "When that jasper rides in there, let him have it. I want to be sure. Wait until he's out of his hull and on the ground."

Two things happened then that made Trent's part in this stranger still. First, he saw someone walk out into the yard below and stand there, waiting, and, as he examined that figure, he made it out as a girl's. Hardly had she stopped before the oncoming rider was in sight, guiding a palomino toward the yard in front of the shack.

The girl walked a few paces to meet the rider, and the man pulled the horse to a stop and swung down alongside her. He was tall, wide of shoulder, and moved with an effortless ease that spoke of boundless reserve of strength. It was too far to see well, but Trent thought that the man took the girl in his arms.

Even before he put the rifle to his shoulder and let it fall into position, he knew who Bill Hillis was paying him to kill tonight. Lining the Winchester was pure bluff, for Trent knew he couldn't shoot.

Hillis suddenly reached out and pushed up the muzzle of the rifle. "Wait, you fool," he whispered. "I don't want the girl cut down."

Trent moved away a little, jerked the gun from the rancher's grasp, and said tonelessly, softly: "Hell, man, I know how to shoot. I won't hit her."

But Hillis's alarm made him reach out and jerk the rifle to one side, and hold it firmly. "You'll do as I say. It's young Stone I want dead, not my own girl."

Trent smiled wryly at the rancher's whispered admission. Here it was, framed in words. Bill Hillis had hired Trent Stone to kill his own son. The girl down there was Barbara Hillis. Kurt Locheim hadn't been wrong.

During the long, thirty-second interval he lay there, watching the two below and hearing the faint murmur of their talk drift up to him, Trent Stone wondered what thing could make Bill Hillis hate Jim Stone enough to want to kill the man his daughter loved. As he waited, a hot panic set up within him. Sooner or later Jim would make himself a clear target and Hillis would call for that shot.

Trent moved his legs slightly to ease the cramp in his muscles. He felt his boot strike something that gave slightly. At the same moment, Bill Hillis, alongside, breathed softly: "Watch him."

Down below, Jim Stone was stepping away from the girl, leading his palomino over toward the corral to tie it alongside the other bronco. Barbara Hillis followed, but left a clear opening for a shot.

"Now," came Hillis's barely audible command.

Trent lined the rifle again, and, as the front sight settled into the notch of the rear, he moved his left foot. Behind him there was a loud rattle as a rock fell off the ledge. It rolled down the slope, loosing gravel.

As that sound slapped sharply out of the stillness, Jim Stone whirled and reached up to his saddle and jumped. Trent fired at the same instant, careful in his shooting, and the puff of dust the bullet kicked up where Jim had stood a split second ago could be plainly seen.

The palomino lunged, Jim Stone hanging low on the off stirrup. Trent shot again just as the girl below cried a warning, but the shot was wide, and two seconds later the palomino was out of sight in the trees.

Bill Hillis came to his knees, cursing, looking below, and, as he remained there, impotent in his rage, Trent looked up and drawled: "And why the hell did you do that?"

Hillis glanced down, choking back an oath long enough to snarl: "Do what?"

"Kick that rock loose. It would have been as easy as shooting down a standing steer."

"Then it wasn't you?" Hillis queried, his rage cooling. He even turned to look above, thinking, no doubt, that something up there had moved to start that rock on its downward roll.

Before he had a chance to speak further, they both heard a sound below that brought their glances swinging down there. Barbara Hillis had crossed the yard and was climbing toward them. She was close enough now so that Trent saw she had a six-gun in her hand.

Bill Hillis saw, too, and stood up where he was,

sighing his disappointment. His daughter looked up, paused, and raised her arm. Hillis called out: "Don't shoot, Barb!"

The girl let her arm fall. "Dad!" she gasped, moving toward them.

In ten more seconds she stood there, facing her father, tall and slim, and with a squarish, fine-featured face that was a softer likeness of her father's and set now in hardened anger. Even in this light Trent Stone could catch a hint of this girl's beauty—of the freshness and strength that must have made his son love her.

She didn't speak for long seconds, and, before her words came, she had looked from her father to Trent, and seen the rifle.

"So you've turned bushwhacker, Dad!" Above the angry passion of her voice Trent sensed a note of unbelief and horror.

"I told you I'd cut down that wolf cub if you ever saw him again. I meant it." Hillis's voice was edged with bitterness.

The girl looked at Trent, her face tinged with loathing. "Do you have to hire a killer to do your work for you?"

"I can't trust myself to shoot straight," Hillis replied. Then, his tone all at once taking on a tenderness, he pleaded: "Barb, can't you forget him? Have you ever known me to be wrong about such a thing?"

She shook her head. "Never before. But you're

wrong this time. Jim Stone is as fine a man as ever breathed . . . as fine as you are."

Once again Bill Hillis lost hold on his anger. "He's the son of a killer. His father . . ."

"That was never proved," she cut in. "Jim doesn't believe that his father killed Frank. Neither do I. Soon we'll prove it."

Hillis nodded soberly. "Trent Stone may come back here. I hope to meet him again." Little was left to the imagination as he spoke these words, for the threat behind them was clear.

"Dad, I love Jim!" the girl burst out, reaching out impulsively to take hold of her father's arm. "I have my life to live the way I choose. I've stayed with you, hoping that someday we could straighten things out, that I could prove Jim isn't behind all that's going on. I could have left you, run away. Don't make me hate you."

Hillis made no reply. He turned, pulling his arm away, and climbed up the slope. The girl didn't follow, but stood there, watching him until the darkness hid him. Then she wheeled suddenly and faced Trent, flaring: "It's men like you that have caused this! Why don't you go in to Jake Troy and hire your guns to him?"

"What cards does Jake Troy hold in this game?" Trent asked. He forced a grin, adding: "He couldn't pay a man a hundred, in gold, for one night's work."

All at once a sob broke from the girl's throat.

The past minutes had built up in her an emotion too strong to check now. She turned and walked quickly away, down the slope, and across to the corral. Trent watched her until she had mounted the pony and ridden into the darkness. Then he followed Bill Hillis.

The two men made most of the ride back to the ranch in silence. As the house lights winked into view across the distance, the rancher, riding ahead, drew rein and let Trent come alongside.

"You earned that hundred," he said. "I'd have paid more to find out what I did tonight. You get your money."

Trent shook his head. "I couldn't take it. It was my foot that kicked that rock loose."

Hillis's eyes stared in brief wonderment before he turned his glance away. They rode on at a walk for nearly a half mile before the rancher spoke again. What he said was a single word: "Why?"

"People told me I'd find Bill Hillis square. What you were headed for up there didn't smell just right."

"You could have shot him, even so," Hillis said.

"I could. But it takes a long life to live down a thing like that. You haven't got enough years ahead to ease your mind."

Hillis looked at Trent once more, his appraising glance frankly open now. "Who are you?" he queried abruptly.

"I said my handle was Quinn, Tom Quinn."

"A while ago you said it was Fred Quinn."

"That's right, I did." Trent smiled.

"You still want a job?"

Trent held back his answer a moment. At length he said: "It depends. First, I'd have to know a few things."

"What are they?"

"Why did you want to kill the man your daughter's chosen?"

"He's a stray . . . no good," Hillis replied, his anger almost choking him. "Fifteen years ago his father shot down my son Frank. That father, Trent Stone, was siding an outlaw, fighting me over grazing rights on four poor sections of grass. It wasn't that four sections alone. They'd have had everything I owned if I hadn't fought back. It was because I fought that they killed Frank. This Stone went to Yuma, but by that time he and the rest had turned every man on this range against me."

"They're still against you?"

"I'll let you decide. Last winter I lost over five hundred head of beef, some stolen, the rest poisoned. The two water holes on my west range have been fouled. I can't use it any more. Every month I hand out a fourteen-hundred-dollar payroll, hiring gun hands I wouldn't otherwise have stinking up my bunkhouse. That can't go on."

"And this young Stone is leading the pack against you?"

"Who else? Years ago it was a wild bunch, the outfit that sided Jim Stone's father. Since then . . ."

"But where's the proof?"

Hillis frowned, considering. "Does a man need proof when he's sure of a thing?" Seeing the uncompromising look on Trent's face, he shrugged, and finally admitted: "I have no proof beyond my own convictions."

"The girl said something about Jake Troy, said if I needed a dry-gulching job to go see him. Who is he?"

"He's a big wind that hides behind a sheriff's badge. If we had the right kind of law on Picket range, this would have been settled long ago."

"Why haven't you elected the right kind of a lawman?"

"Men who go against the law don't want the right kind. Jake Troy won't make a move against these smaller outfits, and they know it. They bring in the votes that keep him in office."

Trent was silent for longer than a minute. As they rode on, the creak of saddle gear and the rhythmic pounding of their horses' shoes on the ground were the only sounds that broke the utter quiet. Finally Trent said: "You're still of the same mind about that job?"

Hillis let out his breath in a gusty sigh. "You may be the man I want. You're a stranger here, and you can find out more than I could . . . or anyone I've hired. I liked the way you played out that hand tonight. If you're still willing to saddle yourself with my troubles, you're hired."

"The first thing I'd do would be to try to get a job with this Jake Troy."

Hillis was puzzled, and plainly showed it in the way he glanced at Trent. "And what good would that do?"

"A man with a badge can go where he pleases. He needn't take sides. Your sheriff may need a deputy. I'll take that hundred dollars tonight . . . as advance wages. Then I'll have a look around."

Later, as Hillis unsaddled at the corral, he asked: "This isn't your fight. Why are you mixing in it?"

"Call it curiosity," Trent said. "I never could be a good saddle tramp. It's too much like a straight beef diet." He paused, then asked a question that had been on his mind most of the past hour: "Why would this young Stone take out on a high lonesome and leave the girl like that?"

The rancher smiled wryly. "Jim Stone knows that only one crew has hung the Indian sign on him. And he knows no man in my outfit would harm Barb."

The next morning in the sheriff's office, when Jake Troy had finished reading the letter he had written Kurt Locheim three weeks before, he looked across at the stranger. "What happened to Kurt?"

Trent eased back in the chair at the front wall and hooked his thumbs in his belts. "Kurt has a crew working a stage road out of Tombstone. He's got too nice a thing to leave."

"He's a damned fool," Jake blustered. "Ten years on a stage road wouldn't get him what he can earn here in the next month."

"Kurt thought otherwise. He offered to let me take his place. I've found the Tombstone country unhealthy."

Troy smiled, and the smile seemed to narrow his eyes with shrewdness and tighten the loose-hanging flesh below his double chin. "A killin'?" he queried.

"Call it a bad run of cards."

An interruption came just then. The door alongside Trent opened and a man stepped in—a young man who stood, straight and tall, with eyes a deep shade of green set wide-spaced in a long, aquiline face. That face was set in sober lines as the man nodded curtly to Trent, and then looked at the sheriff and said without ceremony: "Someone made a try at me last night, Jake, with a rifle."

Troy straightened in his chair, his countenance set seriously. "Did you get a look at him, Jim?"

"No. But it happened on Box H range."

This, then, was Jim Stone. As he sat there, his

face impassive, a flood of emotion coursed through the father as he hungrily studied this man, his son. He liked the look of Jim's face, the set of the jaw. And Jim's shoulders were wide and square, the six-foot length of his body a lean, taut-muscled frame that showed strength in every line. At that moment Trent Stone felt a blaze of pride deep within him, and the emotion wiped out a measure of the bitterness and defeat his fifteen years in Yuma had left in him.

"You want me to swear out a warrant for Bill Hillis?" Jake asked almost eagerly.

Jim Stone shook his head. "I couldn't make it stick without proof. But what I came here to tell you is this. The first time Bill Hillis . . . or any of his crew step out of line with me, I'll use my guns."

"That's puttin' it strong, Jim. Better think it over."

"I've thought about it since I was old enough to think. Whatever's going on here is none of my doing. I've been saddled with the blame for everything that happens on this range. You're the law, and you won't lift a hand to help a man. I'm through. From now on I'll make my own law."

"Careful, Jim." A warning lay in Jake Troy's unraised voice.

But Jim Stone's look didn't soften. "You can make anything of that you like," he said. And he stood there for two tense seconds, letting his words sink in. Then, seeing Jake Troy's manner take on its usual meekness, a violent disgust was mirrored in his glance and he turned and went out, slamming the door behind him.

Trent looked across at the sheriff, and drawled: "Who's the wild man?"

A tide of color crept into Jake's face. "He's a man that won't live long . . . Jim Stone."

"Any kin to the Stone that Kurt framed years ago?"

Jake's glance sharpened as he muttered sharply: "Who told you about that?"

"Kurt. He claimed I ought to know about it, seeing that this younker's old man is leaving Yuma soon. Kurt thought he might be on the prod."

"Trent Stone's already out of Yuma. Maybe he'll come back and try to raise a little hell for us." Jake stopped abruptly, examining Trent with a new light in his eyes. "Kurt's mighty trustin'," he said finally. "What else did he tell you?"

"Enough."

"And you want a job?"

Trent shrugged. "That depends on the money. I want my share, and I'll want to know what's going on here . . . everything."

"You'll get it," Jake assured him somewhat absently. Some inner thought was evidently troubling him. He frowned and muttered, half aloud: "Who would make a try at Jim Stone?"

"I did," Trent announced.

Jake straightened, gripped the arms of his chair, and stared hard at this stranger. Before he could speak, Trent went on: "You told me last night to ride out and see Bill Hillis for a job. Kurt told me to have a look around before I came to you, so I did. Hillis paid me a hundred dollars to go up into the hills with him and make a try at young Stone. It seems he doesn't think much of his daughter meeting Stone up there at that line shack."

Jake's look was incredulous, then suspicious. "How come you didn't cut him down when you had the chance?"

"I aimed not to. From what Kurt said, young Stone is one of your blue chips in this game. We can have him any time we want."

The suspicion went out of the lawman's glance. He smiled, then laughed heartily, and, when he looked at Trent once more, there was a hint of admiration mirrored in his shifty blue eyes. "You'll do, friend." He chuckled. He opened a drawer at his side and took out a deputy's badge, which he tossed across over to Trent. "Pin that on."

Trent pinned the star on his shirt front. "No oath?" he said idly.

Troy grinned. "No lawman in Picket has taken an oath for the past five years. You don't need one, do you?"

"No. What I need is to hear what's behind your play."

Jake settled back in his chair. "You're all right, or Kurt wouldn't have sent you. He was with me when this thing began, fifteen years ago. I was deputy under a sheriff that had about as much brains as he needed to pin on his star. We made a cleanin' in wet beef, one or two stage hold-ups. The way we did it was by makin' this Bill Hillis think the small outfits were fightin' him over a strip of leased land. This Trent Stone, Jim Stone's old man, was in on it with us. One night Hillis's boy, Frank, overheard something from one of Kurt's men that would have spoiled our chances. Frank Hillis died that night. Trent Stone went to Yuma for the killin'."

"Stone was framed?"

Troy said dryly: "That's one thing I'll pass up tellin' you." Trent hid his disappointment behind an unreadable expression as the lawman went on. "We made a good thing of it for two or three more years. Then Hillis ran Kurt and his bunch out of the country. I kept out of it, held onto my job, and was elected sheriff four years later. Since then, things have been quiet until lately. Now they're startin' up again. Kurt's off his head not to be down here and cash in. I could use him."

"And where's all this getting you?"

Jake chuckled. "I have close onto fifty thousand cached in banks within a four-day ride of here. Sooner or later, Bill Hillis will lose his outfit. When he does, I aim to buy it at the right price.

No other man in this part of the country has the money."

"Is that all?"

"All?" Jake was puzzled. "Isn't it enough? Once I've got that toehold, I'll take another two or three years to buy up the rest of this range. I can hire a crew, make my own law, and before I wind up, I'll own the biggest outfit in Arizona."

The man's bluntness, his blind arrogance at the power he would someday possess, brought up a disgust in Trent he could scarcely conceal. "And what do I get out of it?" he asked.

"Name your price."

"A quarter share."

Jake shook his head. "I can't spare it in cash. But after we clean this up, I'll give you title to that much in land. You can sell it."

Trent was puzzled at the lawman's hasty acceptance of such a proposition. "You're handing over big pay for so little work," he said, frank curiosity in his voice. "Why?"

"I need a man I can trust," Jake replied. "What you did last night proves that you're the man. By takin' a shot at Jim Stone, you started the ball rollin'. Between us, we can keep it rollin' . . . which I couldn't do alone. In a week it'll be open war between Hillis and these small ranchers, who'll follow Jim Stone. After that, it's simple. Sooner or later I'll get out a warrant for Hillis on a killin' charge. And I can get a jury that'll hang him. That leaves the girl. She won't come into much money and she'll sell the outfit and get out of the country as soon as she can. It's worth what you ask to pull this thing off."

That was all there was to Jake's proposition. They settled a few more details, and then the sheriff told his new deputy to take a look around the town and let his badge be seen.

As Trent was going out the door, Jake called: "One more thing . . . you'll have a partner! I'm hirin' another deputy, a man who's worked with me before. Name's Walt Peters. Maybe you've heard Kurt mention him."

"Seems like I have," Trent answered, frowning as though trying to remember the name. But deep inside him had flamed a sudden excitement. Here would be his chance to settle things with one more man who had helped frame him fifteen years ago, and here, too, was a chance that Jake Troy would discover a few strange things about his new deputy's story, if Peters met the sheriff before he did Trent. Knowing that, Trent decided he'd see Walt Peters *first*.

But Trent didn't have his chance at a talk with the man who could tell Jake the truth about Kurt Locheim. For Walt Peters rode into town early that afternoon, and not so that anyone knew he'd arrived. Peters wasn't afraid, but cautious. Picket held a memory or two that wasn't pleasant, and, when he sighted the town, he swung off the trail and made a wide circle that brought him in along the alley that ran behind the jail. He tied his bay to a loose board on the wall of the jail's woodshed, and went to the back door and knocked softly.

Luckily Jake was alone in the office. He had a gun in his hand as he opened the door. One look, and his face broke into a smile. "Hell, you ain't dodgin' any Reward notices in this country, Walt. Come on in."

Peters edged in through the door and closed it behind him. He took the chair facing the sheriff's desk, and rolled a smoke. "So we're ready for the pay-off?" he questioned.

"We are. Plenty ready. Kurt sent down a man we've been waitin' for. He's already busted this fight wide open."

Walt frowned, let the cigarette hang from his lip, closing one eye against the curl of smoke as he regarded Jake narrowly. "Kurt sent a man down? The last I heard, he was comin' himself."

Jake shook his head. "No, Kurt claims he's got too good a thing, workin' that stage road out of Tombstone. He didn't want in on this."

Walt Peters whipped the cigarette out of his mouth and threw it to the floor so that it sent out a shower of sparks. He leaned forward in his chair. "Kurt hasn't worked Tombstone in ten years. This jasper's runnin' a sandy . . . a big one."

Jake was a little uncertain now, but he came to

his new deputy's defense. "He had the letter I wrote Kurt." The lawman opened a drawer and took the letter out and laid it on the desk. "Here, read it."

Walt Peters didn't move. "I don't have to. If this gent showed up with that letter, it means Kurt's dead."

"You're seein' spooks, Walt." Jake rose to his feet. "This stranger's square. He's workin' with us."

Peters laughed hollowly. "What did he look like?"

"Old, white hair, a scar along his face. He limps a little."

Walt Peters's laugh went softly menacing. "I talked with a gent from Yuma two or three months ago. He knew Trent Stone. It seems Trent's hair has turned white. Years ago a 'breed knifed him in a riot, and he wears the scar on his face. Jake, you sure took the bait."

Jake Troy sat down suddenly, his face gone loose and a sickly yellow in a look that was for a moment alive with a rising terror. But that look vanished before a slit-eyed glance of quick cunning. "So it's Trent, at last. Well, we'll do something about it."

IV

Jim Stone wasn't a drinking man, but he spent most of that day in the Nugget. It was the quickest way he knew to get the word around. Shortly before noon, after Jim had left the sheriff's office, Charley Wales came into the saloon. He heard Jim's story of the shooting and had a grim look on his face as Jim finished.

"Then this is it," Charley said. "I'll swing up to Dorn's place on the way home and tell him about it. I reckon we'll all hate this, but sooner or later we've got to make our fight against Hillis and it might as well be now. What should I tell Dorn?"

Jim Stone had thought this all out last night. He knew for sure now that he could never marry Barb Hillis. While Bill Hillis lived, he would do everything in his power to keep his daughter and Jim apart, and with Bill Hillis dead it meant that the girl wouldn't be able to put down her loathing of the man who had brought about his death. There was no way out for Jim—no way but to make his fight as a man should. So now he told Charley: "Have Dorn leave a couple of men to guard his layout and ride over to my place tonight with the rest. Get the news to the others if you can. I want twenty men tonight. So long as Hillis lays the blame on us, we'll give him something big to howl about."

"Where are we ridin' tonight?"

"We'll burn every Box H line camp and pull down his windmills and blow in his water holes. Maybe we can drive off a few head of his critters and lose 'em. Later on, when he begins to fight back, we can make a try at firing his house and barns."

"That's a big order, Jim. We'll bring home a few empty saddles." Charley was worried.

"Maybe you'd like to sit by and see him drive you off your place . . . along with the rest of us. That's what it's coming to."

Charley nodded, and a fighting light crept into his eyes as he turned away. "We'll be there," he said firmly.

Jim had his noon meal in the saloon, and in the next two hours he saw three more of his friends and passed on the news. Then, standing alone at the bar and looking toward the swing doors, he saw the white-haired stranger enter who had been in Jake Troy's office that morning.

The stranger wore a deputy's badge. Seeing it, Jim Stone thought a lot less of the man. Strangely enough, the new deputy singled him out and came over and stood alongside. "Have a drink?" he said easily.

"Too soon after lunch." Jim's voice was curt.

Trent nodded agreeably and asked the apron for

bourbon. He downed his drink and stood there, fingering the glass, and all at once he said, low-voiced: "You're making a big mistake, Stone."

Jim's glance darkened. "A mistake about what?"

"Fighting Bill Hillis."

"You figure you know more about this than I do?"

Trent shrugged. "I know a thing or two about that shooting up at the line camp last night. I know what's behind it. There's only two men who can settle this fight . . . you and Bill Hillis. If I were you, I'd ride out there now and see Bill. Tell him Tom Quinn sent you."

"And get a bullet in my back?" Jim laughed mirthlessly. "Not much, stranger."

"All you'd need to do is tell Hillis the truth, that you haven't brought on any of his trouble and that you're willing to help find out who has. Ride in there without your guns. After he cools down, he'll listen."

"Because I say you sent me?"

Trent nodded.

Jim shook his head, his look unbelieving. "I want to live a little longer, stranger. And if Jake Troy sent you to tell me this, go back to Jake and tell him it didn't work."

"He didn't send me. You want the girl, don't you?"

It was the wrong thing to say, for a hot anger flared into Jim's eyes. "A man your age ought to keep his nose out of other people's business." He covered his irritation with a drawl. "Now get away before I decide you need your face worked over. It could stand it."

The words cut deeply. Yet Trent felt no trace of anger. He knew only that he had failed, that he had lost his son's respect. He didn't move away but stood there thinking, wondering what he could say now to change Jim's mind.

It was then that Jake Troy came in, saw his deputy standing at the bar, and stepped over and said affably: "The drinks are on me. Have one, Stone?"

Jim Stone shook his head, and stepped away. And Jake, noticing his manner, asked Trent: "What ails him?"

"He thinks we should be doing something about that shooting last night. When I told him we couldn't, he didn't like it much."

Jake chuckled, and Trent had the feeling that his manner was a little too hearty. "Let him get riled," Jake said. "That's what we want." He ordered drinks from the bartender, and then went on. "Stone's crew is set to ride tonight. They won't dare make their fight in the open. Maybe they'll burn a line shack or two and run off a little beef. Hadn't we better let Bill Hillis know what's comin'?"

"And bust the thing wide open? Why not?" was Trent's reply.

"This'll wind up in a hurry. You're the one to ride out and see Hillis. Start any time you feel like it." Jake finished his drink, saw a friend sitting at a rear table, and went on back to have a word with him.

What Jake had suggested was the logical move for bringing this fight into the open and ending it. It wouldn't be long now before Picket's sheriff could swear out a warrant for Hillis. Trent, knowing the rancher as he did, realized that Hillis himself would be riding with his crew.

He went out of the saloon and down the awninged walk to the livery barn. As he saddled his roan, he was remembering Jake's manner as he had talked a minute ago. Jake had overplayed his hand; something had happened that had changed even the look in the sheriff's eyes, for once or twice during their talk Trent had wondered if he saw a deeper touch of shrewdness and almost hostility than he remembered at their first meeting. And sensing this change in Troy, a wariness took hold of Trent Stone so that he hesitated in riding out to see Hillis.

Then he told himself that he had wanted to see the rancher anyway, and that whatever was on Jake's mind couldn't have anything to do with his errand. So he finished saddling the roan in the corral and was about to get into the saddle when he heard a familiar voice shuttle down the barn's long alleyway.

It was Jim Stone, speaking to the hostler. "Throw

my hull on, Bill. I'll be leaving within the next ten minutes, after I finish at the hardware store."

As Trent rode away and took the south road out of town, he was wondering what Jim Stone's errand at the hardware store could mean. The thought occurred to him that Jim might be down there buying a few cartons of shells, but he put aside that explanation, not wanting for the moment to think of the trouble that lay ahead for his son.

Five miles out along the south trail, Trent saw a buckboard topping a rise a mile ahead of him, coming in toward town. As the rig drew closer, he realized with a sudden excitement that Barbara Hillis was driving the team of bays. He pulled to the side of the trail and waited for her.

When she saw who it was, she was close enough so that he caught the tight expression of anger that changed her face when she recognized him. He held up a hand and she drew rein, the team standing a little ahead of him so that he had to ride on a few paces before his pony stood so that he could look at her directly.

He touched the brim of his Stetson, drawling: "Howdy, miss."

She stared at him coldly, ignoring his greeting. "If you have anything to say, say it."

"You haven't talked with your father yet?"

"No more than I could help. What is it you want?" She lifted the reins and seemed about to start the team again.

"I thought maybe you'd like to know that Jim is headed out the trail here on his way home. He had notions of paying back that little debt he owes your father. Maybe, if you'd wait for him out here, you could talk him out of it."

The anger went out of her eyes as a brief wonder took its place. Abruptly she queried: "Why are you doing this? You could have killed Jim last night, but you didn't. Now you . . ." She broke off abruptly as she noticed the badge on his shirt.

He caught her look, and nodded. "You told me to hire out to Jake."

The fury was alive again in her glance. "The law is against us, like everything else in this country," she breathed in a sort of helpless anger. "For a moment I thought you were on our side. But you aren't." She slapped the backs of the bays with the reins and drew on past Trent.

As she drove away, Trent called: "Better have your talk with Jim!" But he couldn't be sure that she had heard.

V

Walt Peters had nearly a half hour start on Trent. Jake and Walt had figured the thing out in the jail office before Jake went across to the Nugget to have his talk with Trent. And in order to give himself plenty of time for what lay ahead, Walt pushed his gelding hard all the way along the south trail until he came within sight of the Box H.

In these past twelve years, Walt hadn't been in this country for more than a day or two. And twelve years ago, when he was siding Kurt Locheim, he'd avoided men like Bill Hillis—for a man with a price on his head is careful. So now, as he turned into the yard that flanked the house, he didn't hesitate but rode in openly. Bill Hillis wouldn't know him.

He was swinging down out of the saddle at the hitch rail when a man stepped out of a doorway at the end of the house's single wing and stood there on the wide porch, waiting for him. Walt had seen Bill Hillis a time or two, years ago, and now recognized him.

"Howdy," he said. "Is the boss around?"

"I'm Hillis."

"Then you're the man I'm looking for," Walt said, stepping up alongside Hillis. "I hear you're interested in finding Trent Stone."

Hillis frowned, examining this stranger. He didn't like the weak look to the man's receding chin, nor the drooping cigarette in one corner of his mouth, or the pale blue eyes that wouldn't meet his own directly. Yet the mention of Trent Stone's name aroused a curiosity in Hillis that he couldn't put down, so he answered: "If any man's interested in Trent Stone, it's me."

Walt Peters chuckled. "I've heard that. I'm on

my way through this country, ridin' south, and didn't think it would hurt to stop in and tell you what I know. Stone's in town."

The look on Bill Hillis's grizzled countenance changed from one of half curious tolerance to that of pent-up excitement as he breathed: "In town? Are you sure?"

"Would I be here if I wasn't?" Peters reached down into the pocket of his Levi's and brought out the badge Jake had given him, letting Hillis catch only a glimpse of it before he put it back again. "I'm a deputy from up north. I was at Yuma, deliverin' a prisoner the day they let Stone out. And I heard it said that he aimed to ride down here and have it out with you for sendin' him to prison. Then, when I was in Picket today, I had a good look at him. He's on the prod."

Hillis's eyes shone with a fire that hadn't been in them for years. It was easy for Walt Peters to see that his words had carried—that the rancher was already planning his long-awaited revenge for the killing of his son. "If he's wanting to buy into a fight, it won't be hard," Hillis muttered.

Peters shrugged his narrow shoulders. "I thought I'd better let you know. There's talk in town that he's seen his son, that a whole bunch are ridin' for your place tonight. They say the sheriff isn't worried."

"He's never worried. What does Stone look like?"

"White hair, a scar on one side of his face. When I saw him, he was walkin' with a limp. And he's packin' two cutters."

For a moment a look of bewilderment crossed Hillis's face, and he breathed: "It couldn't be."

"Couldn't be what?"

"Nothing," Hillis said. All at once his reserved manner broke. "You've done me a turn that's saved my life, stranger. I'd like to make it up to you some way. Maybe you'd like to lay over here for a day or so of rest and good meals."

Peters shook his head regretfully. "I can't stay. I'll be ridin' on toward the border. There's a sheriff down there that's caught up with a man I'm interested in."

He walked out to his horse and went up into the saddle. Hillis followed and pressed home his thanks. "Any time you ride through here, stop in and call this place home, stranger."

Walt wheeled his pony away and waved a hand as he rode out of the yard.

He wasn't out of sight along the trail to the south when Hillis turned and walked back up onto the porch and into his ranch office. He went to a cabinet behind his desk and took out a matched pair of .38 Colts. He hadn't worn these guns for years, but now he took them down and cleaned them and tested their action. The feel of the hard butt plates in his palms sent a long-forgotten thrill coursing through him, and, when he dropped fresh shells from a newly opened box into the cylinders, it was with a gravity that made the act seem one of near reverence.

He belted on a pair of worn holsters, dropped the guns into leather, and reached for his Stetson that lay on the table. Then he left the house and started down toward the corrals.

He was halfway between the house and barn when he saw a rider coming in along the trail. And as he caught a far glimpse of the white hair under the oncoming rider's Stetson brim, he stopped his stride and stood there waiting, a coldness turning his nerves to a steel-like composure.

Trent Stone saw Hillis and rode across the yard and reined in thirty feet away. He was smiling as he came up, but the look on Hillis's face made his smile fade.

Hillis's face wore an expression as hard as flint. He said flatly: "You saved me the trouble of hunting you down, Stone." And as he spoke, his right hand was moving in a practiced swing toward his holstered .38.

Trent saw it coming. Although he didn't understand, instinct made him wheel his roan around to face Hillis. A jerk on the reins sent the animal rearing onto hind legs. The rancher's weapon lined and exploded. The bullet caught the roan fully in the chest and he lunged wildly and went onto his knees. Trent leaped clear of the saddle, whipping up his gun. He stood there, spraddle-legged, and took careful aim. Hillis shot again and the bullet tore through the muscle of Trent's upper left arm.

Trent fired, saw Hillis's gun spin from his hand as the rancher choked back a cry of pain. And as Hillis stood there, for the moment unarmed, Trent lunged toward him.

Hillis's left hand darted toward his other holster, lifting out the second six-gun. Trent reached him just as the weapon cleared leather. With the edge of his flat, open palm, Trent slashed home a solid blow that knocked the gun to the ground. Then he stepped back and rocked his own weapon into line with Hillis's belt buckle and drawled: "You'll listen to what I have to say."

Hillis's face was pale in cold fury. He looked down at the gun alongside and abruptly stooped to pick it up. Trent Stone's Colt exploded hollowly into the still air, and the gun beneath the rancher's opened hand jumped away a yard along the gravel.

"Hillis, don't move!" Trent snapped out. Then, when the rancher had straightened once more, rubbing his numb, bullet-shocked wrist, Trent went on quietly: "We'll talk this thing over."

Hillis took a step toward his second .38, lying in the dust to one side of him, but, before he could reach it, Trent had stepped in and kicked it out of the way. Trent picked up the weapon, strode over, and picked up the second, ramming them in his belt.

"You're sure as hell a wild man," he drawled. "So you know who I am?"

"You won't live another day in this country, Stone."

Trent was looking beyond the rancher, seeing the three cowpunchers who had just run around the corner of the bunkhouse, forty yards away. "Tell your crew to let us alone. That is, unless you think you need help."

Hillis was a brave man, a little foolish now, perhaps, but Trent's words brought alive a spark of pride within him, and he turned and called to the trio at the bunkhouse: "You three keep out of this!" He faced Trent again, and said, disgust in his voice: "Hand me back my guns and we'll have it out here and now."

"I said we'd talk. After we're through, you can decide whether we'll use our guns."

"You did a lot of talking fifteen . . . years ago. Too much."

"Not enough," Trent corrected. "Because I didn't know enough. Four days ago I met Kurt Locheim on the way down here. Remember him?" He waited until he caught the rancher's brief nod. "Before I left Kurt, I had it straight that I was framed, the way I claimed during my trial. Kurt's dead, buried under a cutbank nearly two hundred miles west of here. He helped frame me."

"You haven't forgotten how to lie, have you, Stone?" The sarcasm in Hillis's voice was biting.

Trent ignored the jibe. "I was in with the gang that started things here, and maybe I had a little of this coming to me. But I didn't bushwhack your son. Remember how he was shot? With buckshot, in the back. Now think, Hillis . . . I'm handy with a cutter, a damned sight handier than Frank ever was. Why would I have used buckshot on him when one slug from my plow handle would have done the job? And why would I let him have it in the back?"

He paused, seeing that Hillis was finally listening. But there was still the same light of impotent fury twisting the rancher's grizzled face, the same hard hatred mirrored in his eyes. Before Hillis had the chance to interrupt, Trent went on: "You'll remember that a jasper named Walt Peters disappeared. I needed Peters's testimony to prove where I was the night Frank was killed. But Peters was paid to leave the country. Kurt Locheim paid him. Do you get that?"

"It's your story, brother. And it hasn't changed much since you left here."

Trent had been even-tempered until this moment. But all at once he saw the futility of this thing, the wall Bill Hillis had built up in his mind against all possibility of reason. A slow-burning passion took hold of Trent. He cursed, long and fluently, cursed Bill Hillis for his bull-headedness, in a drawling, hard-clipped voice. Finally he said: "It's a hell of a lot of thanks I get for coming back to straighten things out. Another day or two without you knowing who I was and I'd have had the proof."

"You'd have skipped the country. I'm damned glad that gent knew you."

"*Who* knew me?" Trent was immediately interested.

"A lawman from the north. He was at Yuma the day you were turned loose."

A suspicion took slow root in Trent's mind. "And when did you see this lawman?"

"He rode away a few minutes before you drifted in. Said he'd heard you were on the prod and rode out here to warn me."

For a long moment Trent considered this, wondering who the man could be that had recognized him. All at once he remembered Jake Troy saying that Walt Peters was on his way in. So he asked Hillis: "Was he short, with light blue eyes that don't stay steady, and a sloping chin? Did he have a cigarette drooping out of his mouth?" He spoke as he remembered the old Walt Peters, and wondered at the same time if the man had changed much in these fifteen years.

"That's him." Hillis's answer was positive.

"Did you ever know Walt Peters, the man that jumped the country after my arrest?"

Hillis shook his head.

"The man you just talked to was Walt Peters. He's here to work with Jake Troy. Hillis, unless we make a play that'll stop 'em, you and every other rancher in this country will be holding a deuce to four aces. You don't know what you're headed for. I do. Listen to this. . . ."

Trent talked, calmly, dispassionately, telling Hillis of Jake Troy's plans. Slowly the hard glitter left Bill Hillis's eyes. At the end of a minute he was listening with all his attention.

"So there you have it," Trent finished. He lifted Hillis's guns from his belt and held them out toward the rancher. "Take these. If you're still bull-headed enough not to believe, make your play."

Five minutes ago Bill Hillis would have snatched those guns out of Trent's hands and used them. But now, frowning in perplexity, he took them and dropped them back into the holsters riding at his thighs.

"You wouldn't be loco enough to do this unless there was some truth in what you say," he mused.

Trent's lips curled to frame a sardonic grin. "So you're coming out of it."

Hillis seemed not to have heard as he muttered: "Maybe we ought to ride in and make medicine with Troy."

"Maybe we had. But we'll have to go about it the right way. Jake's dry behind the ears."

"What's your idea?"

Hillis had unbent this far, and with this scant

toehold Trent started talking and didn't finish until the rancher grudgingly nodded his assent.

"Then let's be riding for Picket," Hillis said, swinging around to walk toward the corral.

VI

Five minutes later Trent Stone and Bill Hillis were riding along the north trail, headed for town. The sun had dipped below the far horizon and the light was fading into dusk.

Once Hillis looked at Trent in half apology. "A man wearing blinders can't help but be a damned fool at times, Stone."

"I asked for it," Trent admitted. Both of them were uneasy, yet both realized that a good measure of the hatred of these past fifteen years was slowly cooling.

Later, as the dusk settled quickly across the far-rolling stretches to the east, they sighted a buckboard far up the trail. Both men watched it until it was close enough so that Trent could recognize the team and make out two figures on the seat.

"That'll be your girl and my boy," he said. "Maybe we ought to let them settle their differences their own way." He cut from the trail at right angles and rode down into a shallow coulée, and Bill Hillis followed. From there they watched.

Barbara Hillis and Jim Stone rode past. The two were talking, but the distance was too great for either of the two men to make out what was being said.

"For all Jim knows, he's stepping into a rattlesnake nest, riding out there to see me," Hillis drawled. "That younker has his share of guts."

A surge of pride filled both these men as they rode on. Each was thankful in his own way for the thing that had happened, for a great measure of the bitterness that had hounded them for these years was now wiped away.

But as the lights of Picket began to glow ahead of them, their silence took on a grimness that pressed in on them both.

Once Bill Hillis said: "This won't be easy, friend."

Trent's only answer was a nod.

At the edge of town they parted, Hillis to ride down the street, Trent to cut obliquely to the left to enter the alley that ran behind the stores. They were acting on the plan Trent had outlined back at the ranch. Hillis rode on and turned in at the hitch rail in front of the jail. He climbed from the saddle, glad to see that a light shone in the window of the sheriff's office.

He crossed the walk and opened the door and stepped in. Jake, sitting behind his desk, looked up in surprise. Walt Peters, tilted back against the wall in another chair and with his feet on the desk, went all at once rigid and took the cigarette from his mouth.

"'Evenin', Hillis," he said nervously. "I left a little unfinished business here and rode back to see your sheriff."

Hillis nodded curtly, tried to hide the excitement running through him. So far Trent's reasoning had been correct. He had said Peters would be here. So now Hillis announced: "Jake, I've just killed a man."

Jake Troy seemed to be having difficulty clearing his throat. Finally he got out: "You've killed a man? Who?"

"Trent Stone."

A look of understanding flashed between the sheriff and Peters, and Jake's loose-fleshed face assumed a severe look as he said: "Stone? But he isn't even in the country."

"He is. He rode out to my place late this afternoon. I reckon he was hunting me, although I didn't wait to ask. I put five slugs through his chest before he had time to say much."

"Then it's murder," Jake intoned, getting up out of his chair and nodding to Peters. He drew a blunt-nosed .45 and lined it at Hillis. "Get his guns, stranger," Jake said. He waited while Peters crossed the room to lift Bill Hillis's .38s out of their holsters. Peters then put the guns down on the sheriff's desk. "Trent Stone served his time in Yuma and was turned out a free man. You'll hang for this, Bill."

Things were going the way Trent Stone had said they would, Hillis was thinking. Aloud he drawled: "A man has a right to fight it out with the sidewinder that murdered his son."

"Sure," Jake agreed mockingly. "But who's to say you gave Stone an even break? Stone was fast with a gun, too fast for you. Maybe we can prove you dry-gulched him."

Hillis gave a sideward glance at the door at the back of the room. That glance showed him that the door was ajar, open a fraction of an inch. Something he hadn't counted on was that they'd take his guns. But in his anger hc gave that little thought as he said: "Jake, I've often wondered if Stone wasn't framed. As he died, he said something about that. He named Kurt Locheim and a gent called Peters."

The lawman's face suddenly drained of all color. "Did he say anything else?" he queried in a hard, flat voice.

Hillis nodded, noticing as he did so that the back door stood an inch wider. "Yes, he said a few other things . . . things that'll count in front of a jury."

"What things?" Jake Troy snarled, grinning wickedly and no longer afraid. Hillis didn't answer, so he went on: "Maybe we'll have to see you don't stand trial, Bill. Maybe we can find

Trent's carcass out at your place and arrange a double killin'. It won't be hard."

For one of the few times in his life, Bill Hillis was afraid. A gleam of madness had edged into Jake Troy's glance, and the rancher was wondering why Trent didn't open the door and throw down on these two. Then, all at once he knew why Trent was waiting. Jake was talking, and Trent was waiting to hear more.

"You seem interested in what Stone told me before he cashed in," Hillis said.

Jake laughed, a laugh that shook his bulging frame. "Why shouldn't I be?" He glanced at Peters. "Walt, you tell him."

"Hold your tongue, Jake!"

"Why should I?" Jake all at once sobered and fastened an arrogant glance at the rancher. "Hillis, you've swallowed the bait. It wasn't Trent that killed your boy. It was me and Walt here. We've built your whole fight for you. A year from now, I'll own your whole damned layout. And a few others along with it."

Neither Bill Hillis nor Trent Stone had been expecting this. A sudden rage at discovering his son's killer possessed the rancher. All the hatred he had nursed these long years toward Trent Stone centered now on Jake Troy in a half-crazed savageness. He took a step in toward the desk, ignoring Jake's weapon. As his hand flashed out and reached for one of his guns, lying on the desk,

Jake stepped in and swung across a hard blow that brought the barrel of his weapon slashing alongside the rancher's scalp. Bill Hillis went down with a heavy thud, the gun falling out of his hand to the floor.

It happened so suddenly that Trent was a split second late in swinging open the door—too late to stop that blow of Jake's. Both Jake and Peters heard the creaking of the door's hinges, and turned. Jake fell back a step, swinging up his gun. Peters whirled and lunged out of line and reached toward his holster. Trent's gun exploded in a blast echoed by Jake Troy's .45.

A panic had taken hold of Jake, so that his bullet went wide, knocking a splinter from the door frame. Trent had aimed surely, with an ease that made the upswing of his gun and the thumbing of the hammer one smooth motion. His bullet shattered the fourth button on Jake's broad expanse of shirt front. The shock of the lead slug made the lawman stagger back and into the desk. His knees gave way and he sat there at his desk, loose-limbed and ridiculous-looking. Walt Peters, crouching beyond the desk, clawed his weapon free and streaked it up. Trent was so intent on watching Jake Troy's sagging bulk that he was nearly caught. But, an instant before Peters's gun blasted outward at him, Trent stepped aside. Peters's bullet took him low, above the thigh bone on his left side, and set up a searing pain along the heavy muscle.

Timed with the gun blast, Trent rocked back the hammer of his Colt and let it slip from under the ball of his thumb. The thunder of his weapon took up that of the other gun and Walt Peters, a bullet through his head, slumped forward onto the board floor. At the limits of his vision, Trent saw Jake Troy move. He wheeled, a flood of panic mounting in him. His eyes whipped around before his hand had moved through the arc that would once more center the gun on the lawman. And Trent found himself staring into the muzzle of Jake's gun. The man, wild-eyed, his thick lips flecked with bloody foam, was making a dying effort to steady his gun. And it was lined true.

Even as his gun hand moved, too late, that instant of time dragged slowly for Trent Stone. He saw Jake's crooked thumb move the hammer back, and then he waited for the shock of the bullet to take him. But from off to his left, ahead of the desk, a gun suddenly spoke, ripping away the two-second silence. There was a stab of flame from there, one that lanced out at Jake Troy.

The burly lawman toppled sideways, his weight leaving the desk as he fell heavily to the floor and rolled onto his face.

Trent took his eyes from Jake's lifeless form and looked across to where Bill Hillis lay on the floor, one side of his face streaked with blood but a smoking gun held steadily in his hand, lined at the spot where Jake Troy had sat a moment ago.

“Close,” Trent breathed, his forehead bathed in fine-beaded perspiration. He stepped over and reached down to help the rancher to his feet. “I’d be lying there now if it hadn’t been . . .”

“Forget it, Trent,” Hillis cut in. “He was my man, wasn’t he?”

They made another ride that night—after the local doctor had taken three stitches in Bill Hillis’s scalp and bandaged Trent’s side and shoulder. They had tried to put Trent to bed for a few days, but he wouldn’t have it that way.

Jim Stone and the girl were waiting at the Box H. Jim had ridden over to his place and called off the raid for that night, for Barbara Hillis was a woman and had her way about wanting Jim to talk to her father before he took to guns to settle what lay between them. There wasn’t much to say, and Trent Stone didn’t say any of it. After Bill Hillis had finished, Jim stepped over and took his father’s hand. And a face, that fifteen years of torture had hardened, went soft.

A BADGE FOR A TINHORN

This story was submitted by the author's agent to *Complete Western Book Magazine* on December 24, 1937. It was accepted for publication on March 19, 1938. The author was paid $91.12. Upon publication in the June, 1938 issue the title was changed to "Ghost-Badge for a Tinhorn". For its first book appearance the author's original title and text have been restored.

I

Six afternoons ago, four hundred miles to the north, Clay Whitehead had lived through the strangest hour of his life. Bill Marsden, U.S. commissioner, had come to Clay's faro layout in the Miner's Luck in Clovis, and asked Clay to step across the street with him to his office. They had talked for an hour, and at the end of that interval Marsden had tilted back in his chair and waited for an answer. And that answer was a mockery to every act of Clay Whitehead's past ten years, for he had said: "I'll take the job, Bill."

Marsden had rolled the butt of a cigar between his thin lips, nodding and saying: "I hoped you would. You've tried about everything but the law, Clay. Virginia City didn't give you anything but a taste for cards and a way with a gun. You hit Tombstone too late to build a stake. Today your pockets are empty and you aren't making more than enough to keep you with your cards. A man crowding thirty ought to lay off raising hell and take a look ahead. Do this thing up right and you'll make your name as a lawman. That's the kind of a name I'd like to see you have."

Clay Whitehead had smiled and drawled: "Two hours ago I'd have choked the man who said I'd ever wear a badge."

"You wouldn't be wearing one now if this job wasn't loaded with dynamite. Supposing I sent you north instead of south . . . up into Halpin county to corral those rustlers."

"I'd quit. There's families up there that would starve without that beef."

Marsden nodded. "Just why I'll never send a man to bring 'em in." He paused, relit his cigar, and went on: "You knew Roy Baker and liked him, the same as the rest of us. You know he didn't deserve to die. Roy was headed for the border on a job. He made the mistake of stopping over in Antelope for a few hours' rest. He was shot that night . . . a bullet in the spine. Poor luck is all it was. Someone thought Roy was sticking his nose into that range war down there and killed him before he discovered anything. It was a mistake. We didn't give one damn about what's going on in Antelope, and still don't. Your only job is to go down there and bring me back the man who murdered a U.S. deputy marshal. And I don't care how you do it."

"Hadn't I ought to know what's going on at Antelope?"

The commissioner shook his head emphatically. "That's county business, not the government's. Get into trouble and I can't help you. They'd skin me alive and nail my hide to my desk if they found out I'd hired a gambler and gunman to do my dirty work for me."

"Then why are you doing it?"

Marsden leaned forward in his chair. "Call it a hunch, Clay. You are the one man I know who can swing it . . . with luck. It's the hardest assignment I've ever handed a man, and you're headed into a pack of curly wolves that won't be tamed." Marsden relaxed, settled back once more. "You can call it something else if you want. I've hated to see a man like you headed the wrong way down a one-way trail. Make good and maybe you've helped me prove a private theory."

Clay Whitehead hadn't asked Bill Marsden to elaborate on that theory. They had cleared up a few last details, and, shortly, Clay Whitehead, whose last ten years had many times seen the law more than mildly interested in him, had walked out of the commissioner's office with a U.S. deputy marshal's badge in his pocket.

The first afternoon, on the thirty-mile ride that took him steadily south, Clay had rooted up his deep scorn at his rôle as a lawmaker and replaced it with the seed of pride. His six-foot frame, long accustomed to slouching over a poker table, straightened at the saddle work and his wide shoulders sat a little more squarely. As Clay made his first camp that night, his lungs felt cleared of all the stale air of the half a hundred saloons and gambling hells that lay along his back trail. He had thought the thing through, seen that his chances with cards and with his guns were slim ones, and given grudging thanks to Bill Marsden for the confidence in him he didn't yet understand. Bill Marsden should have been there to see the visible workings of his shrewd hunch.

Before rolling into his blankets that first night, Clay had pried off the heel of his right boot and gouged out a hole in the leather deep enough to hold his newly acquired gold badge. He was remembering that Roy Baker had worn his badge on his shirt front that day in Antelope, and he wasn't going about the thing the same way.

That had been six days ago. Today, swinging down out of the mountains and onto Antelope range, Clay Whitehead rode with a wariness bred of lean, hard years. Roy Baker had ridden in here from the north, openly. Clay was riding in from the north, too, but not openly. He hadn't followed the trail through the lowest pass that cut between the peaks; instead, he'd swung five miles to the west and taken a higher, untraveled pass that put him above timberline. Sloping down through the foothills, he circled the open pastures, and twice back-trailed to keep out of sight of cabins. He was coming in from the north, yes, but he aimed to be the only one who knew it.

Farther down he came across grass, green and lush and deep, a welcome sign of spring after this long, hard winter. It filled the cañon bottoms and covered the hill slopes; Clay had pictured the Antelope range as bleak and forbidding, not like this. It served as a tonic to his saddle weariness and muscle ache—and it robbed him of a measure of his wariness.

Careful or not, what happened would have happened anyway. Clay, keeping to the tree margins of a high-walled cañon, rounded a bend and suddenly saw before him something that made him rein his blue roan quickly into the trees. Sixty yards ahead three men were grouped about a branding fire, two holding the ropes of a thrown steer, the third hunkered down close to the fire and holding a hot iron in the coals. It was this third who had a flashing glimpse of the roan as it cut into the trees. He surged to his feet with a wild yell, dropping the iron. His two hands came alive and stabbed at his thighs. In a split second he had palmed up a pair of Colt .45s and sent four blasting shots into the trees after Clay.

The first slug of that staccato gun thunder hit Clay's saddle horn with a jarring thud and ricocheted on into the trees with a high, piercing whine. The second knocked a chip of bark from a cedar alongside the roan's head, so that the animal lunged wildly to one side. That nervous movement saved Clay's life, for he felt the air rush of the next bullet fan past his chest.

As he slid the roan to a stop, reaching for the holstered gun at his thigh, he heard the quick, muffled pounding of hoofs. He wheeled around and spurred out of the trees, in time to catch a glimpse of the three riders as they swung down-cañon and disappeared around a farther bend. Two were short, the one who had gone so quickly for his guns tall and wearing a soiled, gray Stetson. Clay remembered the look on the man's gaunt, sun-blackened face, and, remembering, he wouldn't forget.

The fire told him nothing; neither did the unmarked running iron that lay in the red coals. He took the time to inspect the fresh raw brand on the steer's matted hide—a Circle J—before he came to the ground and took off the ropes.

Men on their home range don't brand steers in the spring, or, if they do pick up a stray and put the iron to him, they don't run at sight of the first stranger. And, contrariwise, three rustlers don't waste time on a single animal.

About as clear as Arkansas River water, Clay mused, as he swung into the saddle again and went on.

He was faintly irritated over having been seen, and more than interested in what was to come because of what he had seen. Bill Marsden had said: "If they see you coming in from Clovis way, they may guess who you are. So, if you're spotted, you'd better turn back."

But Clay wasn't turning back; deep down inside him he felt that tense thrill that comes to a man when he holds four aces, or when in a split second he sees that his draw is faster than that of the man he faces. Clay Whitehead was liking this.

An hour later, following a hard-packed road that led east toward Antelope, he climbed a steep grade and rounded a low shoulder of a side slope. There, thirty feet ahead and blocking the trail, two riders sat their horses. One was a girl, outfitted in a man's blue Levi's and a yellow shirt and canvas windbreaker. The other, a spare-framed, stoop-shouldered older man with a limp-brimmed Stetson shading gray eyes a shade lighter than Clay's, held up a hand. But Clay was watching the girl.

He reined in, swinging to the left so that his holstered Colt and his right hand showed openly. It was a friendly gesture; understanding it, the oldster seemed to relax a little.

The girl didn't, for she said sharply: "If you're after a job with Will Jay, you'd better turn back." Her eyes, greener than hazel, flared brightly in unaccountable anger. Her manner was plainly hostile, for she sat proudly in the saddle and her face was too pale for the tan of her neck and hands.

Clay grinned, and answered: "I'm after a job, miss. But this is the first time I ever heard of Will Jay."

The oldster cleared his throat and muttered: "Easy, Mary. You don't know for sure."

Hearing that voice, Clay immediately tried to place it. He had a closer look at the man, and recognition finally came. This was Bede Weld, gambler, gunman, hired killer, lately of Tombstone. Clay was about to call him by name, when Weld stared at him intently, shook his head imperceptibly, and said aloud: "Stranger, your name wouldn't be Young would it . . . Fletcher Young?"

Clay shook his head, but, before he had a chance to answer, the girl flared: "He rides a roan and he's tall. Bede, I tell you he's the one!"

Bede Weld looked at her helplessly for a moment. Clay, regarding the man, was almost taken off his guard. For the girl's right hand suddenly reached across and lifted Weld's gun from its holster. Timed with her motion, Clay felt a flood of warning course through him; he rolled out of the saddle, lit on his two feet in a crouch, and lunged out of the way as the girl wildly swung her gun down and pulled the trigger.

The bullet kicked up a plume of dust at the place where Clay's feet had been a second ago. His lunge took him toward her, on the offside of Weld's horse. The animal shied and took a full stride forward, leaving Clay abruptly in the clear. As the girl swung her six-gun around to cover him, he reached up and knocked it from her grasp.

"You have a queer brand of welcome," Clay drawled. "I don't know as I like it."

He stooped, picked up the fallen weapon, and

looked at the girl. There was still that same hostility in her glance, and her eyes were filled now with tears of bafflement. Clay, above his rising wonder, suddenly realized that she was beautiful.

All at once she spoke, her words full-toned and hard: "You'll die, Fletcher Young. You won't live a day in this country."

And with that she wheeled her bay about and rode down the trail, with never a look behind her. Clay watched her for a few seconds, then turned to Weld, saying tonelessly: "She's strange company for you to be keeping, friend Bede."

"I rod her old man's outfit, Clay. Why in hell did you have to turn up?"

Clay Whitehead had been thinking, remembering the sort of man this was. So now he said easily: "I hear they're paying fighting wages to a lot of men down here. It's a nice set-up for a gambler. I aim to leave this country with my share of their pay."

Bede Weld's glance narrowed in a shrewd look. "Cards? That's penny-ante stuff around here, Clay. Are you open for anything else?"

"Anything with money in it."

Weld was looking on down the trail, all at once impatient to be gone. "She'll wonder what I had to say to you," he said. "Throw my cutter into the bushes off there, so it'll look right. If you're after money, big money, meet me at the Lone Star in town tonight. And be careful, brother. Any man that don't button up his shirt right around here these days gets a dose of slug poison."

He reined his gelding around Clay, lifted a hand in a parting gesture, and started after the girl.

For three long minutes Clay Whitehead stood there, watching the two until they topped the crest of a knoll a half mile ahead. Bede Weld was keeping strange company; and he was doing strange work for a man whose likes ran to liquor and night riding and easy living. His presence here gave an ominous touch to what lay ahead, and Clay suddenly realized that Antelope range must be exactly the sort of country he had expected to find it. Four bullets had been thrown his way a little over an hour ago. And now one more, this time by a girl.

He didn't throw Bede Weld's weapon into the brush, for he was remembering an old gambling debt Weld had never paid. The gun was new, the action easy and feather-triggered, and he found it to his liking. So he rolled it in his slicker tied to the cantle, and rode on.

It was nearly dark before he picked up the lights of the town a mile or two ahead. Antelope was backed by a steep hill, so that only one side of its single street gave onto open country. Even under the veiling curtain of dusk its buildings looked gaunt and ugly. Squat adobes fringed the limits of the street. Farther on were pine-boarded stores, some with false fronts hiding unsightly tin roofs.

No tree showed along the length of the street, and the yards back of the plank walks were bare of grass and littered with rubbish. Here was the home of a people without pride, Clay decided.

He picked out the garish, badly lettered sign of the *Lone Star, Eats and Drinks*, and decided to go there for his evening meal and to see what was on Bede Weld's mind. Beyond it, he made out a hump-roofed barn and pulled in directly before its wide-open double doors to find it the livery stable.

A lame, bearded oldster holding a lighted lantern appeared in the doorway. He had nothing to say, and let Clay lead the gelding inside to a stall, and followed on back with a broken, choppy stride.

"Grain him," Clay said.

"Hell, I know how to feed a jughead. You get on out and let me be."

Clay said: "Have you been feeding on a diet of barb-wire, granddad?"

"Get on out, I tell you!" the oldster growled. "And tell Will Jay I ain't puttin' up any more horses for his sidewinders."

Hearing that name for the second time today, Clay put down his quick anger. "Who's Will Jay?"

"A hog that never tasted swill out of a trough. Now leave me be."

Clay went out the front, knowing that to question the oldster further was like trying to ride a barefoot pony across a *malpais* bed. This was a country of hair-trigger tempers, and Clay was learning.

Halfway along the awning-covered walk to the Lone Star, a man stepped out of the shadows of a store's darkened doorway and queried: "Got a light, stranger?"

With his left hand, Clay reached for a match and flicked it alight. His move was timed to a deceptive quickness, for by the dim light coming from a window across the street he had seen that this man was tall and gaunt-faced and that he wore a soiled, gray Stetson. The man stepped alongside, not in front, for his light, as he should have; he leaned forward a little awkwardly, and put a cigarette in his mouth, reaching for the flame Clay held. The awkward pose, and instant recognition of the man who had fired the four shots at him earlier that day, made Clay instinctively smother the flame and draw back.

On the heel of his move, the brittle, sharp crack of a rifle slapped out from a narrow passageway between two buildings across the street. Clay, halfway turned to face the sound, saw the lancing red wink of gun flame as the bullet crashed through the store window behind within inches of his shoulder. As the clatter of broken glass sounded up from the walk at his feet, he whirled and stabbed a hand at his six-gun. His left hand reached out and took a hold on the tall man's holster aimed arm. Then, with all the weight of his body, he pulled the tall man in front of him and swung up his gun.

"Move, and I'll let you have it," Clay breathed. He thrust out his gun and thumbed three quick shots into the alleyway across the street. Meeting the hollow blast of his gun, the rifle spoke again. And with it he felt the tall man's body shudder convulsively and go limp. The killer's bullet had cut down his partner.

Clay had shot without a target before, but now, a split second after the orange light cut the darkness across there, he threw one more shot. As the gun sound shuttled away down the street's corridor, a piercing, high-pitched scream rode with it.

Clay let go the tall man's arm and watched the killer's body slump to the walk. Then, from out of the Lone Star's swing doors, ran a half dozen men. They looked down the street, saw Clay, and stayed where they were, cowed by the gun in his hand.

Behind him, Clay heard a step on the walk. Before he could turn a harsh voice called: "Drop that iron, stranger! I've got a line on the seat of your pants."

Clay let his six-gun fall to the walk, and only then turned to face the speaker. He couldn't see well into the shadows, but an object on this newcomer's shirt front caught and reflected the lamp glow from the window across the street. And, as the man stepped up closer to him, Clay saw that he wore a sheriff's star—and that he held a six-gun in his fist.

"You're under arrest for murder," the sheriff stated.

The watchers in front of the Lone Star, hearing this, came down the walk in a close-knit group. The sheriff stared on past Clay and said softly: "Get on down to the jail, and make it fast, stranger."

Clay sized up the man—beady blue eyes, corn-silk mustache, a weak, receding chin—and decided he didn't like him. So he didn't move off down the walk as the sheriff directed.

A moment later, Clay turned and faced the group from the Lone Star. Their leader, a short, stocky-framed man wearing a full black beard, looked down at the dead man on the walk and said: "So friend Len got his, eh? Won't Bede Weld love this. Nice work, stranger. I'm Will Jay."

"This man's under arrest, Jay," the sheriff said in a whining voice. "You stay out of it."

Will Jay looked across at the lawman, his brown eyes mirroring a mild disgust. "Put that gun down before you shoot yourself in the foot with it, Moore," he said disrespectfully. And strangely enough, the sheriff dropped his gun into the holster at his thigh. Then Jay went on: "He's not under arrest. Len tried to take him from behind, and some jasper across the street took him from the front. Marsh, go across and see what's in that alley."

A man stepped out from behind Jay and crossed

the street, and Jay said: "It'll be another of Weld's crew. They're the only bushwhackers on this range. Sheriff, get back to your office and polish up that star you're wearing. When you want this stranger . . . when you work up the guts to come get him . . . you'll find him out at my place. He's working for me."

Moore started to say something, but decided he'd said enough. He turned meekly and walked down the street.

From across the street Jay's man called: "It's Hap Small, Will! He's got throat trouble. Looks like he swallowed a bullet."

Will Jay muttered: "This may be a hell of a night." He stopped and picked Clay's gun off the walk and handed it to him, saying: "You've got till sunup to get out of the country, stranger."

Clay Whitehead knew a man when he saw one, and Will Jay fitted the bill. In speaking to the sheriff a moment ago Jay had shown no trace of arrogance; he had known what he wanted and come directly to the point. And his word had carried with the lawman. Clay felt that Jay, alone—without his men to back him—could have accomplished the same thing.

Clay said: "I thought you offered me a job."

Will Jay shook his head. "I offered you a chance to live a while longer. Maybe I ought to have shot you. What you've done tonight does me about as much good as a drink would a drowning man. They'll say I hired you to kill those two."

"Who's they?"

"Bede Weld . . . and his boss, old Bert Ulmann."

"This Ulmann . . . has he got a daughter?"

Jay nodded. "Mary Ulmann."

"And why are they so anxious to hang a killing like this onto you?"

Will Jay sighed, his impatience obvious. "That's too long a story to go into now. If you're ready to leave, stranger, we'll see that you get out of town safely. From there on, you're on your own."

"Someone tried to cut down on me today because they thought I was riding in to hire out to you."

Jay frowned: "So they believed what Weld's saying . . . that I'm hiring guns. Who was it?"

"Mary Ulmann."

For a long moment Will Jay's considering frown held. Then he said: "You've got something on your chest."

"Send these others away."

Jay jerked his head and his men walked away, toward the Lone Star, two of them carrying the dead man. Another pair crossed the street for the man in the alley.

Abruptly Clay Whitehead decided to trust this

man. "I've known Bede Weld for years. He's forked. He was with this Ulmann girl today when she had her try at me. Afterward I had a talk with him. He made me an offer of some easy money . . . said he'd tell me what it was here in the saloon tonight. I'd starve before I let that man put me in the way of picking up a lead nickel."

When Clay hesitated, Will Jay put in: "Weld's easy money isn't news, stranger. What do you want of me?"

"The story of what ails this country. Today, riding in, three men branding a steer Circle J were interested enough in me to throw a little lead my way. The gent that spilled his blood all over the walk here was one of the three."

Will Jay stiffened, and breathed: "Say that again."

"You heard it right."

"Len and Hap were branding a steer Circle J?"

Clay nodded, and waited.

Jay half turned and took one impulsive step after his men along the walk. But something stopped him. He glanced appraisingly, directly at Clay for a long moment, and finally said: "It's signing a death certificate for me to trust a man these days. But if you're of a mind to stay in this country, ride out to see me in the morning. Maybe I can let you have that job. My outfit's the Circle J . . . and my men haven't touched a match to a branding fire for the past four months."

He went down the walk, his stride short and firm. Clay watched him as he stopped at the doors of the Lone Stay and called in: "We're on the way home, gents! Weld's on his way in."

Three minutes later eight riders trotted past the place where Clay was standing. Will Jay, leading them, lifted a hand in a parting salute.

One or two things were clearer now. Mary Ulmann had accused Clay of riding in to hire out to Will Jay only because of the story Bede Weld was circulating. And the three riders who had been branding a steer with the Circle J weren't Will Jay's riders, but Weld's. And Bede Weld's riders had tried to kill the man who had seen them branding that steer. What this all added up to, Clay couldn't even guess. But he remembered Bede Weld's invitation to meet him tonight at the Lone Star, so he made his way to the saloon. Weld wouldn't come yet—not so long as Jay's crew had been here.

Clay had caught three men at the branding fire that afternoon. Two of them were dead. The third, Fred Burns, had been stationed on the roof of a store across the street from Clay during the shooting. Burns had a rifle, and would have used it, but luck played against him, for the walk awning opposite hid Clay from view and he didn't once see his target. When Will Jay and the sheriff and the others gathered about Clay, Burns climbed onto a woodshed off the back of the roof, went to the alley mouth, and softly called—"Hap!"—and got no answer.

Two minutes later he rode a bay horse at a walk down the alley. At length, out of hearing of the main part of town, he spurred the bay into a stretching run. An hour and a quarter later he stepped into Bede Weld's office in the ranch house, breathing hard.

Bede Weld was sitting in a chair with his boots resting on his untidy roll-top desk. He was alone.

Burns said flatly: "He's got 'em both . . . cold. And he's seen Will Jay."

Weld's boots crashed onto the floor and he leaned forward, gripping the arms of his chair. "Both? You mean Len and Hap?"

Burns nodded, his hard face a little pale. "We did like you said, waited for him as he came from the stable. Len stopped him and asked for a light. He caught on, some way, and pulled Len in front of him as Hap shot. He went for his iron and let Hap have it and cut him down. I think one of Hap's slugs caught Len. Anyway, I didn't see much and didn't have a chance. This Whitehead stepped back under the awning."

Weld came to his feet and cursed harshly, tonelessly, with a viciousness that left Burns a little awe-struck. At length, Weld paused long enough to ask: "Did you go to see Moore like I told you?"

"We didn't have the time. This all happened too quick."

Again that string of oaths, only this time Bede Weld took it out on Burns. "I put out a thousand a month on you fake hardcases. I put three of you on a job any one-armed kid could handle. Burns, I ought to beat your brains out with a plow handle."

He was forgetting himself. For now Burns's watery-blue eyes took on a cold light and he slapped his holster with the flat of his palm, breathing: "Try it any time you like, brother."

Weld caught himself, mumbled a gruff apology, and took his Stetson down from a peg on the wall above his desk, and said: "Maybe it would pay us to play along with this Whitehead. I'll ride in and have a talk with him. You take the crew on over to Lonesome Creek and take care of that job on the water hole. And I want it done right. Use a full case of dynamite and open the floodgate. Be back here and in the bunkhouse before sunup."

When Burns was gone, Bede Weld stood for a moment considering what had happened, and what he was to do now. He had a thought that made him go back to his desk and open up a bottom drawer and take out a short-barreled Derringer. He broke it open, tilted out the two shotgun shells, and reloaded it with fresh ones. Then he pushed the weapon down into his boot, blew out his lamp, and left the office.

Two hours later he was entering Moore's office at the front of the single-cell jail.

The lawman wheeled around nervously in his chair at Bede Weld's entrance. Seeing who it was, his face took on a serious frown, and he said with a show of officiousness: "You've got a lot of explaining to do to me, Bede."

In any other circumstances, and to any other man, Weld would have acted differently. But he was playing out a strong hand here, and one of his best cards had so far been the law's backing, so now he said with a show of meekness: "I came as soon as I heard, Moore. I reckon I hired a couple of bad ones."

"And you put me in a hole with Will Jay. I aimed to arrest that stranger, but Jay had his whole crew with him. What could a man do?"

"Lay off the stranger. It was a plain try at a bushwhack. Len and Hap deserved what they got. When a man has to pick a crew of strays, he never knows what'll happen."

Moore was a little surprised. He had expected Bede Weld to come to the defense of his two men. Instead, this ready willingness to assume the blame was baffling. Moore was a weak man in a tight spot; with a range war on his hands it was hard to take an unprejudiced attitude. He didn't like Bede Weld, but he didn't hate him the way he hated Will Jay's calm defiance of all authority. In choosing between the two, he took what he thought was the lesser of two evils, the stronger side, for Bede Weld represented Bert Ulmann and the Flying U had been a power in this country for many years.

"Bede, what's this all comin' to?" Moore queried earnestly. "Jay and his crew were in town tonight, lookin' for trouble. They backed this stranger's play, I reckon, because it was against you. Sooner or later this mess will puff up and bust."

"It's busted already," Weld said. "This afternoon one of my riders, Burns, cut across that north strip of Jay's up in the hills. He spotted a steer with a fresh burn on his hide . . . a Circle J with the old Flyin' U scars still showin'. I want you to ride up there tomorrow and have a look. There may be more."

The lawman straightened in his chair. "Then we've got the proof at last?"

"It's there. Go find it."

"But, hell, Bede, Jay would run me off the place."

"Then take a big enough posse to back your word. Take my whole crew if you want."

Moore considered this, finally said: "Your crew is the only bunch that would ride up there with me. Will Ulmann back our play?"

"He'll back anything I say."

"Then bring in every man you can spare early in the mornin'," Moore said in sudden decision. "I'll make Will Jay take this and like it."

Weld shrugged his narrow shoulders. "You're responsible, I'm not. If Jay carries a chip on his shoulder, one of my men may try to knock it off. There may be powder burned, and I don't aim to take the blame."

Moore tapped his chest with a forefinger. "I'm the law. Tomorrow your crew will have the law behind it. Jay has over-bet his hand, and anything that happens is on his head. That's final."

It was final, too, in Moore's mind. Weld stayed only a minute longer, long enough to drive home his point that he was a tolerant man put on the defensive. When he had done that, he left, crossing the street and walking up to the Lone Star.

Clay Whitehead was standing at the front end of the bar, leaning back against the front wall. It was the attitude of a wary man, and Weld, remembering Clay's Tombstone days, didn't underestimate the job he was taking on.

He walked straight over to Clay and said: "I just heard about it. Thanks for helpin' me get rid of a couple of sidewinders."

Clay smiled, and drawled easily: "And here I thought you'd framed that reception, Bede."

Weld's face took on an injured look. He shook his head. "I need your help, Clay. Why would I sick a couple of dogs like that onto you?"

"Maybe because I caught 'em working Jay's brand onto one of your steers."

Bede Weld chuckled, let a shrewd look take possession of his thin features, and then said softly: "We'll go upstairs where we can make medicine in private, friend. There's plenty to tell you." He stepped off down the bar, and told the apron behind it: "Send a bottle and some glasses up to Number Three, Harry. You don't know we're up there." He motioned Clay to follow, and led the way back to the stairs and up to a hallway on the second floor. He opened a door to one of the rooms, lit a lamp on the table in the center of the room, and pushed back a chair for Clay.

Neither of them spoke until the waiter had brought the glasses and left. Then Bede Weld poured whiskey into the two glasses, raised one in a toast, and said: "Here's to the new half owner of Antelope range." He drained his glass at a gulp.

Clay hadn't touched the liquor. He didn't say anything, but sat there, waiting.

Bede leaned forward onto the table. "That's puttin' it straight. It's gospel truth, friend. When we're through here, we'll have title to every damn' section of this country."

"How?"

"Through Bert Ulmann. He's kingpin in this country, and he thinks I got a pair of wings growin' between my shoulders. It's taken me two years to put the idea across, but right now he treats me like a son. I worked for it, Clay."

"All right, you've got Ulmann. How about these others? Jay, for instance."

Weld laughed mirthlessly, and palmed up his hands. "It was easy. Jay's a small rancher. Years ago he and a few others crowded Bert Ulmann off free range and got title to land Ulmann had been usin'. The old man's never forgotten that. Last year, when he began to lose a few critters, he blamed it on Jay. But he wasn't in shape to force his hand. He's a sick man, in bed more than he's on his feet. Two years ago, takin' a trail herd north, he caught a cold that damned near killed him. It left his lungs weak. Right now he's coughin' blood every day. If he lasts a month, I miss my guess."

"And when he cashes in, the girl gets title to the outfit."

"She hates it . . . hates this war that will last as long as I want it to. She'll sell the minute the old man dies. And I'll be the only buyer. No one else would take over that outfit's troubles."

"You haven't said how you'd lick Jay and his crowd. I met him tonight. He's salty."

"I've made him an outlaw. I've got the story around that he's hirin' outlaws to ride for him. That's what the girl meant this afternoon, thinkin' you were Fletcher Young. He's an outlaw, but he's never heard of Will Jay. Today those three riders of mine changed the brands on a dozen of Jay's critters. Tomorrow I take the sheriff up there to see for himself. And he's takin' my crew along as a posse."

"Jay will fight."

"So will we. I've got money to hire a hundred guns . . . Ulmann's money. Jay hasn't."

The plan would work, and Clay admitted grudgingly that Bede Weld was a man who could force it through. A month ago, a week ago, he would have sided Weld in a proposition like this. But during these past six days he had done some thinking; Bill Marsden had steered that thinking, and it was too strongly rooted to be torn up by the old ways. Thinking of the thing that had brought him here, Clay said: "I heard up in Clovis that a U.S. marshal stopped some lead down here a week or two ago. That was a mistake."

The Flying U ramrod's glance went abruptly unreadable. "Will Jay shot that man."

Weld had played his hand a little too strongly—for the inscrutable expression that masked his features was taken on too quickly. He had the manner of a man on the defensive. Seeing that, half understanding the reason for it, a cold nerveless tension rode through Clay as he drawled: "You've lost your touch, brother. Will Jay wasn't within ten miles of that lawman when he was cut down."

A slow flush mounted up across Bede Weld's countenance. Suddenly he snarled: "How do you know all this?"

It was an admission, as plain as a written confession. Clay knew that his hunt was ended, that here sat Roy Baker's murderer. Bede Weld was the man he would take back with him, dead or alive. This other, the range war, would soon be over once Weld was out of the country. Clay came up out of his chair, his hard glance fixed menacingly on the man before him. "Weld, you're under arrest. A week ago Bill Marsden hired me to wear Roy Baker's badge." As Clay spoke, he reached down and palmed up the weapon at his thigh.

Bede Weld didn't move as Clay stepped over and took his two guns from him. But the color slowly left his face until it was a sickly yellow shade. Finally he summoned words, protesting: "You can't do this to me, Clay."

"Can't I? We leave here tonight. By sunup we'll be across the hills, out of the country."

"But you're a gambler. This is your chance to clean up twice as big a stake as you can ever spend."

"We leave tonight, friend Bede. It'll be your last ride."

Weld's hands were shaking; beads of perspiration stood out on his forehead. He reached up to his vest pocket and took out tobacco and papers, muttering: "Let me have a smoke."

Clay was a little contemptuous of the man's weakness. Bede Weld was unarmed, helpless-looking now, so Clay dropped his weapon in his holster and took the chair across the table from his prisoner, watching while Weld spilled tobacco onto his lap but finally shaped a cigarette.

Weld took out a match and reached down openly to scratch it on the heel of his boot. Suddenly he straightened out of his chair and kicked it out of his way, and his hand arched up and settled into line with Clay's chest. In his blunt fist was the Derringer he had so carefully tucked into his boot two hours ago. Clay went rigid, and stayed that way, his hands on the table.

The cigarette drooped from Weld's down-curving mouth as he rasped: "You should have stayed with your old game, friend. You'd have lived longer."

Clay wasn't watching for his chance; he was wondering how much talking Weld would do before he pulled the Derringer's trigger, blaming the luck that had made him careless.

Weld said: "There's a back stairway out o' here. This time they won't know what happened to their deputy. I know a nice cutbank I can cave in over you."

He made a slow circle of the room that put him behind Clay. Then he gingerly reached out and got the three six-guns—the two of his own and Clay's. Going to the door, he pulled it open and said softly: "You first, tin star."

As Clay went out the door, Weld stepped back

out of reach. Once in the hall he was close behind. He followed Clay through the door that let out onto an open stairway at the rear of the building, then down the steps. In the alley behind, he said: "We'll walk across to the jail and get my horse. Then we'll get into the livery barn the back way and get yours."

It happened that way. Weld was two steps behind all the way across to the hitch rail in front of the jail. After that he was in the saddle, keeping his horse along the walk, less than ten feet away.

The livery barn doors were closed, padlocked. They went around to the back and found the door to the corral open, with a lantern hanging on a nail for the convenience of late customers. Bede Weld leaned against the end of the stall, his gun in his hand, while Clay saddled by the light of the lantern.

Out front once more, Clay leading, Bede Weld said: "I've got a better idea. We'll take the north trail." Then, five minutes later when they had left the last adobe of the town behind, he added the information: "Tonight Will Jay's crew is dynamitin' one of our water holes. He don't know it yet, because my bunch is up there doin' the job, but that's what I've framed for him. Friend Clay, tomorrow the sheriff will find your carcass soaking in the mud of the pond alongside the windmill up there. How does it sound?"

"Like something you'd think up," Clay drawled.

He was remembering the six-gun of Weld's he had rolled in his slicker that afternoon, knowing that somewhere out along this trail he'd find his chance to use it. Weld would take his time about this, for the man's bullying attitude meant that he'd taunt Clay with words and watch him squirm for as long as he dared.

So, two miles farther on, Weld still bringing up the rear, Clay turned in the saddle and said gruffly: "I don't like your weather down here. It's cold."

He reached back and unlaced the slicker from the cantle as Weld answered: "It's goin' to be colder layin' in that muck out at the pond."

Clay moved carefully, a coolness running along his nerves that was blended with a suppressed excitement he could hardly control. The slicker came free, and Clay swung it around. But suddenly the weight of the gun sagged one end of the roll, and before Clay could reach out and catch it, the weapon had slid out the loose end of the slicker and fallen to the trail.

Clay glanced quickly back at Bede Weld. The killer had stiffened in his saddle, not noticing the fallen gun but held in an attitude of tense attention. He snarled—"Hold on!"—and reined in on his pony and raised his Colt and lined it at Clay.

Here the trail skirted a thin line of leafless trees and a thick growth of brush. Off to the left and above both men heard the snapping of a branch, then the slurring sound of sifting gravel.

All at once a voice rang out close at hand: "Drop that iron, Weld!"

It was Will Jay who had spoken. Clay recognized the voice a fraction of a second after Weld. He saw Weld rock back the hammer of the Colt and read his intent. He kicked loose his right stirrup and hunched over his body and threw himself out of the saddle as Bede Weld's thundering shot smote across the sudden stillness. Falling toward the gun he had dropped, Clay felt a searing pain crease the point of his right shoulder muscle. He lit hard, kneeling in the trail, his reaching hand closing about the butt of the .45. He swung it up to line it at the place where Bede Weld had been a moment ago. But Weld was no longer there. Two guns crashed out above him from the edge of the trees. Weld's wheeling pony made a sudden lunge, stung by a bullet. There was a sudden thunder of hoofs, three more shots, and Weld was out of sight in the darkness.

Will Jay called out—"Let him go!"—and came striding out through the tangle of brush not ten feet from where Clay stood.

While the others, four of them, gathered about the pair, Will Jay and Clay stood there, regarding each other. Finally Clay let the breath sigh out of his lungs in a thankful relief, and drawled: "You've got the habit of turning up at the right time, Jay."

"He had a gun on you. What did it mean?"

Clay couldn't help but catch the suspicion in the man's glance, so he told his story, all of it, even admitting who he was. When he had finished, a measure of that suspicion had gone from Will Jay's hard glance. But this man had been through too much lately, and had learned to trust no one. As Clay finished his story and waited, Jay growled: "Let's have a look at your badge."

Clay reached down and pulled off his boot, and took out his clasp knife and pried off the heel. When the badge lay in the palm of his hand and Jay saw it, the black-bearded man seemed to relax. He even smiled thinly as he said: "These are bad times. A man has to be careful." He paused briefly, considering something else. At length he explained: "One of my riders found that fresh-branded steer this afternoon. He met us as we were riding out to the layout. So we swung off here to the west, thinking we'd keep our eye on this trail and maybe find out what Weld was up to."

"Now that you know, what's the play?"

Will Jay was still skeptical, for he queried: "Then you're with us?"

"I'm after Weld for that murder. Siding you is the best way I know to get him."

For once Will Jay seemed to lack that initiative that had made him a leader. For now he said, a little helplessly: "I've got the proof I've wanted. But damned if I know how to use it. What's our move?"

Clay suddenly realized that Jay and these others, now knowing who he was, were instinctively turning to him for help. Bill Marsden had said to stay clear of the Antelope range war, but he was already involved in it, and nothing he could do would change things.

"I'd ride straight for Ulmann's place," he said, working his first impulsive thought. "From what Weld said, his crew is busy dynamiting one of their own water holes, framing you for it. While they're busy, we ought to get Ulmann and that girl off the place. When they're safe, we can smoke out Weld and his bunch."

Jay shook his head. "We'd be outlawed." He swept his arm out in a gesture that included his four companions. "We have our lives to live in this country. So far no man among us has fired a bullet in this fight. Every man here owns his own outfit. To come out in the open, with guns, would wipe away everything we've taken years to build. It's the wrong way, Whitehead."

"You're outlawed anyway. The sheriff's in with Weld. And he won't take your word that Weld is forked."

"That may be right," Jay admitted. "Ulmann still

backs his foreman, and Ulmann's word is better than any man's in this country."

"Then let's tell Ulmann our story."

Studying Jay, Clay could see the workings of the man's mind. These small ranchers had their backs to the wall; they faced losing everything they had spent their lives creating, and open war was something they would use only as a last resort. One of them voiced the opinion of the rest: "Why not ride to town and have our talk with the sheriff? If any of Weld's crew is at the layout, we're liable to bust things wide open."

Jay turned and spoke harshly to the man: "Moore wouldn't throw in with us even if he knew we were right. He's got the guts of a coyote. Ulmann elected him to office and he'll back him for the votes he swings. We see Ulmann, not Moore."

"Not me, Will," the man answered stubbornly. "I've got two kids to raise. I don't reckon I could do it with a bullet through my guts."

Opposition seemed to strengthen Will Jay's decision. This thing had been long in building and now Jay's even temper frayed and he spoke bitingly: "Any man who waits longer is a fool. I'm riding for Ulmann's."

He turned and climbed the slope and reappeared a quarter minute later leading a black gelding. No man moved to follow him—no one but Clay, who holstered the gun in his hand and swung up to the saddle.

A hundred yards farther on the trail, Will Jay pulled in to let Clay come alongside. "You can't blame 'em," he said as though he felt an apology was necessary. "I have to fight. They don't. Weld has aimed this whole thing at me."

They covered the remaining four miles in silence. Only when the lights of the Circle U pinpointed the floor of a valley below them did Clay speak: "What's down there? Where's the house?"

"To the left. The bunkhouse is dark. Maybe we're in luck."

Neither had a plan in his mind, knowing that circumstances would shape what they were to do. So they rode straight into the yard, clear to the hitch rail in front of the house, before a challenge stopped them.

"Speak up! Who is it?"

Clay recognized that voice as Mary Ulmann's. He could see her now, her shape outlined against the piled logs of the house's near wing.

"It's Will Jay, Mary. We're here to see your father."

"Who's with you?" The girl's tone was hard, uncompromising, and suspicious.

"A U.S. deputy marshal . . . the man Bede Weld told you was Fletcher Young. Fletcher Young isn't within two hundred miles of here," Jay said. "And he won't be. Maybe I can explain that."

"What do you want of Father? How do I know you're telling the truth about this man?"

In answer, Clay reached into his pocket and took out his marshal's badge and tossed it across so that it fell at the girl's feet. He said: "I want to ask your father a few questions about Bede Weld."

There was a long, five second silence, until finally the girl said: "Lift out your guns and drop them and then walk in ahead of me. I didn't believe I'd ever see the day when you'd walk into this house again, Will Jay."

Each man unbuckled his shell belt and dropped it into the grass alongside his horse. Jay was the first down, striding toward the door at the wing's end. Clay followed, knowing that the girl had the rifle centered at his back.

They entered a long, low room with massive hand-hewn beams lining the ceiling. It was comfortably furnished—Navajo rugs, a solid oak table with twin benches running along two sides, rawhide chairs, and at one end squatted a broad stone fireplace with a four-foot length of pine blazing on the hearth.

Sitting obliquely toward the fireplace was a wide, comfortable leather couch, and lying on it was the blanket-wrapped figure of a man who raised his head at their entrance. This was Bert Ulmann, white-haired and white-mustached, with a rugged powerful face gaunted by his sickness. His eyes were the same shade of green as Clay remembered the daughter's, and at sight of Will

Jay those eyes blazed with a wrathful, surprised light.

Ulmann cleared his throat harshly and said: "You're more of a fool than I thought, Jay. Do you think you'll live to ride out of here?"

Clay heard the door close behind him, then Mary Ulmann's voice spoke out: "He'll ride away alive, Father . . . after he's told us what he came to say."

A little of the stubbornness went from the old man's glance. It was plain that the girl's word carried with him. "There's nothing you have to say to me, Will Jay."

"Not me," Jay said. "I brought another to do my talking. This is Clay Whitehead, U.S. deputy marshal."

It was a signal for Clay to speak, and he did. For the second time that night he told his story, the story of Bede Weld, of Weld's days in Tombstone, and of what he planned to do on Antelope range.

When Clay had finished, Ulmann was quick to say: "For a man who's traded a pack of cards for a badge, you're quick to turn against your breed. How do I know this is true?"

As if in answer to his question, a distant, muffled thud jarred the foundation of the building. Seconds later came the sound of a far-off explosion, low-noted, ominous.

"That proves part of it," Clay said.

Hardly had he spoken before a window alongside the fireplace, at the back of the house, splintered in a shower of broken glass. Through the jagged opening rode the crack of a rifle shot. Clay moved quickly, stepping across to the table and turning down the lamp and blowing it out. As he moved, he said: "That'll be Weld and part of the crew. He spotted our horses. I reckon he knows what I've told you."

Bert Ulmann had pushed himself up on one elbow. Clay saw him glance toward the door. The next instant the rancher was shouting: "Mary, come back here!" But on the heel of his words the door slammed shut.

Mary Ulmann came in through the door as the second shot from outside whipped into the fire-lighted room, striking obliquely at the table top and burying itself in the opposite wall. She leaned back against the door, a little breathless, holding Clay's and Will Jay's gun belts. Abruptly she held them out in front of her.

"Take them," she said hurriedly. "You'll find rifles in the rack in the next room."

Will Jay was already moving, not toward his gun, but through the door at the far end of the room. As Clay was strapping his belt about his thighs, Jay reappeared carrying three Winchesters and four unopened boxes of .30-30 shells.

Outside, a brittle burst of fire cut loose, and behind Clay the second window shattered, the breeze whipping the drawn blind. But he wasn't noticing this. He was looking at Mary Ulmann, seeing the hard pride ride out of her as she realized the significance of things that had happened the past few months. She was beautiful as she stood there, the blaze from the fireplace striking glinting lights through her tawny hair. She looked at Clay with an unspoken apology mirrored from the depths of her eyes. Then she said simply: "We'll have to move Father."

Together, they pushed the couch away from the light and deep into one corner. Ulmann, in his helplessness, glanced down at Clay and said: "Man, I take back what I said a minute ago. If you can bring me Bede Weld's carcass, I'll feed it to the dogs."

Will Jay was kneeling at one darkened window. Suddenly he whipped his rifle to his shoulder and levered two shots out into the darkness. He got an answer in a piercing distant scream. One of Weld's crew had stopped Jay's lead.

His shots brought a hail of lead pouring in through the windows. Jay was at the back, so Clay took his station at the front, lifting a rifle off the table. First he tried the window, but two rifles from the slope above were pouring a regular, vicious fire through it. Clay moved to the door, released the catch, bellied down on the floor, and then inched open the panel.

Through that two-inch slit he could see a narrow arc of the slope that swept up to the valley rim a hundred yards away. He watched carefully, and three times saw a gun flash wink out from the same location. He thrust his rifle through the opening, lined his sights at the spot where he had seen those flashes, and waited for the next. When it came, he squeezed the trigger.

Against the dark shadow of the slope, he saw a cobalt shadow that was a man's high frame rise up suddenly, stagger a few halting steps, and then fall. His bullet had found its mark.

But, a second later, a whining slug whipped into the sill perilously close to Clay's head. He rolled aside as the marksman on the hill sent in another bullet. Picking up his rifle, he went to the window. When the man out there threw his third shot, Clay's rifle spoke once more. This time he didn't wait to see the effect of his bullet, for he felt a touch on his arm and turned to see Mary Ulmann crouching behind him.

"They'll try the back," she breathed. "Someone ought to be out there."

Clay was on the move before she finished speaking. He had forgotten the look of the house, and only now remembered that this room with its one blank, solid wall faced only three sides. He went to the door Will Jay had used a minute ago, and, as he stepped through into the narrow hallway behind, he turned and saw that the girl was at the window, a rifle held to her shoulder.

He heard old Bert Ulmann say—"Get away

from there, girl!"—as he went down the darkened hall. He came to a door at the end, felt the panel of a door, and reached down and turned the knob and thrust the door open.

Directly opposite the opened panel he made out the dim outline of a window—and framed by the window was a crouching figure of a man crawling through. Clay dropped the rifle and palmed up his Colt in a staccato blast of gun thunder. Above the last echo of those shots he heard a stifled moan, then a thud, as the shape at the window fell backward in a loose sprawl that comes with death.

Clay picked up the rifle and stepped out of line and started for the window. Before he reached it, the darkness outside was swept away before a bursting orange light. Flames suddenly licked above the level of the sill, and Clay, stepping to the opening, had a fleeting glimpse of two figures running across the yard and into the shadows beyond. He swung up the rifle and levered two quick shots at one disappearing form and saw the man stumble and fall headlong and lie still.

Glancing around, he saw that he was in the kitchen of the house. He took one quick look outside and saw that kerosene-soaked straw had been piled waist-high against the logs. A puff of black smoke boiled into the room, and he choked and stepped back, wiping the tears from his eyes.

Remembering his last glimpse of the girl, Clay felt a sudden fear claw at his heart. What if a bullet made her its mark? He considered quickly, decided that the blaze at this end of the house would stop anyone outside from entering. But there were the rooms along the hall.

Clay left the kitchen, taking the key from the lock and closing the door and locking it. He reached for a match, wiped it alight along his Levi's, and in its quick flare he saw that two other side doors opened into the passageway. He opened one of them, and by the light of the blaze outside saw that it was a bedroom.

A cabin of logs burns slowly. When Bede Weld, who was surely one of those outside, found that the only answering fire was from the house's main room, his first thought would be to enter the window of one of these side rooms. So now Clay pushed a massive, heavy oak bureau out into the hall and closed the door and wedged the piece of furniture against it. The room opposite was another bedroom. This time he picked a wash-stand and barricaded the hall side of the door with it, turning the key in the lock.

When he stepped back into the front room, he first heard Will Jay's savage cursing. He looked across at the back window and found Jay sitting alongside it, clumsily bandaging a blood-smeared shoulder. Mary Ulmann was still at the front window, crouching down so that she looked out from a lower corner.

Clay took the time to overturn the big table and

barricade the door. Then he went over to her, took the rifle from her hands, saying quietly: "Get over and help Will. He's hurt."

As she left, she gave him a brave smile that did something to his insides he had never before experienced. In another two seconds he had forgotten it, his glance inspecting the hill slope, now lighted by the blaze at the back of the house. The firing out there had slacked off.

Abruptly a voice shuttled out from the hillside: "Walk out without your guns and we'll let you go!"

Clay thought it was Weld who had spoken but couldn't be sure. A moment later he saw a vague, hurrying shadow making its way along the slope. He let it drop into his rear sight and felt the buck of the rifle against his shoulder as that figure abruptly melted from view. That shot was their answer, and immediately guns out there set up a hell chant that whipped the air inside the room with winging lead. Powder smoke filled the air in a stifling cloud. Clay looked across, at Will Jay, saw that he was crouched alongside his window once more, Mary beside him feeding shells into the magazine of a spare rifle. Clay took this time to reload his own, then crawled over to the door and opened it and looked out.

He was barely in time, for all at once shouts rang out and four riders streaked into view, bent low on the offside of their saddles. Bede Weld had decided to rush the house. Clay whipped up his Winchester and levered shot after shot at that oncoming quartet. One horse went down, and Clay threw a slug at the stumbling rider. Then the other three were in the yard, fanning out in a wide arc. Clay shot one rider from the saddle, swung his weapon around to line it at a second, but he was too late. The limits of the small arc he commanded through his opening soon hid the two remaining riders, and before Clay could get to the window they were safely out of sight, close in to the building's walls, out of range.

Clay waited, hearing Will Jay's rifle speak time and again. He heard Jay mumble a disappointed oath, and then the rifle fell silent and Jay called across: "One man made it to the house back here! Careful, now!"

For nearly half a minute the silence was awful. Suddenly, from beyond the room's hallway door came the sound of pounding. Then there was a crash of splintering wood, and from out in the hall a moment later beat out two blasts that whipped splinters from the panel of the door.

"They're in," Ulmann muttered from where he lay on the couch. "Mary, bring me a gun."

"We're all right, Dad," the girl protested. "We've got the door blocked from the inside."

"Bring me a gun, and come and sit with me," her father insisted. "It's two against a dozen. Our luck won't hold."

The shots from inside were a signal for those beyond the range of light outside. Once more the gun echoes filled the valley with a crescendo of welling thunder. Once more bullets whipped in through the windows. A man would be a fool to try to face that withering fire, and Clay, crouched down below the sill of the window, thought for a moment that Bede Weld had won. But another thought crowded out that first one, and with it he was crawling to the door. Just before he opened it, he looked across at Will Jay, and shouted to make himself heard above the din: "Watch the hall door, Will!" Then he was gone, running through the door and outside in a low crouch.

When the door slammed shut behind him, he was already twenty feet out across the yard. He ran in a weaving stride, expecting the bullets that would come. His move was a surprising one, and he was halfway across the lighted stretch of yard before someone saw him and cried and threw a shot his way. The bullet kicked up dust five feet behind him. He took a firm hold on the rifle and put every ounce of strength into his stride.

That five-second trip into the shadows beyond the circle of firelight seemed an eternity. All the rifles on the hill now picked him out as a target. A bullet brushed his Stetson from his head, another hit the edge of one boot sole and set up a numb-ness in his foot that nearly made him stumble. At last he was hidden in the darkness and slowed his pace, his lungs aching for air. It was then that the bullet caught him, fully in the left shoulder. It's impact made him lose his stride and stagger awkwardly, and the swinging arm set up a bone grating that sickened him.

To his right he saw a low-growing cedar, and ran toward it. Ten yards away, a man suddenly stepped out of the shelter of the tree and swiveled up a six-gun and fired. The bullet creased Clay's thigh, and, as he dodged to one side, he dropped the rifle and clawed at his gun. His swiftly thrown shot was timed exactly with the second from the killer's gun. Clay's bullet jerked the man off balance in a backward stagger and he fell, writhing in pain. He tried to swing his Colt around for another shot, but, before he had it lined, Clay's second bullet centered his chest.

From far off to his right a man shouted some unintelligible word to a companion. Another on the left answered. Clay climbed the slope, keeping to what cover there was—bush, cedar, piñon, and from the shelter of one he waited, listening. From out back, at the opposite side of this narrow valley, two guns were speaking once more. Slowly the three more on this hill slope took up their fire. Five guns were left, more to come, perhaps, when the riders who had blown up the water hole had had time to ride in. And there was at least one in the house.

Clay saw a wink of purple powder flame lance

out from a bush thirty yards to his left and below. He headed toward it, walking soundlessly, his six-gun in his fist. He was soon close enough to make out the figure of the man half hidden behind the bush. He was raising his six-gun, about to line it at the marksman, when suddenly a burst of shots cut loose inside the house.

Clay hesitated, and in that brief interval the man below turned and saw him. He straightened up, tall and stoop-shouldered, and Clay recognized Bede Weld.

Bede wheeled around. He had been clutching a rifle. Now he dropped it, his two hands streaking to the guns at his thighs.

Clay raised his weapon and said flatly: "Don't make me kill you, Bede."

Weld had plainly lost, and knew it, for his hands abruptly froze in their gesture, and then he slowly raised them.

Then, from far above and well into the distance sounded the hoof mutter of running horses. Weld jerked up his head, listened intently, and Clay thought the man's face took on a strained look. Clay was listening, too, feeling a nausea at what he knew was coming. These were more of Bede Weld's traitorous crew, and it threw the odds against Mary and her father and Will Jay far out of balance. Clay had his man. He could shoot him and escape before these others began their search. His job as marshal was finished. Yet he couldn't leave. Knowing that, he took two steps toward Weld and said: “Call off your dogs and I’ll take you in alive. And make it quick, Bede. Shuck out your hardware.”

Weld was acting strangely. Clay, closer now, could catch the half frantic look on the man’s twisted, gaunt face. Slowly Weld’s hands settled to his sides. He carefully took hold of the trigger guards of his guns and lifted them out. Then, holding one out toward Clay, he said lifelessly: “You win, lawman.”

Clay’s left arm was throbbing with pain. Each time he moved it he had to hold his breath to keep from crying out. Bede Weld must have seen the blood on Clay’s left shoulder and known that Clay would have to reach out with his right to take the guns. For, as Clay held out his right, his six-gun a little out of line as he reached for Weld’s weapon, Weld flipped his gun back into his palm and thumbed back the hammer. It was timed to a half-second motion. Clay jerked his arm back, but Weld’s shot broke the smoothness of that play of muscle. It drove Clay back in a broken stagger.

Clay fell, and Weld’s second bullet missed. As he hit the ground in a breathtaking jar, Clay let his thumb slip off the hammer of his .45. Its solid, whipping buck was too much for the weakness in his wrist to control, and it jumped out of his grasp and whirled into the dust alongside. Then, expecting to have his sense wiped out by Weld’s next bullet, Clay waited, a torture of pain burning like a white-hot iron in his chest.

That expected bullet never came. For Bede Weld's right hand fell limply to his side and he choked back a groan and his knees suddenly gave way. He fell stiffly, like an uprooted tree, so that the force of his fall carried him onto his back and left his arms spread-eagled at an inhuman angle.

Weld was dead. Clay knew that much. But crowding out his small thankfulness at this turn of luck was the earthly pound of running horses. Those riders couldn't be far away now. Locating the sound, Clay rolled over and raised his head and looked up the slope.

Four riders were streaking down the trail. Clay tried to reach out and get his .45 in his hand again, but he lacked the strength. So he lay there and watched the riders pour down off the slope in a smother of dust. They didn't stop, but made straight for the house.

Abruptly Clay realized that the two rifles across the valley were no longer firing. Then he heard a faint shout from across there and looked down at the cabin in time to see a man jump from the window of one of the side rooms and run across the yard. One of the riders pulled up and swung a rifle to his shoulder and fired one shot—and his bullet knocked the runner off his feet. Only then did Clay realize who these riders were—Will Jay's friends.

He tried to shout down to them, but his voice rose only above a whisper in a feeble moaning sound. He watched, saw the riders round the house, and ride up the far slope. There were shots up there. Once he heard a man scream. Then, from close at hand, came the sounds of a running pony cutting out along the trail. Bede Weld's only remaining gun partner was hitting a hitch lonesome out of the country.

Later, when Clay was trying to keep his eyes in focus and not lose control of his senses, they found him. Mary Ulmann and Will Jay were together, Jay holding a lantern.

When Mary saw Clay's huddled form on the ground, she sobbed out a stricken cry and ran over to kneel beside him. Jay strode over and had one look and pushed the girl gently aside and lifted Clay onto his shoulders.

Jay called to the others, and two more men came over and helped him carry Clay. They took him down to the house and put him on a broken bed in the room Weld's men had entered. Mary sent one of Jay's friends to the kitchen, where the fire had burned itself out, and a minute later the man was back with a pan of boiling hot water from the range reservoir.

Will Jay himself rode to town for the doctor, killing his horse as he swung into Antelope's street. He was back with the medico in an hour and a half.

Doc Walker was a blunt and a hard man. He took a look at the hole in Clay's chest, looked at Clay, and said: "It's going to hurt like hell."

"Get on with it," Clay whispered.

The sawbones took off his coat and rolled up his shirt sleeves. "I'll want someone with a strong stomach to lend a hand."

"Let me." It was Mary who spoke.

Walker took one look at her, then turned to the others and growled: "The whole pack of you clear out."

Will Jay stormed into the front room and paced restlessly in front of the fire as two of his men did what they could to board up the broken windows and clean up the room. Bert Ulmann, his couch pulled close in to the fire once more, looked across at Jay and finally said: "I reckon this all falls on my head. I'm as sorry as a man can be, Will."

Jay stopped his pacing and stared across at the old rancher. "That's done with," he said quietly. "But I reckon, if anything happens to that man, we'll all be murderers. This wasn't the job he was sent here to do."

Ulmann was silent a long minute. Finally he raised his head in a slow nod. "He won't die. That girl of mine can pull him through."

Two days later Bert Ulmann's prophecy came true. Doc Walker had been there all that time, and

Mary Ulmann had slept less than two hours out of the forty-eight. It was morning, and Bert Ulmann was dozing before the fire, Will Jay sitting along-side in a rawhide chair, staring into the flames with a grimness only one thing could explain.

Mary came in through the hallway door, and Ulmann stirred, and Jay came up out of his chair.

"Any news?" Jay asked gruffly.

Mary held out a sheet of paper. "Clay wants you to ride to town to send this telegram for him."

Jay took the sheet of paper and read Will Marsden's name across the first line. The rest of the message Jay read aloud: "Job finished. The man you wanted was Bede Weld. If you say so, I'll ship his body to you along with my badge. A married man shouldn't be a law officer."

Bert Ulmann lifted his head and looked across at his daughter in alarm. A tide of color mounted to Mary's face, and suddenly all the worry and defeat that had robbed her of her beauty disappeared.

"Did I hear right? Is Clay a married man?"

"Not yet," the girl answered, low-voiced. "But by the time that Bill Marsden gets that message he will be."

All Will Jay could do was grin. Bert Ulmann lay back on his bed, deciding that if Clay Whitehead could pull through a thing like this, he could, too.

EVEN MONEY HE DIES AT NOON!

Finally a Peter Dawson story that kept his title. "Even Money He Dies at Noon!" was submitted to *Star Western* on December 3, 1939. It was purchased rather quickly, on February 12, 1940, and the author was paid $57.30. It was published in the May, 1940 issue.

I

To anyone with a sharp eye and an understanding of the country, the thing that happened along Apache Butte's street that morning built up into something unmistakably ominous. Mike Shaw, barkeep at the Oriole, saw all the signs, and by 10:00 he was laying even money against Bill Nichols's living beyond noon.

First, a few minutes short of 9:00, Guy Mooney and four of his Slash M men came into the street off the west trail, the last man in line holding the rope to a lead horse packing a bulky tarp-wrapped weight roped to a double-rigged saddle. Mike Shaw, who happened to see all this from the window of the Oriole Saloon, thought he knew the saddle, for there weren't many like it on the bench. He wasn't sure what was roped onto the saddle until the Slash M men stopped at George Hill's, the undertaker's. Then he knew it was a body. He watched while the ropes were taken off and the body carried into Hill's. Then he saw Guy Mooney and the other pair come on down the street and stop at the jail, Mooney going into the sheriff's office alone.

In five minutes Mooney was swinging his huge frame up into the saddle again, smiling wryly at the warning the sheriff called from his office doorway: "Get me proof and I'll make the arrest, Mooney. Without it, you haven't a leg to stand on against Nichols. Remember that!"

Mooney drawled: "Safford's dead from a bullet in the back. That's all the proof I need. Better keep your nose out of this, Ed." And Mooney was big enough, his outfit powerful enough, to make that warning carry more weight than any man in this part of the cattle country.

Mike Shaw wasn't much interested in the news of Safford's death, since Safford was a new hand at the Slash M. But he was interested in this other—this mention of Bill Nichols's name and what lay behind it. He watched the Slash M men dismount at the hitch rail before the hotel and, with pointed casualness, take stations along the street.

Mooney himself went up onto the hotel verandah and sat in a chair there, boots cocked on the rail. Mark Booth, Mooney's blacksmith, sauntered up the awninged walk toward the Elite Café while Rusty Ryan, top hand, went to the window of the hardware store alongside the hotel and showed an uncommon interest in a new galvanized water trough displayed in the window. Jeff Conklin crossed the street with Ted Fisher, and the two of them took chairs on the upstreet side of the Oriole's swing doors.

Mike noticed that Fisher, newly hired by Mooney, wore two guns, and he wondered why the sheriff hadn't gone through his old Reward dodgers on the chance of collecting a bounty, then he remembered that Mooney's votes had kept the sheriff in office for ten years, and thought he understood why the gunman went unmolested.

Mike was curious enough over what happened on the street to go out back and climb the ladder to the Oriole's roof. From up there, he could see out across the sage-studded flat, his hand shielding his eyes against the brassy glare of the sun. Far out on the trail that climbed up out of the Whippoorwill Creek bottom, the wind lifted a banner of dust that told him a rider was heading in toward town. Then he saw a buckboard drawn by a pair of blacks turn into the far end of the street. Mike came down off the roof in a hurry, in time to see the sheriff hail Morg Foote as he passed the jail.

What was said between the sheriff and Morg Foote while the blacks tossed their heads nervously under tightened reins was something Mike Shaw didn't learn until later. But the fact that Foote drove the buckboard into the feed barn instead of leaving his team on the street was significant. And when the homesteader's gaunt figure trudged back up the walk and turned in at the sheriff's office again, Mike had his inspiration. He went to the bank, drew out his savings, borrowed his next month's pay from his boss, and started making his wagers. In less than twenty minutes the word had made the rounds, and he had no takers for his last $100.

Forty minutes after that, Bill Nichols walked his sorrel gelding down past the end house of the street. He made a tall and lean shape in the saddle, and his blue cotton shirt, vest, and Levi's were powdered with dust. The eight-mile ride in from his Whippoorwill Creek homestead had been made in a hot wind that came in off the desert. He hadn't paid much attention to the heat and the dust, since the errand that brought him to town marked a milestone in a two-year struggle. Two years ago he'd taken a long shot, gambled $400 in savings against his ability to make a worthless creek-bottom homestead earn him a living. He'd worked his guts out, ditching water, leveling land, damming the stream, and investing every dollar of his money in cattle. Last year a few others had followed his example—Morg Foote, his nearest neighbor, Bob Streit, and Red Owens. Now Whippoorwill Creek was flanked by four paying outfits, and Guy Mooney, who'd always ignored the land as worthless graze, was beginning to show signs of becoming a range hog.

Bill forgot Mooney in the knowledge that, from today on, he could stand on his own feet financially. Last year he'd borrowed $1,000 at the bank. Today he had $500 in his pocket—enough to convince the bank that he was responsible and merited a bigger loan. With the new loan he'd buy a windmill, hire a man who would file on adjacent graze, and add to his small holding. Here, finally, was his chance to build a sizeable brand and lay the foundation for his future.

He was abreast the jail when Morg Foote's hail stopped him: "Nichols, hold on!"

Bill said—"Howdy, Foote."—seeing the grave expression on the homesteader's gaunt face and not understanding it.

Morg Foote ducked under the tie rail and came out into the street, glancing up toward the hotel as he stopped at Bill's stirrup. He said soberly: "Better not go to the bank today."

Bill spent a moment studying the man, wondering, as he had many times before, what Morg Foote's past might be. Always silent and taciturn, always outfitted in this unpressed black suit and the flat-crowned black Stetson, the pallor of his face and the gun he invariably wore low along his thigh had gained him a certain quiet respect. Morg had never been overly friendly, yet it hadn't occurred to Bill or anyone else to want to pry beneath his shell. As a neighbor, Foote had been helpful whenever called upon. Yet he never asked any return favors.

Bill's wide-shouldered frame bent indolently on arms folded across the horn of his saddle as he considered Foote's warning. Then he asked: "Why not?"

"Guy Mooney's down there at the hotel waitin' for you."

"That so?" Bill's deep blue eyes traveled down the street before his glance went again to Foote. His weathered face took on a thin smile. "What's wrong this time? Last week he had me setting out strychnine for his sheep dog."

"Someone ran off another bunch of his critters last night. That new man, Safford, was shot in the back tryin' to stop whoever did it. He was ridin' fence."

An expression of obvious surprise crossed Bill's face. Then he queried bluntly: "You're not trying to say I did it, are you, Foote?"

"No. But Mooney is."

"Thanks," Bill said, and lifted his reins to go on.

Foote said: "I came in to raise hell with him about that drift fence bein' down. The sheriff stopped me and told me what's up. Mooney's got his crew with him."

"Then I'd better get down there and not disappoint 'em," Bill drawled.

Foote abruptly reached down and unbuckled the shell belt from his waist, untied the holster thong, and held the weapon up, glancing significantly at Bill's empty waist. He said: "You'll need this."

Bill looked at the gun, shook his head. "I reckon not."

"But I tell you Mooney's on the prod!"

"He'll cool down." Bill rode slowly down the middle of the street and didn't look back.

It was barely fifty yards to the hotel, where the five fly-worried Slash M broncos stood at the tie rail. In covering that distance, Bill wondered if he shouldn't have taken Morg Foote's gun. Today might bring the showdown between him and Guy Mooney. This was the fourth time in the last six months that Slash M cows had been driven off into the badlands, and each time Mooney had indirectly blamed Bill. Now that Mooney had lost a man, it looked as though he was ready to do more than talk.

As he went along the street, Bill saw the way Mooney's men were placed to cover the hotel from front and sides. He saw Ted Fisher, the new hand Mooney had hired a few weeks ago, and he wondered, as he had before, how fast Fisher was with his guns. As he came abreast the hardware store where Rusty Ryan stood, he was prompted to a recklessness that hadn't been in him since he'd stopped his wandering and settled down here.

He called to Ryan: "Nice day for an inquest, eh, Rusty?" He was answered by a stony look.

He turned in alongside the Slash M horses, ignored Mooney, threw his reins over the rail, and stepped up onto the walk when Mooney's curt—"You, Nichols! Come up here!"—stopped him.

He swung around slowly and gave the Slash M

owner a long look. Then he drawled: "Supposing you come down."

Mooney's underjaw was thrust out belligerently, but he came on down the steps and almost within arm's reach of Bill. They were equally matched in tallness, but Mooney was much the heavier man. Bill wondered idly where he would hit Mooney first. Then he heard steps coming along the walk behind him and remembered where Mark Booth had been standing, and knew the odds were against his being able to hit Mooney at all.

The Slash M owner said: "You're sort of puffy around the eyes, Nichols. Miss your sleep last night?"

"I don't miss anything," Bill drawled, and moved to take his weight off a broken plank that had tilted up as he stood on it. Beyond Mooney, he saw Rusty Ryan saunter past the alleyway between hotel and hardware store.

Mooney waited, allowing Mark Booth to close in behind Bill. Then: "Safford died before we found him."

"That's too bad. Know who shot him?"

Mooney went on tonelessly: "We rode over to your place. You weren't there."

"That's a fact," Bill drawled. "I took a bedroll and a fly rod up into the hills yesterday afternoon. Caught a nice string of rainbow."

"Anyone see you?"

Bill shook his head.

Mooney's lips twisted down in a sneering smile. He said—"Take him, Mark!"—at the same time lifting his right hand up along his thigh toward his gun.

Instinctively Bill tensed as Mark Booth's hand closed on his arm from behind. Then, pivoting around against the blacksmith's unyielding grip, he threw his weight onto the broken plank of the walk.

Its broken end tilted upward in a quick swing that caught Guy Mooney on the point of the elbow. As Mooney cried sharply, Bill wrenched his arm from Booth's hard grip and chopped a short hard blow that took Mooney across the wrist. He caught the heavy .45 as it spun from Mooney's hand.

Stepping back out of reach, he rocked the gun into line in time to freeze Mark Booth with his weapon half drawn. Down the walk, Rusty Ryan came to an abrupt stop, too surprised to lift his hand. Mooney stood in line with Conklin and Ted Fisher, who were halfway across the street.

Bill drawled: "The picnic's over gents. Unload the hardware!"

Mooney swung around to face him, boots planted wide and left hand clutching his numb right elbow. He said: "You won't leave here alive, Nichols."

"If I don't, you don't." Bill thumbed back the hammer of the Colt. He nodded to Booth. "Make your play or drop that iron, Mark. You, too, Rusty."

"What'll it be, boss?" Mark asked, his voice hollow with anger.

Mooney eyed the rock-steady gun lined at his chest, said: "Better do as he says."

Booth dropped his gun to the walk.

As Ryan was drawing his single weapon, Ted Fisher made a lunge in from the street that took him behind the horses at the hitch rail. Bill caught the beginning of that move, and rocked his gun away from Mooney. His shot echoed flatly along the false fronts and his bullet took Fisher in the calf of the leg, knocking the leg from under him. Fisher rolled into the dust, blurring up both his guns with a speed that justified Mooney's boast of hiring the fastest gunman in the county when he hired him. Bill's stomach tightened at the expected impact of a bullet as Fisher fired his first shot from beneath the belly of the nearest horse. But all Bill felt was a faint tugging at the side of his opened vest. He hadn't wanted the thing to go this far, but now, seeing Fisher's gun fall into line with him again, he shot by instinct. The gun's solid pound traveled up to his shoulder, marking the jerking spasm of Ted Fisher's prone body. It was over then. Fisher's head dropped into the dust; his Stetson rolled away, showing a blue hole that centered his forehead.

Mooney called: "Rusty! Jeff! Keep your heads! Let him go!"

Ryan's gun slipped from his hand to the walk, and out in the street Jeff Conklin's .45 made a splash of dust as it fell from his fingers. Bill backed away from Mooney, stooping to pick up Mark Booth's weapon. His spurs jingled as he crossed the walk, stooped under the hitch rail, and climbed into his saddle. He waited until Ryan and Conklin had moved away from their guns, then reined out until he was abreast Mooney.

He looked up and down the street, saw that the walks were clear, then said: "I didn't want to kill Fisher, Mooney. He asked for it, and I'd do it again. I didn't run off your critters, and I didn't put lead in Safford's back. But damned if I won't find the man who did. Meantime, you can swear out your murder warrant and try running me down."

"I'll do that," Mooney answered briefly.

Bill raked the sorrel's flanks with his spurs. He looked back once as the animal's stride lengthened to a run. Mooney was running into the street to pick up Jeff Conklin's gun. The store doorways were spilling men onto the walks that had a moment ago been deserted. He reined his sorrel aside as he saw Mooney lift the gun and take aim. The bullet went wide and a moment later he was heading for the hills, two miles away.

II

At 9:00 that night Bill put the sorrel up the creekbank and followed a little-used path through the willow brakes toward Morg Foote's layout. There were no lights in the cabin. The place was empty, the remains of a cold supper on the kitchen table. Bill was disappointed. He had hoped to see his neighbor and find out what had happened in town today after the shooting. He also wanted to see Foote about something else, a plan that—if it worked—would prove his innocence.

The last ten hours had changed Bill Nichols. Shortly before dusk, as he was hiding his sign by keeping to the middle of Whippoorwill Creek, a dull rosy glow far out on the flats was an ominous reminder that he was a wanted man. That glow, brightly splotching the sky as darkness came on, marked the burning of his house, barns, and outbuildings. He told himself that he should have thrown down the gun and let Mooney take him when Fisher had made his play, but that hadn't been in the cards, either, for he was a stubborn man, and Mooney had crowded him too far.

Looking back over his two years here, he could trace step by step the building of Mooney's hatred toward him. It began when he was the first to homestead along Whippoorwill Creek; it was his misfortune to file on land Mooney could have used if he'd had the brains to improve it. Then Ruth Channing had served as the next prod to Mooney's anger. Bill didn't yet know whether he or Mooney would be her choice in the end—probably Mooney, now that Bill was wanted for murder. And with Mooney's influence, it would be suicide for Bill to give himself up and stand trial on grounds of self-defense in today's shooting. They had rustling and another murder charge against him, and Mooney could make them stick.

The rustling had been going on for nearly eight months now. In that time neither Guy Mooney nor any of the Whippoorwill Creek outfits had been able to get a shred of evidence pointing to the guilty party. But this afternoon, while hiding his sign from the posse he was sure followed him, Bill had hit upon a startling idea. Mooney, goaded by jealousy and greed, might have stolen his own herds—even killed one of his own men—to put the blame on the small ranchers, particularly on Bill. It was this hunch that Bill needed Morg Foote's help in following.

With Foote gone, Bill turned back down the creek trail and rode the two miles to Bob Streit's place. There were lights in the windows of Streit's cabin.

Streit muttered a surprised oath when he recognized the sorrel and its rider. As Bill drew rein, the rancher said grimly in a hushed voice:

“Goddlemighty, you want to drag me into this? Mooney and the sheriff was past here less’n an hour ago.”

“Then I’m safe for a few minutes.” Bill drawled, wondering at the edge of hostility in the rancher’s words. “I’m hungry, Bob. Got anything left over from supper?”

“You’ll have to eat it cold. The missus is in bed and I don’t want to wake her.” Streit turned and trudged back to the cabin, leaving Bill to get down out of the saddle and stretch his stiffened limbs, still wondering at his neighbor’s lack of friendliness.

Streit was back in less than two minutes with half a loaf of bread, a handful of jerked beef, and a tin cupful of lukewarm coffee. “The fire’s out and that java ain’t all it should be,” he said as he handed the food across. “Somethin’ I forgot to tell you. That Channing girl was past here, lookin’ for you. Said to tell you she don’t think you’re guilty.”

A slow flare of excitement welled up through Bill. To conceal it, he started eating. To know that Ruth Channing still believed in him was even better nourishment that this much-needed meal. There was something besides the smear on his name worth fighting for now.

When he had finished wolfing the food, he asked Streit: “What happened after I cleared out of town?”

"Mooney's crew fired your place," Streit said bluntly.

"I saw that. What else?"

"He's slapped a reward on you. Five hundred."

Bill smiled wryly. "It ought to be worth more'n that to him to keep me on the run."

Streit was silent a moment, then flared: "Bill, damn it, look at this thing from my angle! Your bein' here right now might buy me more trouble than I could ever take care of. I got the missus and the kids to think about."

Bill eyed the man's face in the darkness, seeing the dogged set of the features and the bright look to the eyes that was half anger, half fear. He understood then that he was alone, that his neighbors would all be like Streit, wary of him, looking out for themselves, possibly believing him guilty. Men with families and responsibilities couldn't be expected to throw in with him—a hunted fugitive, an outcast who could only bring them trouble and even perhaps death. Yesterday Streit had been a friend, but now that this thing had come out in the open, he was perfectly willing to let Bill take the fight on alone, protecting his own future.

Bill had intended asking Streit to help in the same way he would have asked Morg Foote to help. But now he put that to the back of his mind, drawling: "I need a rope and a rifle, Bob, if I'm going to travel far. You can have a couple of my critters as pay."

Streit said: "You got me wrong, Bill. I don't need pay for doin' a friend a favor." He turned into the cabin and was back almost immediately, a Winchester in one hand, coiled lariat in the other. As he gave them to Bill, he said hopefully: "Headin' out?"

To save argument, Bill nodded and climbed into the saddle. He thrust the rifle into the scabbard under his right leg, then wheeled the sorrel toward the gate, asking as an afterthought: "How did Morg Foote take what happened today?"

"They say he talked pretty salty to Mooney in town. I don't know for sure."

Riding north from Streit's place, Bill took hope from this last piece of information. Morg Foote no longer remained an enigma, but a lonely man whose loyalty he could trust. Foote was the kind who could see that Bill's frame-up was only a prelude to Mooney's clearing out the small ranchers from Whippoorwill and claiming it as his own. Foote would have the sense to know that all their futures were being undermined by Mooney's guile.

Bill turned north from Streit's place, rode past Foote's layout, and came to the corner of Slash M's fence to set about doing the only thing that seemed to offer him any lead on what had happened. Hours ago, coming down out of the hills, he had asked himself what the next move would be against him. The answer was undeniable.

Framed for rustling in the beginning, whoever had framed him had only one thing left to make the case against him complete—if another of Mooney's herds disappeared, it would look as though Bill had audaciously struck back in a last gesture before the law ran him out of the country. It was Mooney himself, of course, who would drive his own herd down into the badlands.

Turning north, Bill set about the task of covering the seven long miles of the Slash M's west fence. It was more than a one-man job, but this was the only logical thing that came to his mind.

Doggedly he rode to the end of the wire, turned, and started back again into the south. To the westward, the faint starlight revealed a down-dropping and tangled series of jagged hills and twisting cañons that ran on to the waste of desert. That maze of torturous rocky badlands separated the desert from this higher, richer bench where enough rain fell to nourish grass and let him work out a good and honest living.

Looking out across the badlands, Bill was sobered, by the knowledge that down there, somewhere in the obscurity, lay the answer to his destiny. Each raid on the Slash M had seen the herds driven down over the rim and deep into the breaks. There rocky going and endless cañon turnings obliterated all sign and made pursuit as fruitless as the efforts of one or two misguided souls who had tried to dry-farm the small patches of topsoil to be found in some of the cañons. Sheriff Ed Potter, even Bill himself, had made more than one try at riding out the mystery of the vanished herds. But the sheriff, with his keen eye and his fifty years of experience at working sign, had failed just as Bill had failed.

The near, sharp ring of a shod hoof striking against rock jerked Bill alert. He slid from the saddle and reached out to clamp a hand over his gelding's nose in a move that was purely instinctive. He stood rigid a moment and the next saw the shadowy shape of a rider come abreast of him, close in to the fence. And then he recognized that rider as Mark Booth, the Slash M blacksmith.

Mark seemed to slow the deliberate walk of his horse to pause and look directly at him. It was a good quarter minute before he passed on out of sight and in that interval Bill's right arm was tensed for a downward slash to the holster at his thigh. Perspiration cooled on his face and down the small of his back and left him shivering against the sudden chill of the night air. He knew that, once discovered, he would have had to use his gun, and Mark Booth, in his gruff and hearty way, had been friendly enough these past two years. Bill had no wish to see him lying dead from one of his bullets.

He waited until the last muffled echo of Mark's going had died on the still night air before following the line of the fence in the direction opposite the one taken by the blacksmith. Mark's presence here puzzled him. For the most logical solution to the rustling had been that Mooney was responsible for it. Why, then, would he make a pretense of having his crew ride guard on his fences? Was he keeping his crew in ignorance of what he was doing? Or had this been a wrong guess from the beginning?

He pulled in on the sorrel and sat for long seconds, catching a far-off, muted sound and trying to define it. It would die on the stillness a moment, come back stronger the next. Suddenly he knew that a large herd was on the move far to the south. Instantly he touched his spurs to the sorrel and was streaking along the line of the fence.

Soon, within three minutes, the sound welled over the rush of wind and the rhythmic beat of his pony's hoofs. Once or twice he caught distinctly the bawling of cattle. Then, as suddenly as the sound had come, it was gone. He reined in again, listened. All he could hear was a faint murmur, seemingly farther away than when he had first caught it. He was puzzled, undecided, but he went on.

Four miles below the point where he had met Mark, he came abruptly on a wide break in the fence. A broad swath of hoof-churned earth, darker than the rest of the sage-studded grounds, was a clear sign of the herd's passage. It cut an unmistakable line straight for the nearest drop of the rim into the badlands. And now Bill knew why the herd had disappeared so suddenly and completely from his hearing. Once over the rim, less than half a mile away, the sound of the herd's going had been shut off completely.

He looked at the fence and his first impulse was to ride the four miles across the bench to the Slash M. But his conviction that Guy Mooney was in back of this ruled out the possibility of finding help there. He would have to go on alone, follow the herd down into the cañons, and take his chance on uncovering the hide-out and getting back to town for help.

He reined the sorrel out from the fence when the sharp explosion of a .45, close to his left, swept away the silence, and the bullet whined past his head. He loosened his body, rolled from the saddle and hit the ground hard on his shoulder, his gun under him. Then, because he would have to roll over to reach his gun, because the shot had sounded too close for a second miss, he lay still. His muscles were knotted in expectation of a bullet slamming into him.

Bill raised his head slowly when the second shot failed to come. He was in time to see two indistinct shapes edge out from behind a stunted cedar fifteen yards away, on a line with the fence.

One made the outline of a horse, the other that of a tall man, arm raised and hand holding the reins close. The rider started toward him.

Bill recognized the horse first. It was Morg Foote's black gelding with the white stockings and the broad white chest blaze. And that tall thin shape could belong to no one but Morg. Bill's cocked muscles relaxed. He opened his mouth to call out and pushed himself up onto one elbow.

Morg Foote exploded sideways in a lunge. His Colt shattered the stillness once more, the bullet kicking up a geyser of sand that whipped into Bill's eyes.

Bill called hurriedly—"Morg, it's me . . . Bill Nichols!"—as Foote was rocking his gun into line a second time.

Foote hesitated as Bill came to his feet, then said sharply: "What the hell are you doin' here?"

"Maybe the same thing you are. Looking for a lead like this to work on. I dropped by your place earlier to ask you along. You'd already gone."

Morg said suspiciously: "Where'd you come from?"

"North. I came up here on a hunch and was riding fence. I heard the bunch moving from three or four miles above and hightailed down here."

Only then did Morg Foote's menacing attitude desert him. His gun dropped into leather in one swift flow of motion. He reached back for his reins and led his black in to where Bill stood. Bill saw that he was smiling crookedly as he said: "Either you're the luckiest man alive or I'm the poorest shot. It must have been the light. I had you pegged as one of the gang stayin' back to cover the rear. Glad I missed."

"So am I." Bill felt a keen relief sweep over him. Here was Foote, the man he would have chosen before all others to help him, and yonder was the first tangible evidence he had found to prove his innocence. He nodded toward the badlands. "Think we can work it between us?"

Morg Foote turned toward Bill's horse. "If we hurry."

Four hours later they led their horses warily through a narrow cleft in the sheer wall of a deep cañon many twisting miles down in the badlands. In those four hours Bill and Morg Foote had uncovered all but this final link in the chain that had so mysteriously bound the disappearance of the Slash M's herds. Soon after leaving the rim they had ridden within hearing distance of the fast-driven herd. But for that they would have lost it long ago in the rocky twisting cañon mazes that lay behind, for there were many turnings and for miles the going had been across bare rough rock swept clean by the winds that whipped in off the desert.

Once they had guessed wrong. Facing a branching in a shallow cañon, momentarily out of hearing of the herd, Foote had insisted on taking the right-hand fork. A mile's fast riding hadn't brought them upon the herd and they'd ridden back and taken the other branch, the one that led them to within hearing of the herd again a few seconds before the cattle turned abruptly into this narrow slit in the wall that now gave no sign of leading anywhere. It had been close, and it was only because of Bill's insistence that they push on fast that they hadn't lost the herd altogether.

"Not bad, eh?" Bill drawled as they walked around a hidden shoulder that took them beyond the back wall of this seemingly boxed and shallow offshoot. Ahead lay a narrow gorge striking crookedly back through the heart of what had looked from the main cañon like a flanking high mesa. And, as abruptly as they made the turning, they picked up from ahead the faint bawling of the cattle.

"Not bad," Morg Foote conceded. "Now what?"

"We'll go on."

Foote frowned but made no objection. They climbed into their saddles again and rode on at a walk. Within a hundred yards, in which the rocky floor of the narrow offshoot descended perceptibly, Bill slowed enough to let Morg come alongside, saying: "They've stopped. This must be the hide-out."

Morg nodded, since he had already noticed that the herd wasn't drawing away any longer. At that moment, something else seemed to take his attention. His head lifted sharply, and he pointed up the wall to the left, saying softly: "Something moved up there."

Bill made out the gray line of a ledge that climbed steeply up the wall from a point almost abreast of them. His glance followed the line of the ledge but couldn't pick up what Morg had seen. "What?" he asked.

"Couldn't tell. Let's take a look."

Morg reined his pony across to the beginning of the ledge, and, as Bill came up, he said doubtfully: "It might be a trail. See what you think."

Bill swung aground and knelt at the spot where the ledge began its upward climb. He struck a match, shielding its flare by his cupped hands. In the brief glance he had of a thin patch of topsoil, he saw the imprint of a horse's shoe. He stood up. "There's been someone along here."

"Reckon we'd better follow it?" Morg asked. "Looked like a man up there."

"We'll go along careful," Bill agreed. He started walking up the line of the ledge, leading his sorrel. Morg followed closely.

The ledge varied from a ten foot width to a narrowness that made Bill involuntarily catch his breath when he looked down into the shadowed void toward the cañon floor, dropping steadily away as they climbed. The imprint of the horse's shoe below had looked fresh, made probably during the last twenty-four hours. Had Morg seen someone moving up here or was it his imagination?

Bill's eyes were scanning the trail ahead when he saw the pinpoint glow of a burning cigarette end wink barely thirty feet upward from him. He stopped dead in his tracks as a man cradling a Winchester under his arm stepped out onto the trail and called: "Who's with you, boss?"

From behind Bill, Morg Foote's sharp-edged voice drawled: "It's Nichols. Heist 'em, Bill!"

Bill's right hand had slid up two inches along his thigh when the guard spoke. Morg's answer froze that gesture to a quick paralysis. Lifting his hands outward so that they were in plain sight and away from his gun, Bill wheeled slowly around. He saw the satisfied sneer on Morg Foote's gaunt face, caught the dull glint of starlight reflected from the blued barrel of a gun lined at his stomach. He raised his hands to the level of his shoulders, his left still holding the sorrel's reins, his right empty.

A flood of understanding came over him. Hadn't this guard just called Foote "boss"? Hadn't Morg tried to lead him the wrong way out in the main cañon, tried to throw him off long enough for the herd to gain the sanctuary of this hide-out? As the guard came up on him from behind, Morg Foote said: "It's a good thing they slapped a reward on you. Now you disappear, you won't be missed. I might even try and collect. . . ."

Morg's thin body suddenly jerked. A second later the hollow burst of a rifle back of them and below laid racketing echoes along the narrow chasm. Morg swayed in the saddle as another gun exploded to add its echoes to the first. The rifles had spoken from the foot of the ledge trail. Morg's gun dropped out of line as his left hand came across to clench his right shoulder.

"What the hell, boss!" the guard said sharply from behind Bill. "There's someone down there!"

Bill chose that moment to throw all his weight against the sorrel's reins, letting his knees go from under him as the horse shied violently back against Morg's black. The black pitched as Bill went to his knees, palming up his gun, turning around. The sorrel was now between him and Morg Foote. His swiftly rising gun beat the downswing of the guard's Winchester by a split second. His .45 exploded and drove the guard back to the ledge's edge. The man's hands opened, the rifle fell, and for a moment he stood balanced, hands frantically flailing the air for a hold that wasn't there. Then, slowly, he tilted over the rim. His shrill scream came up to them as he fell off into space.

Behind Bill the black's quick-striking hoofs

sounded into the echoes of the scream. The sorrel lunged suddenly in on Bill, threatening to trample him, as guns below spoke again. One bullet struck rock above Bill's head, ricocheting off in a buzzing whine. Morg Foote's black bolted into the clear and up the trail past Bill. As he swung past, Morg tried a snap shot at Bill; his bullet slit the brim of Bill's Stetson. Then, a moment later, he was gone from sight around an outthrust shoulder of the rocky wall ten feet above. The clatter of his pony's hoofs slapped back loudly by the opposite wall as he raced on up the trail.

The guns below were setting up a rhythmic fire now. The sorrel winced under the sting of a bullet that scorched him across the withers. Bill came to his feet, caught the reins, and ran on and around the rock shoulder. He glanced ahead and was in time to see the light in a cabin's window dim and go out. Then, from up there, rifles added their sharp explosions to the ones from below and lead from both directions cut the air past the rocky buttress behind which Bill stood. Morg Foote was no longer in sight. He had had time to reach the cabin.

It was fully a minute before Bill understood that he and his horse could not be seen in the impenetrable shadow of the rock shoulder. Out on the trail, his shape outlined against the light gray face of the cliff had made him a target for the guns below. Now he was safe from them. And the shadows in this small pocket were deep enough so that those above couldn't see him. But he was also nicely trapped.

Daylight, two hours off, would reveal his hiding place to the men in the cabin above. He couldn't hope to go back along the trail and give himself up to the marksmen below; they would think him one of the rustlers and shoot him before he could make himself known. Strangely enough, the sound of a shout from the foot of the ledge trail told him the identity of the men down there even before he had asked himself who they might be. The voice that shouted belonged to Guy Mooney. Mark Booth must have discovered the break in the fence and routed out the Slash M crew and brought them down here.

Soberly fitting together the last piece of this amazing puzzle, Bill saw how cleverly Morg Foote had played his hand. Building up the animosity between Bill and Mooney—big rancher against homesteader, their rivalry over a girl—Morg had kept in the background behind his cloak of friendliness to start this feud. He, least of all, had been suspected of the rustling. He had even gone so far as publicly to defend Bill against Mooney. It was plain what he would gain in the end. Since his fences footed Mooney's and therefore made the lower reaches of Whippoorwill inaccessible to the Slash M, Foote could name his own price on buying out the small ranchers once he had made it too unhealthy for them to stay in the country. Because Bill was the only logical homesteader to put up a fight, Foote, the only single man besides himself, had framed Bill first to get him out of the way. The rest could easily be taken care of. Once Whippoorwill was clear of the small outfits and Foote had title to its ten-mile length of graze, he could enlarge the ditches Bill and the rest had slaved to throw up, perhaps build a dam to catch the spring floods, and have an outfit that would rival Guy Mooney's in acreage and worth. From then on Morg Foote would be kingpin of the bench, and now for the first time Bill understood that Guy Mooney was only a stubborn and hard-working man, fighting to stay on his feet, his shrewdness no match for Foote's.

The winking flashes of muzzle fire at the window of the cabin were a grim reminder that Bill couldn't hope to go up along the trail without being spotted. Foote's men would expect him to make the try and be waiting for him. Going back down the trail would be as suicidal as going up. Even if he could make himself heard and talk to Mooney, no one would believe his story. Mooney would gladly put a bullet in him, thinking him one of the rustlers trying to talk his way free. He couldn't expect Mooney to give him a chance, for Mooney's enmity had been bred on months of annoyance, suspicion, and now hatred. Nor could Bill stay where he was, hidden by the darkness and waiting the outcome of the fight. Mooney would, of course, wait until daylight before trying to force the trail. He would logically send a rider to town for reinforcements, working on the hunch that there was no back trail away from the hideout. As soon as it was dawn, the whole reach of the trail would be easily seen from the cabin. And the guns of Morg Foote's men would be turned on Bill. He was more nicely trapped than he would have been had he given himself up to Mooney in town today to face the frame-up for murdering Safford.

Staring intently up the trail, Bill could make out the cabin's shape near the edge of the rim made by the end of the ledge. Above the ledge the cañon's higher rim fell back, leaving a depres sion shaped like the broken half of a saucer. Behind the cabin, up the slope of fallen and rotten rock that was dotted with huge boulders, Bill could see a pole corral but no trail leading up to the rim. Evidently Foote and his men had no other way out of the cañon than the one he and Bill had taken in, the one Mooney and his crew now guarded.

The insistent ragged firing of the guns below told Bill that Mooney's crew had found cover. The answering fire from the cabin slanted downward past the buttress, the bullets droning with the constant reminder that to step off of the buttress' thick shadow was to meet with instant death. A feeling of hopelessness, then anger rode in on

Bill. He told himself that he wouldn't die here like a trapped rat. He had too much to live for. Today, riding the hills alone with a posse on his back trail, he had accepted the inevitable fact that he would have to lose his ranch, everything, and leave the country. The odds against him—Mooney's power on this range, the evidence the past six months had built up—had been too heavy to fight. Now the odds were even heavier against him. But another thing had happened to outweigh all this. Ruth Channing's message to Bob Strcit had formed a tie Bill wouldn't see broken. He and Ruth had never spoken seriously of their feelings toward each other simply because Bill didn't know how to go about it. But tonight Ruth had swept away all the barriers in her word to Bill's neighbor. She was worth fighting for.

He put down the feeling that he was living out his last hours and calmly, dispassionately tried to think of a way out. The trail was blocked at both ends by men who would kill him on sight. The guard's prolonged scream as he fell from the ledge was proof enough that the drop was too sheer and deep to be reached by climbing down Bob Streit's fifty-foot length of rope, still tied to the sorrel's saddle. There was only one other possible way out, and that was up the wall to the rim. His first glance upward momentarily wiped out this last hope. But then he picked out a slender overhang deep in the shadow of the climbing buttress behind which he stood. The overhang thrust out at a right angle from the wall a good thirty feet directly over his head. It was a third of the way to the rim. He couldn't see what lay beyond it, above, for the shadows up there were too dense for him to pick out details. But if he could get that far, he might go farther.

He wedged the sorrel's reins tightly under a heavy rock, then untied the lariat from the saddle, and shook out a three-foot loop. He wondered grimly if that upward throw was as impossible as it looked, but didn't give himself time to form a real doubt in his mind. The suppleness of the manila responded to his hand as he spun the loop, the rope held loosely coiled in his left hand. He gave it half a dozen quick turns and made his cast. The loop disappeared into the gloom overhead. His left hand closed on the knotted end. He crouched, expecting the rope to fall back at him. A six-foot length of it did. Then it quivered and hung there, swaying.

When he eased his weight against the rope, he knew that he had made a perfect throw. The noose had caught on the overhang. He let it hang while he took off his belt, made a sling for the Winchester, and looped it over his neck, the weapon hanging down his back. He started up the rope, hand over hand, boots braced against the wall. Mercifully the rising bulk of the buttress' shadow line hid him as he climbed.

Four minutes later he was lying belly-down on the slender outcrop, coiling the rope again, looking upward along the wall as he worked. There was nothing directly above that would have held his rope. But ten feet out of line, upcañon, a break in the sheer upward tilt of the wall offered a jagged edge of rock that would hold the rope. It was a shorter throw than the first, barely twenty feet, but he made three throws before the loop caught and held. He braced his boots against the wall to keep from swinging outward too far and managed it nicely, although the rope burned his hands once as a boot slipped and he dropped half a dozen feet before he caught himself. Finally he was standing on the narrow shelf, leaning back against the wall, his lungs dragging in air as he stared downward at the sickening drop to the trail.

He stopped looking below. When his glance followed up to the rim, it seemed deceivingly close. Far to his left the rim made a downward dip. He had the thought that he could work across that way and shorten his climb by one stage. Hardly had the thought come to him than he saw he had only one choice. A stunted cedar grew from a cleft in the wall thirty feet to his right. There was no other outcrop or ledge within throwing distance that would hold the rope. He could secure the noose to the cedar but doubted that the roots would hold. And, if they did hold his weight, he would have to swing downward and out, pendulum-like, and across to a narrow ledge immediately below the depression in the rim if he hoped to catch another foothold. If he missed that ledge, he would hang at the rope's end until the cedar's roots pulled loose or until he became too exhausted to hold on any longer. But there was no other way. The insistent racket of the rifles below warned him of that.

This time his throw was sure, as the first one had been. He spent a full minute shaking the loop over the branches of the tree until it hugged the lower end of the trunk, close in to the wall. Only when he put his weight against the rope and straightened, ready for the jump, did he realize that his downward swing would carry him out of the shadow of the turning of the wall that was now at his back. Morg Foote's men could see him if they were looking in that direction. And certainly Mooney's men would see him from below, since they were looking upward across their rifle sights.

He hesitated one brief moment, considering his chances. Then he let himself fall. His downward swing was swift, breathtaking. His long frame arced beyond the vertical and started the upward swing; the far wall underneath the rim was blurring past, the ledge dropping toward him. Then his swing slowed unbearably, the ledge hanging above and out of reach.

IV

In one last supreme effort, he pulled himself up as far as he could on the rope and kicked his boots upward in a twisting reach to get a toehold on the ledge. His left boot scraped the edge, dragged away. Then his right caught and held. He was lying flat, his hold on the rope supporting his upper body, his toehold the only thing that kept him from falling back. The rifle hanging from his neck was an awkward weight that threatened to mean the difference between life and death.

Someone below at the cabin shouted. A rifle-bullet nicked a shard of rock from the wall's face. The splinter gashed Bill's left cheek. The convulsive jerk of his body hard on the heel of the blinding pain in his face lifted him up and put him belly-down on the ledge. He was exhausted, gagging for breath. A second bullet, slapping the outer edge of the shelf and whining away into the night, brought him to his feet and sent him climbing upward along the series of precarious hand- and footholds directly below the rim. Once a bullet burned his right thigh; another time the Winchester lying against his back slammed against his spine as from a sledge-hammer blow. Then he was pulling himself over the rim, rolling away from it, safe.

A surge of wild hope hit him the instant he came to his feet and looked across the tableland backing the rim. He was standing on a high and twisting narrow bench, gashed on one side by the cañon he had climbed out of, on the other by a second chasm as sheer-walled as the first. Morg Foote and his men were trapped in the cabin. There was no way out, as he had at first supposed, across this broken mesa.

Before he knew exactly what he meant to do, he was running up along the rim toward the cabin. He was remembering the abrupt slope behind it that climbed steeply to the rotten, boulder-strewn, jutting rim. Close in to the rim he had a brief glimpse of the cabin almost directly below now. He judged the distance, the slope, and moved twenty feet farther on, in behind a waist-high rock seemingly balanced on a flat shelf. He put his shoulder to the rock, threw all his weight into the drive of his body. The rock tilted slightly, then fell back into place. He straightened, unslung the Winchester from his neck, and pushed again.

This time the rock seemed more stubborn. It wouldn't move. He finally put his back to it, chose two shallow depressions in the rocky slope for the heels of his boots, and pushed again. At the first tough straightening of his body, the rock tilted over and was gone; he lost his footing and was rolling down the slope after it. Before he could stop his downward roll a prolonged roar rose above the sound of the guns below. He spread his legs wide, slid for ten feet on his belly, and finally stopped and looked below. What he saw was a thin fog of grayish dust forming a line down the slope toward the cabin. The shapes of rolling boulders and small rocks showed through the blur. A roar of blended sounds, some sharp as the explosions of guns, filled the cañon as the avalanche gathered momentum. Bill shuddered as a man's scream echoed into the din. The earth trembled beneath his feet and he stared in fascination at the spot where the cabin should be.

It was out of sight in a smother of dust and flying rock. Suddenly, as the dust cleared momentarily, he saw tons of broken rock roll down over the lower rim and into the cañon. The cabin was no longer there; it had been swept away with no trace of even its foundations marking the spot where it had been. A roar, more prolonged and mightier than the first, rose up between the cañon walls as the avalanche's plummeting weight struck the solid earth two hundred feet below. Then, gradually, came silence, awesome and complete, except for the faint bawling of cattle from somewhere downcañon.

Bill's knees sagged weakly under him. He sat down, hearing vaguely the echoing pound of running horses climbing the ledge trail. It was over now. Morg Foote and his crew were gone, crushed beneath tons of rock. And Guy Mooney and his men were on the way up.

He saw Mooney and his men round the turning behind which he had been hiding a scant quarter hour ago. Ten riders were strung out behind Mooney, who led on his bay horse. They swung in off the ledge, hesitated a moment, then started climbing toward the corral several rods below and to Bill's right. He stood up and started down to meet them.

It was lighter now, the sky to the east graying with the false dawn. In this stronger light he could recognize Mooney's big shape, that of Mark Booth and Rusty Ryan. All at once something moved far to his left, on the upslope of the saucer-like depression. His glance went over there in time to see two men picking their way upward, out of sight of Mooney and his men, crouching as they ran from boulder to boulder. One shape was tall and thin, stooped over in an awkward run. The other was stocky, unfamiliar.

Bill dropped the Winchester and was running the next instant, on a line that would intercept the pair. He dodged in behind the cover of boulders and outcroppings. He covered sixty yards, seventy, before Morg Foote's tall frame straightened in an attitude of attention. Bill stepped out into the open, his right hand brushing the thonged-down holster.

Morg motioned to the short, stocky man who strode at his heels, saying dryly: "He's mine, Len.

Don't interfere." Then Morg was striding toward Bill, arms bent and hands clawed above a pair of holsters. His man followed him.

Morg stopped ten short paces away, drawling: "You asked for it, Nichols."

As he spoke, his hands were moving upward in the effortless fluid motion of the practiced gunfighter. Bill's draw was instinctive, unhurried, but fast. He turned sideways quickly as he threw his .45 into line. Morg Foote's first bullet, well before his own, struck him a hard blow low along his ribs on the left side, prolonging his turn. Then his gun was in line. He squeezed the trigger, saw Morg's body stiffen, and fired again. Morg's hands opened. His head rocked backward and he went rigid. He crumpled suddenly and fell backward, spinning around so that his long body went into a tight roll. Len, behind, tried to step out of the way. But one of Morg's boots tripped him and he fell to his knees as his right hand was dipping toward holster.

"I wouldn't!" Bill commanded, and the urgency in his voice made Morg's understrapper lift his hand away from his gun.

Behind Bill a pony's shoes racketed against bare rock. Others joined it. Guy Mooney's voice bellowed: "Drop your irons, or we'll blow you in two!"

Bill let his .45 fall to the ground and lifted his hands lifelessly, for now that it was over, his side was aching with a burn like the prodding of a red-hot iron. Len, cornered and knowing he would live only long enough to be taken out of the badlands to be strung up to a limb of the first big cottonwood the Slash M crew could find, suddenly lunged to his feet, whipping out his gun. A rifle exploded behind Bill. Len's knees buckled and he slumped lifelessly to the ground.

Mooney said: "Nice work, Mark. We've still got Nichols."

He walked from behind Bill to go across and kneel beside the two bodies. Bill plainly caught his gasp of surprise. Mooney's head jerked around and he looked at Bill intently in a puzzled stare.

"So Morg was in on it, too?" he grated. "Who started this slide on the cabin?"

Bill said—"I did."—all at once unable to keep Mooney's face in focus.

Mooney laughed mirthlessly." Double-crossin' your partners, were you? Thought you'd hide out up here until we'd gone!"

Mark Booth, who had come across to stand beside Mooney, suddenly looked down at Len and said: "Looks like we'd have two of 'em to hang, boss."

Bill tried to blink away the fuzzy curtain of wavering light that came down over his eyes. He knew he was falling sideways. He tried to reach out and steady himself, but his muscles wouldn't respond. He felt his head strike sharply against a rock edge and knew no more.

It was forty minutes later that Bill's eyes came open and he stared dully up into Mooney's face without recognition. But in a few seconds he could see Mooney, and, strangely enough, he saw that his old enemy was smiling.

Mooney said: "Feel better?"

Bill nodded, tried to sit up, and couldn't. It felt pretty good to lie back against Mooney's arm.

Mooney drawled: "Take it easy. Jeff ought to be back with the sawbones pretty quick." His glance changed perceptibly, the smile fading. "We've only got one man for noose bait now."

Bill said weakly: "There's no use asking for a chance to talk, is there?"

Mooney shook his head soberly, his face grave. "No use in your talkin'."

Somewhere out of Bill's range of vision, Mark Booth coughed nervously and said: "Hell, Guy, what's the use in raggin' him? Tell him he ain't the one."

Mooney's rugged face couldn't keep from smiling at Bill's look of bewilderment. "That's a fact, Bill," he said. "Foote's understrapper's the one we'll fit the necktie to. Mark's slug knocked him out but didn't hurt him much. We kinda persuaded him to tell us what he knew. He cleared you." Mooney was uncertain for a moment, his voice gruff. "It looks as though I've been barkin' up the wrong tree. Accordin' to what Len says, we've got you to thank for savin' all our hides."

As Bill realized what an admission this was—Mooney's blunt and gruff way of putting a sincere apology—all the torment and hopelessness that had been in him vanished. Mark Booth stepped into sight, his face lit with unconcealed pleasure.

"Ain't you sort of glad, Bill?" he asked.

Bill nodded, not trusting himself to speak for the emotion that was in him.

Mooney misunderstood his silence. He said hastily: "If it's killin' Ted Fisher that's got you worried, forget it. Len claims Fisher was Morg Foote's man, hired out to me to work from the inside. I'd give plenty to have cut him down myself. Another thing, about that fire we touched off last night at your layout. Hell, don't worry about it. I'll give you a couple of men and you can build it over again, better than before. I was thinking, too, you might like to take over Foote's outfit from the bank. I'd be glad to go on your note."

"That's white of you, Guy," Bill managed to say.

Mooney seemed even more embarrassed than Bill at this sudden turn of events that was threatening to change their enmity to friendship. It seemed that each was recognizing in the other a strong man, one to be respected, trusted.

All at once, Mooney said gruffly: "Mark, go

take a walk. I've got something private to talk over with Bill."

"Wouldn't be about a girl, would it?" Mark drawled, and laughed as Mooney shot him an angry look. He sauntered away.

Moony's face had flushed a brick red at Mark's question. But when his crewman was out of hearing, he nodded down at Bill, saying: "Mark knows. He was with me day before yesterday when I stuck my neck out."

Bill frowned, making little sense of what Mooney was leading up to.

Mooney went on: "I proposed for the first and last time, Bill. She wouldn't have me."

"Ruth?"

"Ruth."

Mooney got to his feet, cuffed his Stetson lower over his eyes so that its shadow hid his expression. "Better try and get some rest until Jeff gets here with the sawbones. You've got a hole in your side but nothin' you can't get over."

As Mooney walked away, Bill closed his eyes, letting his new and unreal world settle into place. He didn't feel the pain much any more. Ruth Channing. For many months now she had never strayed far from his thoughts. But this was different, still unreal. Idly he wondered how long they'd have to wait for a preacher to come through so that they could be married. . . .

BULLETS ARE MY DESTINY

It wouldn't be until 1949 with the serial, *Renegade Canyon* in seven parts, that Peter Dawson graduated from pulp magazines to *The Saturday Evening Post*, the highest paying slick magazine at the time. In the 1950s many of his Western serials would appear in this magazine and, except for two short stories in the digest-size pulp magazine, *Zane Grey's Western Magazine*, virtually all that Peter Dawson wrote was now published in higher paying periodicals. However, in late 1946 his agent, Marguerite E. Harper, had made a multiple-story deal for Jon Glidden to write Peter Dawson short stories for Popular Publications' pulp magazines, these stories appearing primarily in *Fifteen Western Tales*. "Bullets Are My Destiny" was one of these, sold in February, 1949 for $110.00, and published in the August, 1949 issue of that magazine.

I

They let the small herd drift along the timber margin and cut obliquely out to the rim, Steve driving the chuck wagon, Nels forking his dun gelding. They reined in and had their long look at that low country, a half-moon sweep of emerald lush grass paling across its five-mile width into a tawny waste of desert. This was a warm spring day, with a cool breeze slanting off the peaks to temper the sun's bright glare. From a strip of jack pine, immediately below, came the scolding voice of a jay and, farther out, a flock of crows rose lazily from the crooked willow-bordered line of a creek.

"Nicest stretch of grass I ever saw." Nels Olds slacked his stocky weight against the off stirrup, his dark eyes brightly interested. "We'll plant ourselves right in the middle of it, fella."

Steve Ash's long length was slouched lazily in the corner of the wagon's seat, one boot hanging from the brake. He pushed his wide hat onto the back of his blond head, his lean face wholly serious as he drawled: "There's nothing I'd like better. But you heard what they told us."

"Did I? I forget." Nels's grin was rash and for the moment his eyes were alight with a devil-may-care look. Then he caught Steve's soberness and a bright anger touched his gaze. "Who's this Jackson and his Crow Track? Damned if he tells me what to do."

"He meant it, Nels." Steve was too used to his partner's headstrong and reckless ways to be anything but patient now. "He had three men with him, which means his Crow Track's a big outfit."

"Look, Steve, we checked those maps in the Land Office yesterday. Everything outside a fence below this rim is wide open for homestead."

"And the agent told us Jackson and these other outfits had always run settlers off this strip."

"Sure . . . farmers. We're running cattle, Steve"

"Not here. They won't let us."

Nels frowned now, eyeing Steve in mock seriousness. "Scared?"

"Hell, yes. Those gents back there this morning were loaded down with iron. Jackson said to clear out. He meant it."

Nels laughed, slapped the holster at his thigh. "Powder comes just as cheap to me as it does to him. We got our chance here, Steve. Every damned nickel to our names is in those fifty white-faces. I aim to turn those nickels into dollars. We can do it down there."

"Not me."

"Then we split up right here."

Steve hadn't been expecting this. He thought about it soberly now, looking back across the six years he and Nels had sided each other, working for a spread across the desert. He remembered all the fun they'd had and these past three years how they had saved their wages with only this one idea in mind—of quitting when they got enough and having a herd of their own. They had made a start now, stretching their savings by buying sound underweight culls from an agency herd. And here, disagreeing for the first time, Nels was threatening to pull out.

"Nels, there's other country to go to." Steve knew that his one hope was to make Nels think through his bull-headedness. "Fifty miles across there we'll run onto grass."

"Not like this."

"Then why don't we do what they said we could, throw our stuff out there beyond that bar wash?"

"And fight the desert? Watch our grass burn out in another thirty days? Not me. I'm going straight down there onto the best of it, Steve. Let 'em try and throw me off."

They measured each other seriously, Steve thinking: *When he cools down, he'll make more sense.* So he smiled meagerly and shrugged. "OK. Down we go."

That was the end of it, then.

And they did go down, right onto the best of it, as Nels had said they would. He was the one who pointed out the way, the one who picked the spot for that night's camp alongside a creek not two hundred yards from the line of a four-wire fence. They turned the cattle out onto grass that was fetlock-deep and picketed the horses on the richest stand of it.

"Tomorrow we go in and file on this," Nels said as they were finishing supper.

Steve glanced pointedly into the darkness toward the line of the fence. "What'll our neighbor say?"

"Who cares?" That ready, cocky smile came to Nels's blocky face.

"Maybe this is Crow Track fence."

"Still who cares?"

Steve shrugged, seeing the futility of arguing. Tomorrow or the next day Nels would get to thinking this over and see how they were only asking for trouble. He'd give in gradually, and, if they could keep out of trouble a few days, they would soon be moving on. Steve was sure of this.

He went to the chuck wagon for his bedroll now and started away from the fire when Nels called: "Where you going?"

"Out here a ways."

"Why?" When Steve made no answer, Nels drawled: "Scared to be near the fire?"

Steve sauntered over and stood staring down at his friend. "That's the second time you've used that word today."

Nels moved his eyes away. "Forget it. I didn't mean it. But you're damned spooky, friend."

"Just careful. Maybe you ought to try it."

"Yeah, I will someday. When I get ready to grow that long white beard."

Steve carried his bedroll over a low rise, away from the creek, and spread his blankets close to the squat shadow of a cedar, more amused than angry at Nels's remark. He supposed he was being foolish, keeping away from the camp like this. But that had been a hardcase quartet of riders they had met this morning. Jackson hadn't said much but it was plain to Steve he had been deadly serious. He regretted this misunderstanding with Nels, but he knew that these first few weeks of their partnership were to set the pattern of their future, and, if he gave in to Nels on this thing, he would forever be giving in to him. Good judgment counted now as it never had before in their association and it was up to him to blunt Nels's impetuous and unthinking ways.

He was in his blankets before he got to thinking about his .45. Maybe he should have dug it out of the chuck wagon and brought it across here with him in case of trouble. *But nothing's going to happen,* he told himself. He was thinking that as he dropped off to sleep.

A shot blasting across the night's stillness two hours later jarred him awake. He had rolled from his blankets and was pulling on his boots, seconds later, when another explosion rode across from the direction of the camp. Some instinct prompted him to throw his blankets in under the cedar before he ran up the slope. He threw himself belly down behind another stunted cedar at the crest of the rise. He had barely made out the glow of the fire toward the creek when the quick pound of a running horse drummed over the stream's steady murmur. Gun flame winked redly, twice, from beneath the vague gray blotch of the chuck wagon's tarp. A rider's hurrying shape momentarily streaked before the fire's glow and the next instant a heavier explosion boomed hollowly. It was a shotgun. And now Steve could dimly see the rider come to a sudden halt alongside the chuck wagon.

"Spread out! Get the other one!" the man down there shouted.

He got Nels! Steve lunged, half erect, knowing he had found the only answer to the rider's having stopped so near the fire. That had been Nels, a moment ago, shooting from beneath the chuck wagon. As the fury mounted in him, some wild instinct made Steve want to run down there, find his gun, and kill.

He had moved out a step from the obscurity of the cedar when, abruptly, he heard a second rider trotting up the slope toward him. That sound worried him, stretched him full length and hugging the ground once more. A man's high bulk took form against the star-studded sky, passing within ten feet of him. And as the horse moved away, Steve lay paralyzed by an impotent anger, whispering a curse over and over again, knowing that, if he had argued, really argued with Nels this afternoon, they wouldn't be here now. But it did no good to think back on what might have happened. The stark reality of what was going on around him now fully held his senses; what he saw and heard these few minutes might decide certain things later on.

Presently he heard the man below give a sharp whistle and shortly three others rode in on the camp. He caught the low murmur of voices, unintelligible over the muffled roar of the creek. Then he saw shadows shifting around the chuck wagon and slowly its gray shape moved in toward the fire.

They pulled the wagon over on its side, briefly blotting out the glow of the fire. The tarp caught at once, its sudden blaze throwing a flickering light that let him see those four riders lined out downcreek, going away. He lay there and watched the chuck wagon start burning, afraid to move, thinking they might be out there in the darkness, waiting to turn their guns on him.

At first he just watched. Then his anger heightened suddenly, uncontrollably. Before he quite realized it he was on his feet and running down the slope toward the pyre. Something—the sight of everything he owned going up in flames, the wild hope that he might be able to use a gun if he had one, the thought of Nels—had snapped the thread of his carefully ordered reason. He dodged from side to side as he ran. The heat of the blaze struck him like a blow. He ignored it, throwing himself in under the tilted-up bed of the wagon. It was so hot under there that it scorched his face. He held his breath and dragged one of the two big stores boxes clear. One end of the box was burning but he forgot that and crawled in for the other. A sudden burst of flame drove him out without the box and he stood a moment, staring helplessly, as the fire mounted to a roar, suddenly beginning to eat into the grain bags.

Sanity returned to him then. He realized he had been standing here in plain sight for maybe a quarter minute, that no shot had come. He dragged the box to the creek now and put out the red glow that was eating through the panel at one end. Then he walked over to find Nels.

It didn't take him long. He was thankful that a clump of alder cut off most of the light. There was nothing left of Nels's face—the job had been thorough.

He went back to the fire to pull a shovel from the toolbox on the unburned side of the wagon bed.

During the forty minutes it took the fire to burn down, Steve Ash squatted there in the deep shadow of the alders alongside the body and thought things through in his careful ordered way.

He kept telling himself: *There were four of them this morning and four tonight.* He kept remembering Jackson, remembering the Crow Track brand he and Nels had seen on those four horses this morning. And one more thing he tried to seal clearly in his mind was the voice he had heard here tonight.

While he was concentrating on each remembered inflection, his mind made itself up. In the end he knew what he was going to do. Nels had wanted to settle here. He had died because of that. To move out now would somehow be betraying their partnership—betraying himself. So, Steve decided, he would stay. But he would go about it his own way.

It took him most of the night to dig the grave. The winking gleam of the stars was paling before the false dawn when he carried the last armload of rock up from the creek and heaped it on the mound. He thought about a prayer. But then he remembered Nels's ways and said simply—"God, he was a good man."—before he sauntered down off the knoll and took stock of what he had saved from the fire.

There were tools, shoes for the horses, nails, a .40-70 carbine, some canned goods, salt, wheat and buckwheat flour, jerky, little else. Cooking his breakfast, he decided to leave the camp as it was.

His saddle had burned and his .45 lay there somewhere in the ashes. The last thing he had done before burying Nels was to take the heavy shell belt from his friend's waist and buckle it about his own narrow hips. As he finished his coffee now, he drew the weapon and looked at it in the strengthening light. Its handle was of antelope horn and Nels had carved it. It was hair-triggered, a .38, and Steve could remember Nels once saying: *It'll outrange your Forty-Five and shoot a damn' sight straighter . . . kill a man just as quick.* Steve supposed Nels had been right, although he couldn't be sure. He had never carried a handgun much, never used one except on rattlesnakes or potting at coyotes, and once to turn a stampeded herd out of the path of a grass fire. But from now on he would carry this Colt and one day he would use it. He was sure of that. Therefore it seemed right that it should be Nels's. Wearing it would take some getting used to.

He left his breakfast fire in the strengthening dawn, carrying a bridle and rope, knowing it would take him some time to find a horse. Whoever had fired the camp would certainly have run off the small remuda, maybe even the herd.

Half a mile down the stream he sighted a stock black of Nels's, grazing up a side draw. He roped the animal, rode him back to camp, and threw on

Nels's saddle, admiring the turquoise-set silver *conchas* dotting the swell and skirt. Nels had been vain in a lot of ways and had thought as much of this saddle as he did of the finest horse. Steve had to let out the stirrups a couple of holes and re-lace the straps. Finished with that, he stood deliberately, considering his first move.

They had passed below the town of Arrowhead early yesterday morning. There would be a sheriff back there, he knew, for the town was the county seat. But something about Jackson's arrogant manner yesterday, the lack of any reservation in the man's warning, told Steve now that he could accomplish little by going to the law. If people around here showed the law much respect or fear, such a thing as last night's raid on this camp couldn't have happened. So he decided that when he left camp it would be to ride down the stream.

First he picked up a couple of horses, a few minutes later a small bunch of four steers. He took his time and, in the next hour, covered less than two miles of the stream's length. By then the sun had rimmed a pass between the peaks and the night's chill was gone. It was another fine spring day.

Just short of 10:00 his count was thirty-two on the cattle, four on the horses. That, he decided, would have to do for now. The rest of the herd wouldn't stray far from water and he could work this part of the range later, tomorrow, the next day, or a week from now. He began pushing the herd on out toward the desert, occasionally stopping to take a long look back toward the rim.

Twenty minutes later he made out a faint haze of dust off to the north of the stream, and presently saw two riders angling in toward him from the foot of a hill spur to the north. From then on he didn't look back, just kept the herd moving.

When the quick hoof rhythm of trotting horses sounded across to him, he did look around. The man in the lead was Jackson. The one close behind, slat-bodied and dour-looking, wore a five-pointed star on his open vest

Jackson came to within ten feet of Steve before reining in and, as the sheriff halted his horse, said civilly: "'Mornin', stranger." Then, without preliminary, he added: "We see you had some bad luck last night."

Steve only nodded.

The sheriff's beady eyes were studying him and now the lawman asked: "That a grave we saw back there by your camp?"

"My partner."

"See here," Jackson was quick to say. "I'm damned sorry you ran into trouble. But it wasn't my crew that did that, stranger. You think I'd be here now if it was?"

"Did I say I thought it was you?"

Jackson seemed relieved. "Well, after all, we did have that talk yesterday. And I warned you off. I brought the sheriff out this mornin' to tell you to keep movin'. We had no idea of what happened to you."

Again Steve let a nod take the place of words.

The sheriff leaned out and expertly emptied his cheek of tobacco juice. His left eye was squinted as he gave Steve a glance that was purposely severe. "Where you goin' now, mister?"

Steve tilted his head at Jackson. "He said there was open range out a ways."

"You aim to file on it?" The sheriff reached in under his vest and scratched his ribs. The gesture fit his seedy, dirty look. He probably hadn't shaved for three or four days, for his gaunt face was covered with a short growth of gray whiskers. His vest was grease-spotted from spilled food and Steve noticed that his boots were cracked and badly run over at the heels.

"Thought I'd look it over and maybe take out papers if it was worth it," Steve answered.

"Well, son, it ain't. Save yourself the trouble and keep right on goin'. I'm powerful sorry them fools shot you up and burned you out last night." He made a point of adding: "Whoever they was."

Jackson looked around at the lawman now. "Len, you'd damn' well better find out who it was!"

"Sure, I aim to. You see anything that might help, stranger?"

"Not much. I counted four men. The one that got Nels used a shotgun on him."

"The hell! Remember that, Len. Check every shotgun you can lay hands on. You can start right now with my layout. Go on back there and tell Harvey you want to see every gun on the place."

"What's the good of that? All I need is your word your crew didn't do it, Bill."

"And last election we were told Len Hammer was the smartest man for the job," Jackson drawled with a thin sarcasm. "How do I know but what some of the boys decided to take things in their own hands last night?"

"Yeah, you're right."

"Then start lookin' around. This man's partner was murdered. You just goin' to say you're sorry and let it go at that?"

The lawman's eyes brightened in anger. "You run Crow Track, I'll run the sheriff's office, Bill," he murmured. He caught himself then and seemed to regret his outburst. "Hell, I'm jumpy this mornin'," he growled. "See you later." He reined his horse around and headed back the way he had come.

Jackson drawled acidly, as Hammer went away: "If the holes in Len's head were any bigger, sparrows would be nestin' between his ears." He shrugged, turning to Steve. "I'll send a couple men across to help you, neighbor. Lord, I'm sure sorry about this! Sure you can't remember anything that might help us track down who did it?"

"It happened too quick." Steve had carefully listened to Jackson's deep voice but it hadn't told him anything. "Much obliged for the offer, but I'll just mosey along on my own. Now I've got plenty of time. If you run into any A Bar O stuff mixed in with yours, you might let me know."

Jackson was a big man, as tall as Steve and heavier. He now thrust out his barrel chest and ran thumbs inside his belt, pushing his shirt down. "I'll do that. But you're makin' a mistake to go out there. It'll look nice at first. There's grass now and Small, the last man that tried it, left a cabin and a tank where he dammed up the wash. There'll be water in the tank. He even dug a well and there may be water there, too. But about thirty days from now your grass will die off and some fine morning you'll find your tank and well gone dry."

"Maybe I'll just hang on a week or so. Give my beef time to put some weight on."

Jackson nodded agreeably. "Now you're talkin' sense. Lay over a while and then head on south. Down there where the hills give out you'll find plenty of open range. Not the best, understand, but good enough to get by on."

Steve was thinking of something. "You say this man put down a well? How deep?"

"Only twelve, fifteen feet. Dig down any where along that wash and you'll find water in spring and early summer. Small always claimed this creek here ran underground out there. Guess he proved himself wrong. All it does is thin out until finally it runs dry."

"Doesn't sound too promising."

"It isn't, friend. Sure you don't want help?"

"No, thanks."

"Come on up to the place if you need anything. God Almighty, man, that was a mess back there. You must've lost 'most everything."

"Just about. But I had some luck." Steve's wide grin was deceivingly pleasant. "They didn't get me."

"I wondered about that. How come?"

"I'd walked off a ways to sleep. It was too dark for them to find me."

Jackson smiled slowly, broadly. "You must carry a rabbit's foot." He lifted a hand, wheeled his horse around. "Be sure and let me know if there's anything I can do."

"Sure will." Steve sat watching him ride away, wondering if it was his imagination that made him think Jackson's voice had something of the same tone as that voice last night by the chuck wagon. *There's a way to prove it!* he suddenly told himself. A tightness ran along his nerves as he sat there, letting Jackson ride almost a hundred yards. Then he took a deep breath and shouted: "Where do I find that cabin?"

Jackson stopped, turned in the saddle. "Keep

right on down the creek!" he shouted. "It runs into the wash. You can't miss it."

It was *the* voice—there was no mistaking it. A wave of rage stiffened Steve. His hand dropped to the holster at his thigh. Then an inner voice warned him—*Too far!*—and his hand slowly lifted to the swell of the saddle. It was a good thing, he decided, that he hadn't laced on the scabbard and brought along the carbine. Nothing would have pleased him better right now than to put a bullet through Jackson's back. *But there's a better way. There's got to be,* he thought.

The thought dammed the flood of his fury and he sat there, watching Jackson go away, turning the beginning of an idea idly over in his mind.

Small's cabin was a sorry sight as Steve rode in on it. Wind and snow had nearly ruined it. Better than half the slabs of its walls had warped as they dried and pulled loose, a few fallen at one end, so that Steve could see daylight through the one-room shack from any side. The corral on the lip of the wash was in about the same shape. Some of the peeled aspen poles were down, others were broken. Several were gone, the charred coals of a fire nearby telling Steve that someone had made firewood of them. The well was the biggest disappointment of all. It lay at the foot of a path leading down the ten-foot wall of the arroyo. Small had used more slab to shore up the sandy walls of the hole but a good many of these had rotted through, letting sand and gravel fill in the bottom, until all Steve saw as he peered down into the well was a greenish scum, covering a small puddle.

Not much was what he told himself as he climbed the path back to the shack. Nine out of ten other men would have decided that the place wasn't worth bothering about. But Steve had always been a steady thinker and last night's violence had ripened his purpose, and so he judged that Small's place would suit him as well as any other, perhaps better. And because he was anything but lazy, he at once began the job he knew must come first.

He had pushed the horses and cattle as far as the pond, then let them drift, knowing they wouldn't leave the water. Up at the shack he had spotted two rusty buckets. Now he brought them down to the well, took off his jumper and boots, and dropped into the hole. The moist sand felt cool to his feet. He began scooping out the sand steadily, for better than an hour easily throwing it out over the lip of the hole. By the time he rigged his rope to the pulley on the crosspiece above, he was standing in cloudy water that reached to his calves. He would fill both buckets, tie the rope end to them, then climb out, and dump the sand.

An hour before sunset the buckets were lying alongside the pulley brace and he was looking down at the water seeping into the clean hole, knowing that by morning there would be three feet of clear, sweet water down there.

He saddled the black once more and started back upcountry to the camp and the burned wagon. On the way he caught up another of his horses, and as dusk was settling he loaded the spare animal with grub and tools and packed them back down to the cabin, reaching it long after dark.

He slept in the open that night. But it was a long time before he closed his eyes. He was thinking about Nels, trying to keep down the bitterness and anger and make sense of certain things. He was remembering particularly what Jackson had said about the creek and Small's well. And presently he was looking back four years, recalling in detail the digging of a deep well on a ranch where he and Nels had been working. For a week or so they had worked the well rig and it was the mechanics of the thing he was trying to picture now.

The next morning he was up before dawn, his breakfast fire burning a rosy hole in the blackness. By sunup he was in the hills high above the rim, keeping clear of trails and following out the cañons that cut back toward the high country.

Four times he looked down on ranch buildings lying along those cañons, and not until the fourth time was he impressed by anything he saw. The first three layouts were just ordinary, the size of their corrals marking them as small outfits. But the fourth was something different. It lay along a creek in the widest cañon, heading a two-mile sweep of rich, open grass. The house was L-shaped, big, built of stone. One small corral and two big ones lay out behind the huge hump-roofed barn and a cluster of smaller buildings. Steve knew it was Crow Track even before he slanted down through the timber to read the brands on the steers grazing the upper edge of the meadow.

He dropped back down to the rim trail finally and, as he headed north toward Arrowhead, drew certain conclusions about what he had seen this morning. Crow Track was big, prosperous, and had the best of the graze along this slope. Crow Track's neighbors were poor and, from all appearances, just getting along. And Steve revised his opinion of Bill Jackson to a small degree. He had thought that somewhere he would be able to find help in what he had set out to do. Now he knew he wouldn't find it. He was on his own.

Mark Wheeler looked at his watch and, seeing it lacked eight minutes of being noon, decided to take advantage of those extra minutes. He had risen from his desk and was reaching for his hat when a stranger came up to the rail beyond the desk, drawling: "They tell me you're the man to see about a loan."

Wheeler smiled in his good-natured way. "I'm the one. Come on in." He was inwardly impatient to leave the bank and go on home to dinner but didn't show it.

Steve stepped on into the small enclosure behind the bank's street window, holding his hat. He shook the banker's hand when it was offered, gave his name, and then took the chair alongside the desk Wheeler indicated. His instinctive distrust of bankers was slightly disconcerted by Mark Wheeler's straightforward, honest look. The man was tall, thin as a rail, his face hawkish and tanned deeper than any townsman's had a right to be, his hands work-worn and calloused. He looked to Steve more like an ordinary cowpoke than the president of a bank.

"I have fifty head of cattle out on the flats I'd like to borrow three hundred on," Steve said.

"Shouldn't be hard to arrange that. When can I see 'em?"

"The sooner the better."

Wheeler nodded, already liking Steve's directness. "One o'clock suit you?" The banker waited for the tilt of Steve's head, then queried: "How far out are they?"

"Do you know Small's homestead? They're there."

Mark Wheeler's look was puzzled. "Not for good, I hope."

"For good."

Wheeler folded his hands on the desk, made a tent of his thumbs, and, carefully regarding them, said: "You must be new here or you'd know better than to try that place. There's no water on it."

"There will be."

The banker looked up sharply. For a moment he studied his customer's angular face. It was a young face. But there was a solid look in the pale blue eyes. He was impressed. He said: "Cattle are cattle and it's your look out where you're headed, Ash. How long do you want the money for?"

"Thirty days."

Wheeler made a mental note: *He'll have grass for just about that long.* He got up from the desk and reached his hat down off the rack by the window. "I'll be here at one."

He walked out to the street with Steve, shook hands with him, and took the opposite direction along the uneven plank walk.

Mark Wheeler, in twenty-two years of banking, hadn't made as much money as even the average resources of this country should have allowed him to make. Intelligent, shrewd to a point, he had tried to worship money as did some men of his calling, but had failed, finding it easier to make friends than enemies. And during these past few years he had put aside the ambitions of his early manhood and decided to enjoy life and his friends. As he left Steve, he was curious enough about him to stop in at the Land Office, to discover that Small's quarter-section had been filed on by the stranger. The matter still didn't concern him beyond the point of protecting his investment. Since it was to be for only thirty days, he saw little risk in making the loan.

He went on along the awninged walk, flanked by the weather-beaten false-fronted stores, thinking, as he always did on walking this street, that this was a sorry-looking town, but liking it all the same. He'd been born and raised here; it was home to him and he was loyal to the town and its people.

He was sauntering past the feed store when Les Anders hailed him from the doorway and stepped out alongside him.

"Mark, what do you know about a man named Ash? Ever heard of him?"

"Just," Wheeler said. "Why?"

"He was in to see me about leasin' my well rig. Wants me to haul it out to Small's place and set it up and haul some wood to feed the engine. Wants to drill the well hisself. He's willin' to pay my price."

"I'll know by tonight if he's good for it, Les. He's borrowing on some beef."

Anders was frowning thoughtfully, seeming almost uninterested in what the banker had told him. "What gets me is this idea he has of hittin' water. He claims it's goin' to be artesian, Mark."

Wheeler's eyes opened wide in quick surprise. He thought about it, said nothing, and shortly Anders drawled: " 'Course, it ain't my affair whether he's wrong or right. But if he's right, he's got a gold mine by the tail."

The banker nodded. "He certainly has."

"That soil out there would grow anything if it had water. You reckon he's on the right track?"

Wheeler was a long moment saying: "He could be. Give me time to think it over. I'm going out there this afternoon with him. I'll have a better idea tonight."

Anders nodded. "You're the only man around here that knows a blamed thing about gee . . . geol . . . whatever you call it."

"Geology, Les."

"Yeah. Well, Ash claims there's a limestone bench breaks off there along the rim and takes up farther out, along about where Willow Creek goes underground. It's his idea he can drill through to a regular underground river."

The idea made such an impression on the banker that he breathed a low whistle. Then, impatient to be gone, he said—"I'll let you know, Les."—and went on up the walk, hurrying now.

At the house, he went straight to his bedroom upstairs, to a shelf of books hanging above his dresser. There were fourteen books in all and six of them were on geology and mining. He took one out and was thumbing through it when his wife called up the back stairway from the kitchen: "Mark, your dinner's hot."

"Be there in a minute, Carrie."

But she had to call twice again before he finally came downstairs and sat at the table, propping the book up by his plate and reading as he ate. All through the meal he was silent, deeply absorbed by his reading. Finally his wife gave up trying to talk to him.

On the way back to the bank he stopped in at the courthouse, a hunch taking him to the sheriff's office. He had never felt anything but a well-hidden contempt for Len Hammer and it was his intention now to be as brief as possible in his call on the sheriff. But he had no sooner mentioned Steve Ash's name than Hammer started a long-winded yarn about the stranger. With but little prompting from Wheeler, the lawman had presently told the whole story of Ash and his partner, of the killing and of his own meeting with Ash, accompanied by Bill Jackson, yesterday morning.

"So you don't know who killed his partner?" the banker asked finally.

"Mark, there ain't a prayer of findin' out. I cut back to where they burned the wagon and tried to follow sign. But it was all messed up by then. From what I could make out, them four jaspers circled, rode the creek upstream, and made for the hills."

"Think it could have been Crow Track?" Wheeler, over the years, had formed his private opinion of Bill Jackson, and now that he saw the possibility of Jackson's being involved in an out-and-out murder he was more excited than he usually let himself get.

Len Hammer laughed at the question. "Why would Bill have come in to get me to kick them two off his range if he'd done it, Mark?"

"His range, you say?" Wheeler tried not to show his irritation.

"Well, it's the same as his, ain't it?"

"So it is," Wheeler drawled wearily. He had learned a great deal more than he had hoped to as he went to the door now.

"What was it you wanted to know about Ash, Mark?"

"Nothing much. He's come in for a loan."

"Borrowin' money? What for?"

"To put down a well."

Hammer's cackling laugh came again. "He sure come to the man that can tell him what a fool idea that is, eh?"

Wheeler was on the point of agreeing, for his noon reading had settled the question in his mind. But now, because there were things about this he didn't even begin to understand, he gave the lawman a strange answer. "I don't know, Len. He thinks he can bring in artesian water. Maybe he's onto something we've all overlooked."

"The hell!"

Mark Wheeler nodded and, knowing he had

planted a seed of strong curiosity in the sheriff's mind, left the office.

All the way down the street to the bank he was thinking of Crow Track. And when he saw Steve waiting by the bank's tie rail, he was struck by the thought: *Maybe Bill Jackson's pushed one man a little too far*.

He went to the livery barn for his horse and ten minutes later he and Steve were headed out across the grass flats below town toward Small's cabin.

Neither of them said much for a time. But presently Steve decided that something needed explaining. "Mister Wheeler, this morning I claimed this herd was fifty head. Right now it's closer to thirty, with the extras scattered off there along the creek above the place."

"I heard about that," Wheeler said.

Steve was surprised. "And you'll still make the loan?"

"Why shouldn't I?"

He's being honest, I better . . . was Steve's thought as he drawled: "Well, for one thing, they might try to run me off again."

"From Small's place? I doubt it. That's too sorry a layout for even Crow Track to bother with."

Steve sensed a veiled sarcasm in the banker's words. That somehow encouraged him. "Suppose I give 'em a reason to try and run me off?"

Mark Wheeler looked across at him, smiling

faintly. "It'll take more than talk of artesian water to give them a reason, Ash."

Once again Steve was strongly surprised. Wheeler, it seemed, knew everything he'd done in town and he wondered now how much the banker had guessed of his plans. Yet something about the man's directness encouraged him to ask: "Suppose I give 'em more than talk to go on? What then?"

"You'd have a fight on your hands."

"They'd try and kick me out?"

"They would."

"Who, Mister Wheeler? I've been trying to figure that. Crow Track casts a mighty wide shadow. Who else is there?"

"You've got three other outfits using this range along with Crow Track. But only because Jackson lets them," Wheeler couldn't help interjecting dryly. "There's Olson and his O-on-a-Rail, Milt Crosby who runs Double-Tree, and Akers, owner of Wheel. There's just about enough grass here outside Crow Track fence to keep them going."

"Then it could have been any one of them that shot us up?"

"Could have been. But it's not likely. Any one of the three would have talked it over with you first."

Steve thought about that a moment before saying quietly: "You're the same as saying it was Crow Track."

"Am I?" Wheeler looked at Steve seriously. "If you ever claimed I said that, I'd have to call you a liar, Ash."

Once more they rode on in silence, Steve idly noticing that the banker seemed quite at home on a horse. They reached the creek and followed it on west and, with Small's cabin finally in sight, Wheeler spoke again.

"I don't know how much you know about water, Ash. But you haven't a prayer of getting it out here. Artesian or any other kind. Anders said you hoped to run onto that limestone fault that gives out along the rim."

Steve gave a slow grin. "I was counting on nobody taking me up on that."

Wheeler nodded. "So I suspected. But when you make a brag on something you don't know too much about, there's always at least one man that can trip you up. I'm the one man here, Ash. The only one."

"So you'll spike my story?"

The banker glanced obliquely over at Steve, his eyes wholly grave. "No . . . I don't think I will. I don't know what you aim to prove, son. But it's your affair, not mine. Go ahead with it, whatever it is. And if someone's going to get hurt, I can only hope it won't be you."

Steve would have liked to thank the man. He didn't know quite how. So all he said was: "We'll see how it turns out."

It took Steve three days, with Les Ander's help, to set the well rig and get the drilling started. The steam engine was balky at first, but Anders knew its peculiarities and that second day, after they got it going, Steve had caught onto its crankiness.

"Sure you don't need me?" Anders asked when they quit work that third evening.

Steve shook his head, grinning sheepishly. "Guess I'm just trying to nurse the nickels, Les. We'll see how it works out. Chances are I'll be running in to you every day."

"Well, I ain't makin' no charge for what I can do. Fact is, I'd work full time for nothin' to see this come through."

"You could file on that quarter-section below me," Steve said. "If it pans out, there'll be more water than I can use."

Anders frowned and explained awkwardly: "Hell, I got all a man needs to live on. But if you could make a fool of Bill Jackson, you'd please me and plenty others around here. If I was you, damned if I wouldn't take a box of shells up there and wait along that Crow Track trail some moonlight night."

"They'd hang you, Les."

The well man chuckled. "Guess they would.

Well, you know what you're doin', Steve. So long." And he started off to the corral for his horse, having told Steve an hour ago he had to be back home in Arrowhead at suppertime

Steve thought a moment before calling after him: "Les, you'd be doing me a favor if you did file on this bit west of me! You might mention the idea to Wheeler, too. He could take up that stretch to the south."

"Too much bother," Anders answered.

"Wouldn't take you ten minutes to do it," Steve urged.

Anders frowned thoughtfully, his look puzzled. "You mean you want me to, even if I never take it up?"

Steve nodded.

"You got a reason, ain't you, fella?" Anders eyed Steve questioningly, then at length gave an offhand shrug of his bony shoulders. "All right, if it'll help you, I'll do it." And he left.

Anders reached town at dusk and, on his way home, stopped off at Mark Wheeler's house, telling the banker of Steve's idea. The next morning Anders and Wheeler visited the Land Office. Shortly after they had left it, the agent put on his coat and hat and walked up to the courthouse. As a result of his stop there, the sheriff left town around 10:00 and rode out along the rim trail.

Mark Wheeler had barely hung up his hat after

getting back to the bank from his noon meal when Bill Jackson came in and over to the rail by the desk, saying affably: "Hello, Mark. Makin' any honest dollars?"

"Damn' few." Wheeler had a certain smile reserved for men he didn't particularly like, one that had deceived several of his acquaintances over the years. It accompanied his words now.

Jackson reached in under his black suit coat and took out two cigars, tossing one across to the banker.

Then Jackson said: "See I've got a new neighbor."

"Ash?" Wheeler paused to draw on the cigar. "He's done some business here. Borrowed on his herd so he could put down a well."

Jackson's hearty laugh rang back along the room. "So you'll soon be in the cattle business?"

A thoughtful look crossed Wheeler's dark face. "I'm not so sure, Bill. He may be able to pay off that note easier than I could."

"There's no water out there."

"So we've all thought all along. But Ash is going at it a different way. He's after deep water, artesian."

Jackson tried to look amazed. "You been eatin' locoweed, Mark?"

Wheeler lifted his shoulders, let them fall. "Sometimes I wonder. But I've looked up a few things on artesian water"—it was with real effort that the banker controlled his expression of gravity—"and there's a typical formation for it showing along the rim. Then Willow Creek drops underground with all that water."

"Dries up, you mean."

"Maybe so, maybe not. That's what Ash is gambling on."

"And you think enough of the idea to gamble along with him?"

"No. I'll get my money regardless. But I filed on the quarter-section south of him this morning."

Jackson chuckled, forgetting to appear surprised. "You'll never prove up on a homestead, Mark."

"If that water comes through, I'm turning the bank over to John Byard and building a place out there," Wheeler said in honest seriousness. "I've always wanted a place out of town."

Jackson tried to laugh off the idea and for a few minutes they talked on. Then Jackson took up some minor business, and presently left the bank.

It was just past 3:00 that afternoon when Steve spotted a lone horseman coming in on the cabin from the direction of town. It didn't take him long to recognize Jackson's massive bulk and a wave of excitement hit him.

He was stoking the boiler with lengths of cedar when Jackson rode up. Steve used the steady, clanking pound of the rig to conceal the fact that he knew anyone was around. When he straightened and appeared to see the Crow Track owner for the first time, his head jerked up in astonishment.

"You're makin' a lot of noise, Ash," Jackson said as he swung off his horse.

Steve wiped the sweat from his forehead and to all appearances his smile showed Jackson a strong welcome. "Nearly drives me crazy sometimes," he said loudly over the pound of the engine.

"How far down is she?" Jackson asked, eyeing the moist muck heap on the far side of the rig. The mound was capped by a gravelly showing of limestone rock.

"Haven't measured lately," was Steve's evasive answer.

He was hoping last night's trip up to an isolated spot along the rim would pay off now. He had packed four sacks of limestone back here, roped to the makeshift saddles of two lead horses, and it had taken him until 2:00 this morning to break up the rock and dump about half of it on the muck heap. Yesterday he had hit rock, an obstacle Steve knew would sooner or later stump him. He knew nothing about rigging Les Anders's drill cores to get through the rock. Anyway, he didn't have to drill through it. The only thing that mattered was that the muck heap looked as though he was bringing up limestone. Now, with the rig set only so it was pounding on the rock shelf exactly twenty-eight feet below the surface, he was going to find out how convincing he had been in his deception.

He saw the interest liven briefly in Jackson's eyes. "Much farther to go?" Jackson asked.

"Not much. You can see how wet that stuff is." Just ten minutes ago, he had used two buckets of water he'd kept handy for just this purpose, dumping them on the top of the muck heap.

Jackson sauntered around the rig now to the muck heap, resting one boot on its muddy slope and picking up a handful of the powdered limestone. He turned to Steve, fingering the mess in his hand, looking down at it. "What's makin' it so wet? Surface water?"

Steve shook his head. "No. Didn't run into any of that water that feeds the well. The hole was dry as a bone as far down as the rock." This much was true and for the first time Steve's conscience was letting him give Jackson a definite answer.

"Then where's the water comin' from?"

"It could be that pressure from below is forcing it up through the rock." Steve shrugged. "But I wouldn't say for sure." He was going to let the Crow Track owner decide this for himself.

That enigmatic look of Jackson's was fading before an eagerness he couldn't keep out of his eyes. "You mean there's enough pressure so that it pushes the water clear through the rock?"

Steve let a broad smile come to his face. He was really pleased at seeing the way Jackson was swallowing the bait. "If you got an ear for this thing, you can hear water sloshing around down in that hole right now, Mister Jackson."

It was up to Jackson, Steve decided, to read anything he wanted to into the thumping of the rig. And, watching the man, Steve saw a look of amazement slowly cross his face. "Then it really will be artesian water, Ash?"

"It'd be bad luck for me to say it before it happened, wouldn't it?"

Jackson shook the muck from his hand, took a blue polka-dot handkerchief from his back pocket, and carefully wiped his fingers. Abruptly his glance lifted to Steve. "How much would you take for this place, Ash?"

Steve sobered. "Well, I . . . fact is, I hadn't thought of selling."

"It'll take money to develop this. You haven't got it."

"Maybe I could get the money. Just as you came up I was wondering if I hadn't ought to knock off and go in for that casing Anders has got loaded for me. If this thing blows before the casing's down, it might mean I'd have to drill a new hole."

"But we were talkin' about money, Ash," Jackson said impatiently. "You could cash in without the bother of developin' this place."

"Developing it won't be hard, Mister Jackson.

The bank ought to be willing if I hit what I'm after."

Jackson didn't appear at all pleased. He stood looking at the muck heap, thinking. Finally he looked around at Steve, drawling: "Have you thought of another thing?"

"I've thought of a lot of things."

"But has it struck you that whoever killed your partner that night might make another try at you? Especially when he finds out what you've run onto."

"Why would he?" Steve queried in seeming innocence. "All he wanted was for us to get off his range, whoever he was."

Jackson laughed. "You don't know these men around here. Take Slim Akers, for one. I've had nothin' but trouble with him for years. He's got it in his craw that I once hogged him off twelve sections of hill graze behind his place. The truth is he'd never thought twice about the land until I put a fence around it."

Steve appeared to think this over a moment. "But I'm not taking anything from Akers. I've got a legal right to be here."

"Look, my friend, you've got something here that's worth more in cold cash than any outfit there in the hills, not countin' mine. If you met with an accident, what's to keep any one of those jaspers from movin' in and takin' this place for their own? Akers or Olson or any of the rest?"

"I hadn't thought of that."

"You don't need to think of it. Just say the word and I'll give you two thousand in cash for the place."

"It's worth more than that, Mister Jackson. Besides, I wouldn't want to sell."

Jackson's manner changed abruptly. He laid a hand on Steve's shoulder, saying affably: "Maybe I wouldn't sell if I was you, either. But just remember the offer, Ash. In case you want to get rid of it later."

"I'll do that. Much obliged."

They talked a few more minutes, Steve mentioning the balkiness of the rig and the hard time he was having operating it alone, and presently Jackson rode away. When he was out of sight, Steve closed down the boiler, saddled a horse, and started for town. The excitement was still running high in him.

He rode alertly, warily, remembering Jackson's mention of an accident. He had never before knowingly faced the actual danger of anyone deliberately setting out to kill him. But now he instinctively attuned himself to that danger and his riding showed it. He studied the ground ahead, skirting likely places of ambush. And as the miles dropped behind him, he was planning what he would do tonight.

On reaching town, he went straight to Les Anders's house and arranged for the casing to be loaded onto a wagon, saying he'd call for it after supper. He avoided as well as he could any detailed discussion with the well man about the progress he was making on the job, telling him only that he thought the casing should be ready when he needed it.

Leaving Anders's place and riding on down the street, he saw Mark Wheeler coming up the walk on his way home after his day's work. He cut across the street to meet the banker, suddenly remembering one more detail that had almost slipped his mind.

" 'Evening," he drawled. "I was on my way to see you. It's about money again."

"How's the well coming?" Wheeler seemed eager for Steve's reply.

"I'm hauling out the casing tonight," Steve answered noncommittally. "There's a lot extra I can use above ground, piping the water where I want it to go. What I wanted to see you about was getting me some credit with the hardware store. I want them to order an extra thousand feet of four-inch pipe for me."

Wheeler looked as though Steve had idly remarked that the ground was splitting open under his feet. "You can't do that," he breathed.

"Why can't I? I can still borrow a lot more on the herd. By the way, I make a count of forty-seven now."

The banker stepped off the walk and close in to

the horse's shoulder, gravely looking up at Steve. "Son, you're throwing your money away."

"Money never did me a bit of good until I spent it," Steve drawled, adding as an afterthought: "Jackson paid me a visit this afternoon."

"I knew he would. Anders and I filed on that land next to you this morning. Jackson came in to see me. He'd heard about it some way."

"He wants to buy the place as is, Mister Wheeler."

The banker smiled gladly. "What's his offer?"

"Two thousand."

"Then take it and get out."

Steve shook his head, drawling tonelessly: "He'll pay more. A lot more."

"He won't have to pay it if anything happens to you. Don't take any more chances, Ash. Sell out to him. That's what you've been after all along, isn't it?"

"Maybe I have. But I'm not through for a while yet. Will you give me more credit?"

"Of course," Wheeler said glumly, finally seeing the futility of arguing. "But be careful. If anything happened to you, I'd never forgive myself."

"Jackson mentioned a man named Akers this afternoon. Said he was a curly wolf. Said he might be the one that killed Nels."

Wheeler snorted. "Slim Akers is about the same kind of a curly wolf I am. Does that answer your question?"

"It does. Thanks." Steve lifted a hand and reined back out onto the street, going on.

His visit to the hardware store caused a flurry of excitement. Bates, the owner, was as curious as he was garrulous and Steve had a hard time not saying too much. But he held his tongue and, after ordering the pipe, ate his supper at a restaurant.

He was swinging into the saddle once more at the tie rail in front of the restaurant when a man he had never seen before came to the edge of the walk and called to him.

"Hear you've brought in a hell of a good well, Ash! I'll be your neighbor to the north. I heard about your luck and made the Land Office just before they closed."

"Better go easy," Steve drawled, once he could speak over his surprise. "Better wait until it's a sure thing."

The man laughed, really pleased at something. "There's no use trying to run a sandy, Ash. 'Most everybody in town knows you've struck it rich."

IV

By 11:00 that night, when the waning moon slipped below the far flat horizon, Steve was within three miles of the cabin. Anders's two teams had plodded steadily along for the past three hours and Steve felt reasonably safe, for the moon gave enough light so that he could see for several hundred yards. But now, with the obscurity gathering deeply about him, he moved down off the high perch of the seat.

He had pretty thoroughly thought out this possibility of not reaching the cabin before the moon went down and for most of the past quarter hour he had been down off the seat, ahead of it, working with the reins tied to a seat brace. He had scanned the night shadows about him uneasily as he shifted the center lengths of the heavy ten-foot casing back a couple of feet from the head board of the wagon's bed, leaving a cavity big enough for him to drop down into, well out of sight. The one thought that made him uneasy was the hunch that he might have made a mistake in leaving his horse and saddle back in Les Anders's barn. He might, just possibly, need the horse now before he reached the cabin.

He came to the wide place in the wash where Anders's wagon had crossed several days ago. And as the two teams dropped down the slope, the sand deadening the grating of the wheel rims, he caught a stray sound shuttling in out of the night. Instantly he dropped down off the seat. His legs were catching his weight when a heavy explosion boomed close by. He heard the impact of a bullet through the backboard of the seat, as the reins tightened suddenly and the wagon lurched ahead while the frightened teams slogged into a slow run.

He pulled on the reins, keeping low between the two racked stacks of casings as three more shots cracked out, two of them swift-spaced and from one gun, the last from a second on the other side of the wagon. One of the bullets clanged against the iron pipe and went screaming away. The sounds now made the horses bolt.

Steve held the reins in his left hand and drew his .38. The wagon tilted sharply, gave a violent lurch, and then settled back on its wheels as the teams pulled up out of the wash. Other hoofs pounded close by. Some instinct made him crouch lower and the next moment a gun's staccato thunder beat across the night. And once more a length of iron clanged loudly against the impact of a bullet.

When the gun went silent, Steve came suddenly erect, guessing that the marksman had emptied his weapon. He saw a rider's vague shadow swinging off into the obscurity, lifted Nels's .38, lined it carefully. An instant after the gun bucked against his hand he saw the indistinct outline of man and horse change shape. A high scream rode in over the hoof thunder of his two teams. The next moment the second gun opened up against him from the other side of the wagon and he dropped quickly to his knees.

The teams were really running now. The wagon lurched crazily, once threatening to go over. But Steve tugged hard on one rein, swinging the teams sharply to the side where he felt the wheels lift. They hit the ground with a jolt that bruised his knees.

All at once the bottom seemed to drop from under the wagon. It swayed sharply up on the left wheels and Steve sensed it was going over. He dropped the reins and drove up and outward. Falling clear, he crashed through the branches of a piñon, lit hard on one shoulder, and let his body go over in a roll. He came to his feet, saw a mound of pipe spill from the wagon, rolling toward him, and lunged away. Then he lost his footing along the steep side of the wash and fell headlong into it, scrambling up the far side as lengths of iron clanged downward into it.

It was over then. Even the teams were quiet now, no longer pitching against the traces of the overturned wagon. Then from far behind, Steve caught the fading sound of a horse being ridden away fast. *Where's the other?* he at once asked himself, knowing that two riders had shot at the wagon.

But before he could even begin to think about that, he heard another sound, quite like the first, this time from the opposite direction, toward the cabin. As it strengthened, it took on the definite rhythmic beat of horses on the run. He looked around, saw a low shadow nearby, and walked over to find it a waist-high clump of greasewood. He was kneeling there behind it, Colt in hand, when two riders came in on the wagon and pulled down to a quick stop. Then a voice hailed him loudly.

"Ash, you there? Sing out!"

It was the same voice that had shouted that night when Nels had died, Bill Jackson's. Steve could make out the two figures plainly and now he deliberately lifted the .38 and lined it at the biggest of the pair. Then a small voice of caution and of curiosity spoke to him and he dropped the Colt out of line. He wanted to see how Jackson was going to play this. So he answered: "Over here. Who is it?"

Jackson and his companion reined over as far as the lengths of casing that lay strewn down the far side of the wash and the Crow Track owner called out again.

"You all right?"

"Right as rain." Steve was still kneeling there, out of sight.

"What the hell happened?" Jackson wanted to know.

"Someone made a try for me. There were two of 'em. Maybe I got one."

There was a moment's silence before Jackson queried: "How sure are you?"

"Not at all sure. We can take a look back there a hundred yards or so."

Steve heard Jackson say to his companion—"Light a fire so we can see something, Milt."—and then Steve saw him ride away in the darkness along the faintly visible line of the wagon tracks.

"Any brush across there?" the Crow Track rider called to Steve.

"I'll have a look."

Steve was careful as he moved, walking away from the wash and far enough to be out of sight of the Crow Track man. He started gathering dead branches from several nearby bushy cedars, but, as he worked, he would stop every few seconds and listen. He didn't feel even halfway safe until he saw the flicker of a small blaze cut the darkness back near the wagon. Then he watched Jackson's man carefully, and didn't walk in on the fire with his armload of wood until Jackson was back, dismounted alongside the blaze.

Jackson saw him crossing the wash and called: "Didn't find anything! If you got him, he's lyin' off there somewhere in the brush. We can look again tomorrow."

Steve came up and dropped his wood alongside the fire.

"Did you get a look at either man?" Jackson asked.

With a shake of the head, Steve grinned wryly. It was important just now that he appear perfectly at ease. "It was black as the inside of your hat."

Jackson looked at his crewman. "What's your guess, Al?"

"Slim Akers," the man said deliberately, not looking at Steve.

"Damn! Wish you'd got at least a look at one," Jackson said, eyeing Steve. He drew in a deep sigh. "Well, here's the trouble I warned you about. Maybe you'll feel different about sellin' now."

"No, I'm just cussed enough to want to stay worse'n ever."

"I might up the price a little, Ash. Here's your chance for some quick money and a whole hide."

"I can think it over," Steve drawled.

Jackson seemed to dismiss the matter as he turned to survey the wreck of the wagon. They walked over and looked at it. One front wheel and that axle were broken, the brake arm was gone, and some of the sideboards were split.

"Anders'll love me for this," Steve said ruefully. He was unhitching the teams, taking the harness off one of the wheelers so he could ride him to the cabin.

When Steve was ready, Jackson said: "We'll ride on back with you."

Steve managed somehow to lag behind the pair when they started out. The fact that his horse was worn out from the run helped and most of the time he had both Jackson and his crewman positioned so that he could keep an eye on them.

Presently Jackson offered: "You're loco not to wish this all on me, Ash. I've got men enough to handle whoever's makin' a try at you."

Steve was thinking—*He wasn't expecting it to*

turn out this way.—before he drawled: "I'll stick it out a while longer."

Jackson reined over closer to him. "This is disappointing as hell. When I found you weren't at home, I decided to wait for you if you took the whole night gettin' here. I came across here to buy, regardless of price. All you've got to do is name your figure and I'll meet it, providin' you don't want the gold out of my teeth."

Steve chuckled softly. "You could've saved yourself the trouble. Besides, I'm not at all sure yet you'd be buying anything but a hole in the ground."

"I'll take my chances on that. To the tune of four thousand."

Steve whistled. "That's considerable."

"Sure it is. You better take it."

After a long moment, Steve said: "We can talk when the well comes through."

"Why wait for that?"

"Hell, mister, I'm not swindling any man."

Crow Track's owner said nothing more, and, as Steve rode along, his right hand lay on his thigh, his fingers now and then nudging the holster. Once he asked himself: *Why don't I use up a shell now and get it over with?* And the more he thought of it, the more tempting the idea became.

But then he realized he was getting more than a little satisfaction out of stringing Jackson along, watching him grow anxious. The man's mind was obviously toying with all the possibilities that lay open if he could buy the well. He would be thinking how he could develop this long stretch of fertile land edging the desert, mile upon mile of it. Perhaps he was already planning on sending his crew in to the Land Office to file on neighboring quarter-sections. Or was he simply counting on drilling more wells, bringing in water enough to supply twenty or thirty sections of this land? He could make more selling water than he could clear raising crops and planting orchards. And it would be quick money, while the men who worked the land would have to develop it to make their profit. The thought of all these things, that were never to be, made Steve laugh softly.

Jackson heard that laugh and said: "Damned if I could see anything funny if this had happened to me."

Steve thought quickly. "I was just wondering how much Anders would charge me for that well rig of his."

"Why? You going to buy it?"

"If this well comes through, it wouldn't be a bad gamble to drill a couple more, would it?"

Steve had said enough, just enough. He let it go at that, knowing that the reason Jackson made no comment was because he was too absorbed by the possibilities of the idea. And, by the time they climbed their horses out of the wash in front of the cabin, Steve guessed that the Crow Track owner was still mulling it over in his mind.

"Much obliged for all your help," Steve said as he slid from his horse alongside the cabin.

"You think over my offer, Ash." Jackson reined out to join his crewman.

"I will."

"Let me know if the well comes through. I might even be able to lay hands on a little more money."

"I'll do that, too."

The pair of Crow Track men said good night and started away and Steve at once went into the shack, keeping an eye on their fading shapes. Then, just to play it safe, he stepped out through a hole in the cabin's back wall where a slab had fallen off. He ran out and lay behind the engine platform of the well rig until all sounds of their going had died.

Later, after he had gone back to the wrecked wagon for the three other horses and brought them in to the corral, he carried his blankets far out onto the flat and went to sleep the moment he lay down. He had made a mental note to wake up early, very early. For he knew that the coming day would decide this. There was a lot of work to be done. He'd been waiting, holding off, wanting more proof against Jackson. Now he had it, for there wasn't the slightest doubt in him about that try for him tonight. Crow Track had made it.

• • •

By dawn the next morning Steve had already put in two hours of work. He had made two trips up the wash to the point where the wrecked wagon lay and, unbolting the rear axle, had used it and the two sound rear wheels to move the heavy lengths of iron pipe to the cabin. For a time he thought of caving in the bank of the wash on several lengths of pipe and burying it, hiding it. Then he remem-ered that no one but Les Anders would know how many feet of iron he had hauled out here.

As the light strengthened, he fired up the boiler, watered it, and then hauled three barrels of water up from the well. When he had steam enough, he winched the cable up out of the hole until the core drill hung suspended over it. He took the drill off, packed it with some of the pulverized limestone, and laid it aside. Then he emptied his barrels into the hole and made two more trips to the well with them.

Finally the water gushed out over the rim of the hole and filled the depression around it, making a shallow pool. Then Steve used the engine to lift the first length of casing and drop it into the hole. He was working fast now, his restless glance time and again shuttling upcountry for any sight of a rider. He didn't want to be seen doing this.

He dropped that first length of casing into the hole, rigged another. He waded into the muddy water carelessly, slopping it up over the front of his waist overalls. He got the second section down, and then the third. It was the fourth that stuck out of the hole, its end barely above the surface of the pool. This last length was different from the others, its upright end threaded.

Anders had sent along a gunny sack full of elbows, Ts, and caps. Steve took one of the caps and used a big wrench to tighten it down on the end of the casing. He put all his strength against the wrench. Finished, he dumped a bucket of water over the cap and stepped back, inspecting what he had done.

The luckiest thing that had happened to him, he saw, was the way that last section had gone in. He hadn't planned it this way, but the cap was half under water. It really looked as though the pool was being fed by leakage from the casing around the cap. Now he could take his time, even sit down. Nothing but the waiting remained to be done. Every so often he would have to dump another barrel into the pool to keep up its level. But that was all.

He went across and built up his burned-down fire and brewed a second batch of coffee. He thought about cleaning up, wiping the caked mud from his boots, and putting on a clean pair of pants. But then he realized that his grubby looks made the whole thing more convincing. So he squatted by the fire, shivering a little against the dampness of his legs and feet until finally the sun was high enough to warm him.

V

Bill Jackson had his first good look at the well rig from half a mile away. He had stopped twice and listened for the pounding, hadn't heard it. That fact had already made him curious, for it was past 10:00 and he knew Ash must have been up and working for hours. Now, as he eyed the rig, he could see that it was shut down. There was no smoke coming from the chimney of the boiler.

He's done it! Jackson raked his gelding's flanks with spurs the instant the thought came.

He didn't let the animal break his run for a second of the time it took him to reach the wash. There he roughly hauled in on the gelding, suddenly thinking he mustn't appear too anxious about this. But the memory of Ash's stubbornness finally convinced him that any subterfuge would only work against him.

Steve saw him coming and left the fire, his second steaming cup of coffee in hand. By the time he walked in on the rig, Jackson was already out of the saddle and staring at the pool, his eyes showing his excitement, wide in disbelief.

"Looks good, eh?" Steve asked as he approached.

Crow Track's owner swore. "She's pushin' right out around that cap . . . a real artesian!"

Steve said nothing, and shortly Jackson became

aware of this, looking across and asking: "Don't you feel worked up over it?"

"Some. But I've been counting on this for so long I kind of wore it out of me."

Jackson said recklessly: "Name your own figure and I'll meet it."

"But I don't have any notion of what it's worth, Mister Jackson."

"See here . . . you've stalled me long enough. Four thousand was my offer last night. I'll double that right now."

Jackson reached to the inside pocket of his coat and took out a wallet that bulged. "Right this minute. Here's eight thousand. All you have to do is ride into town with me and sign the deed."

Steve eyed the man calmly for several seconds. Then he drawled: "I got to thinking about it last night. This isn't my game, Mister Jackson. All I know is horses and cattle. If I could walk away from this thing with a stake big enough to buy me a nice layout somewhere, that's all I'd ask."

"Eight thousand will do that."

Steve shook his head. "No, it'd take more to swing the deal I'm thinking about." This morning, over breakfast, he really had been dreaming about a certain outfit he knew was up for sale down in a valley of the Sawtooths. There was a girl down there, too, and for some time he'd been thinking of her, off and on. The girl and that hill layout somehow went together and only this morning he had remembered how they had both been at the back of his mind when he and Nels went in as partners. Then it had seemed out of the question that he could ever own the ranch, let alone ever take the girl to it. But now, quite suddenly, he saw that it was possible.

Jackson spoke to interrupt his thoughts. "How much more?"

"This place I got in mind, they're asking ten thousand for," Steve said.

Jackson's eyes lighted up with eagerness. "Then that's your price?"

"That or nothing."

A slow, satisfied smile eased the tightness of the Crow Track man's blocky face. He softly laughed. "I figured you'd make me pay through the nose, Ash. But hell, what's money for, if it ain't to use?"

He thumbed a sheaf of bills from the wallet, counted them, stepped over, and thrust them into Steve's hand. "Here's all of it, to the last dollar. Mark Wheeler once told me I was a fool to keep this kind of money in the safe at the house. And I told him there might come a time when I'd need a big wad of it." He laughed again. "That's once I outguessed him."

Steve deliberately folded the money and pocketed it. "She's all yours, Mister Jackson. All but the herd and those nags. I'll move 'em off today if you say."

"Take your time." Jackson was so delighted that he couldn't help smiling broadly. "Where's the deed?"

"They said it would take about a month for me to get one. But we can go in to the Land Office and I'll sign it over to you."

"Fine, fine." Jackson turned away at once, walking over to his gelding. "Let's get it finished right away. On the way in we could swing up to my place while I tell Al to move some men out here."

Steve was willing enough. He didn't even mind the prospect of having to ride bareback, didn't even think of his saddle being at Anders's place until he was down in the corral putting a bridle on a horse.

Later, on the way to town, Steve came to an abrupt realization. This bundle of money pressing along his thigh didn't seem to have eased his mind much. Ten thousand dollars, or twice ten thousand, wasn't enough to wipe out the memory of how Nels had died, how he had looked as he lay there by the alders with the flickering light of the burning wagon playing across what was left of his face. Ever since Jackson had given him the money, Steve had had some vague thought of leaving Arrowhead on the afternoon stage. But now he knew he couldn't leave.

When Mark Wheeler heard about it, he left the bank and started looking for Steve. He found him bellied up to the bar of the Catamount, staring glumly at a full glass of whiskey.

The banker nodded to the barkeep and said nothing until a bottle of whiskey and a shot glass slid to a stop in front of him. He filled the glass, lifted it, and said: "Here's to the smartest man I've met in many a day." He emptied the glass.

Steve made no comment, didn't even look around at him, and presently Wheeler drawled: "The stage is making up down at the corral right now. Better be thinking about getting aboard."

Steve's glance came around. "Not this trip, Mister Wheeler. Later, maybe."

If Wheeler was surprised, nothing in his look indicated, it. He said, with a touch of anger: "You're a fool, Ash. You've taken a big chunk from his hide. Get out while you can."

Steve asked mildly: "If you were me, would you get out?"

"If I were you, I wouldn't have had the guts to do even as much as you already have. Yes," Wheeler added stubbornly, "you're damned right I'd get out."

Steve smiled a little. Then he thought of something and reached to his pocket, taking out the big roll of bills. He handed them to the banker. "Hang onto this for me, will you? And if you see I won't be needing it, use it any way you want . . . so it'll do someone some good."

Wheeler knew enough about human nature to

realize that he was talking to a man whose mind was set hard as bedrock. Silently he took the money and pocketed it. Then he poured himself another drink and downed it as he had the first, at a single gulp.

"Steve, you've let yourself in for something."

"I knew that before I started."

"He's got his crew and he owns the sheriff, body and soul."

"I know that, too."

Mark Wheeler wondered what he could say to penetrate the hard shell of Steve's obstinacy. "Look, son. Your partner's gone. What good will it do for you to follow him?"

"Maybe I won't."

"How do you think Jackson got where he is now? I know of at least three men he's killed. That gun's a part of him, Steve. Unless you're fast as a rattler, you don't stand a chance."

Steve reached for his glass, took a little of the whiskey, set the glass down again. "A man's got to cash in his chips someday. Mister Wheeler, I could never live with myself until I'd made a try at this. I'd keep seeing Nels in my dreams and it'd get me in the end. I couldn't put up with it."

He had spoken gently, softly, and now Mark Wheeler understood. "You know more about this than I do. If you see it that way, go through with it."

"I aim to."

"Then give yourself as much of a chance as the odds will let you. First, get away from this place. Come on over to the bank. Or go loaf down there at the stables where you can watch the street."

Steve took that in, laid half a dollar on the counter, and turned from his unemptied glass. "Thanks for reminding me. Guess I wasn't thinking."

Wheeler stood outside on the walk, watching Steve saunter away. He watched him cross the street a hundred yards down and step over to the big open maw of the livery barn and take a chair alongside it. And as he stood there, he looked back over many things, reaching a decision he knew might influence the rest of his life. Bill Jackson, he was thinking, was what was wrong with this country. It was because of Crow Track that Arrowhead was the kind of town it was, anything but prosperous. Jackson's outfit had gradually, through the years, hogged so much of the best range that much of it was lying waste now, not producing enough—what it did produce was going into only one pocket. Crow Track wire closed in enough graze to support twenty or thirty families, men and women and kids who would trade here in town and spend enough money to make Arrowhead the prosperous town it should be. Jackson was only accumulating wealth, spending no more than was necessary, as his father had before him. Mark Wheeler took a long look at the odds against him. Then, because he had always hated Crow Track—and because he hated what was happening to a good man, Steve Ash—he knew he was going to do what he could to keep it from happening.

He went up the walk and turned in at the hardware store. He found Cass Bates at the rear, waiting on a customer.

When the customer finally left, Wheeler said: "Cass, I want to buy a Thirty-Thirty. And a box of shells."

Bates frowned. "You got a carbine, Mark."

"I know. This one's for the bank. Wrap it up and I'll take it out the back way."

"What about that shotgun you keep in the back cage?"

"We might need to take a long shot one day, Cass. A shotgun's no good for that. Come on, I'm in a hurry."

Somehow Les Anders had found out about what was going on. He came out across the street after Steve had been sitting there in the sun by the livery barn's door a good hour. He walked straight up to Steve and, his face set seriously, asked: "Where do you want me?"

Steve knew at once that Mark Wheeler must have talked to the well man. Grateful as he was for Anders's concern, he didn't want anyone else involved in this. So he said: "I'll handle it on my own, Les."

"No one man could," Anders told him roughly, almost angrily. "He'll have his crew with him. Then there's Hammer." His look suddenly brightened. "Maybe I could help there. Someone ought to keep an eye on that forked law of ours to keep him from cookin' up a story."

Without waiting for Steve to answer, he turned on up the walk.

It was another three quarters of an hour before Steve noticed anything. Then it was a thing that might have had no meaning. Al, Crow Track's foreman, came in off the rim trail and slowly rode the length of the street, apparently with no object in mind. If he saw Steve as he passed, he gave no indication of it. He went on down past the stores and Steve saw him turn into a lane beyond a house down there. And Steve was thinking: *It'll come soon now.*

It did.

Ten minutes after Al had ridden out of sight, he appeared once more at the head of the street. This time two others were with him. Jackson was the biggest of that pair.

The palms of Steve's hands became moist now. He was keyed up, his nerves so tight he could feel them drawing, tensing him. He came up out of the chair and stepped into the open doorway of the barn, glancing back along the runway to make sure no one was behind him. A youngster, the hostler, was forking fresh straw into one of the back stalls and his lazy movements, his thin whistling told Steve that no one could have come through the back corral during the past few minutes.

The three Crow Track riders stopped in mid-street in front of the saloon, a hundred yards above. Steve, leaning idly there in the doorway, felt Jackson's glance settle on him, move away. Even at this distance he could catch the sullen, angry set of Jackson's ruddy face. Though he could have guessed it, here was the proof that Crow Track had uncapped the well. Jackson knew the well was dry.

Steve was puzzled a moment later when Jackson and one man swung in to the tie rail before the saloon. At the same time Al came on down the center of the street, riding the way he had before, leisurely taking his time. He was abreast the barn's ramp when he tightened rein and turned his horse to face Steve.

"Ash," he called, "the boss wants to see you!"

"Well, here I am. It isn't far for him to walk."

Al's narrow face betrayed no surprise. "That water you poured around the hole soaked in, Ash."

"I figured it would."

Al eyed Steve a moment with a pitying expression in his eyes. "You dumb knothead," he drawled. He reined on around then and started back up the street. The gun slanted at his hip was what took Steve's eye as he rode away.

Al dismounted in front of the saloon and went inside. And now a slow and indefinable restlessness seemed to wake the street from its midafternoon quiet. Men would saunter down the walk past the saloon, turn and look in Steve's direction, and then be hurrying as they crossed the street or continued on.

Steve didn't see Bill Jackson until he had ducked under the tie rail and walked out between two of the horses standing there. Then, knowing that the next minute would probably decide this, a strange calm settled through Steve. He pushed out from the doorway and walked down the plank runway into the dusty street. He turned, faced Jackson squarely, and stood there waiting.

Jackson hesitated a moment at sight of this move. Then a smile came to the Crow Track man's face and he called: "Don't make me come and get you, Ash!"

Steve didn't bother to answer. He heard Jackson laugh, saw him turn and say something to a man standing on the walk, where a crowd was gathering close in to the saloon wall.

And now Jackson started toward him.

He wanted to reach for the gun, Nels's .38, wanted to start reaching for it now because he knew his draw would be slow. Then suddenly he was remembering something: *It'll out-range your Forty-Five and shoot a damn' sight straighter, kill a man just as quick.* It was as though Nels stood here beside him now, talking to him.

He moved the next instant, lifting his hand along his thigh and the Colt clear of leather as the knowledge came to him that the distance separating him from Jackson was too great for accuracy with a .45. A moment's panic nearly unnerved him as the Crow Track man's hand blurred toward his weapon, for he was only guessing that Jackson's Colt was a .45.

Sunlight glinted from the barrel of Jackson's gun as it streaked into line. Steve, the .38 only half raised, lunged to one side. The thunderclap of Jackson's shot rode down to him between the false fronts of the stores and he saw a geyser of dust spurt up ten feet ahead of him, in line with the spot where he'd been standing. And now he doubted that he was close enough to hit Jackson even if he had all the time there was to aim his shot. But still he kept remembering what Nels had said. He leveled the weapon and sighted along the barrel as Jackson shot again. A hard blow struck his left forearm, swinging him half around. Then anger steadied him. The weapon bucked upward. He brought it down again. Something was bothering the Crow Track owner, for his gun arm was slanted downward.

At the moment Steve was ready to tighten once more on the trigger, Bill Jackson's wide shape dropped out of his sights. He looked over the .38's dropping barrel. Jackson lay sprawled now, a haze of dust settling about him.

Mark Wheeler's strident shout echoed down to him. "Stay set, Crow Track!" And, unbelieving, Steve saw the banker step out from the opposite walk with a rifle half raised to his shoulder.

The next minute was packed with confusion for Steve. More men than he had known were on the street left the walks and the shelter of doorways now to join Mark Wheeler there on the street and crowd around Jackson's body. A couple of riders left the saloon tie rail and pounded away up the street. Les Anders appeared from nowhere and, ignoring the crowd, ran down to Steve and pounded him on the back, saying: "You done it, Steve! I saw it hit. Dead center, it was. Here, give me a look at that arm."

It was while he was rolling up Steve's left sleeve and looking at the shallow trough in the thick muscle of his forearm that Mark Wheeler walked down to them.

"Well, we've spiked our sheriff's guns," the banker announced solemnly as he approached. "At least a dozen of us jumped right down his throat when he mentioned an arrest."

Now for the first time he noticed what Les Anders was doing and took Steve's hand, looking carefully at the wound. Finally he said: "Not near as bad as that Crow Track man Jackson brought to the doctor's on his way in a while ago." He looked up sharply at Steve. "You wouldn't know about that, would you? This man's pretty bad off with a hole through his shoulder. Won't say how he got it. Neither would Jackson."

Steve nodded, remembering last night and the shot he'd taken at that one man just before the wagon turned over. Then he happened to think that he hadn't told Anders about the wagon. He was groping for a way to begin telling them about it when the banker spoke again.

"Son, you had us all fooled." He looked down at Steve's holstered Colt. "Why didn't you let on you were good with that thing? It would have saved us a lot of worry."

In that moment Steve was thinking only of Nels, wishing Nels could hear this. His arm was beginning to throb. But somehow this violence had lifted a weight from his mind and he was feeling better than he had for days. Nels's being dead was as right as it could ever be.

He had a thought then that made him say to Wheeler: "That money goes back where it came from. I'll take out enough to pay Les for busting up . . ."

"The hell you do!" Wheeler said indignantly. "It's yours, every last dollar of it! You didn't make claims for your well, did you?"

"Not a one. But . . ."

"Then the money's yours. Besides, who would you pay it back to? Jackson didn't leave a family. And you saw how his hardcases lit out the minute he went down. By tomorrow there won't be a man left at Crow Track. They've kicked too many people around to risk staying. The courts will probably auction off the outfit, split it up like it should have been years ago. Steve, this is the best thing that ever happened to us. And by the way, we've got an election coming up. All you have to do to get yourself a sheriff's badge is say the word."

Steve smiled and gave a slow shake of the head. "No, I'll just head back where I came from."

Now he was wondering if he ought to send a telegram, just to make sure that the layout in the Sawtooths wasn't sold from under him.

LONGRIDING LAWMAN

Western Fiction Magazine in 1938 was one of the Red Circle Magazine group that included *Complete Western Book Magazine*, *Western Novel and Short Stories*, *Best Western*, and *Western Short Stories*. Jon Glidden's Western stories appeared regularly in these other magazines, but "Longriding Lawman" was one of only two stories by Peter Dawson ever to appear in *estern Fiction Magazine*. On the contents page of the (11/38) issue it was classified as a "dramatic action novel". The author was paid $45.00.

I

Blaze Hefflin was no coward. But there are limits to the things a man can stand. As far back as Las Vegas, New Mexico, eighteen days ago, Blaze had sighted the man on the bay who dogged his back trail. At first Blaze hadn't been sure that the stranger was following him. To make certain he had swung a hundred miles to the north, across the Sangre de Cristo range and up to Fort Taos. He waited in Taos two days and on the second day had his second look at the same man.

Blaze was fairly fast with his guns but his critical inspection of this stranger made him hesitate in taking his chances in an open shoot-out. The stranger was tall and lean and even in his walk had a certain economy of motion that warned Blaze of what he could expect.

At the feed barn, the oldster who had saddled the chestnut on which Blaze was leaving, wiped out the last small doubt. "Stranger here lookin' for you a while back," the oldster announced only when Blaze had climbed into the saddle. "He was askin' for a red-headed gent forkin' a chestnut horse. It weren't none o' my business so I told him I'd never set eyes on you. That all right?"

Blaze fished into his pocket and flipped down a

silver dollar. “Stick to your story,” he said as he rode away. Blaze’s hair was a fiery red and anyone who had ever seen the chestnut would never mistake the animal for another.

Halfway the length of Taos Cañon, coming down off the high mesa and into the valley of the Río Grande, Blaze decided to get this over with. He climbed high into the cover of the boulders flanking the steep trail and waited, his Winchester within easy reach and his chestnut horse staked out a safe quarter mile away. He was a dead shot with a rifle and wasn’t particular about his target being either a man’s chest or back.

He waited there the remainder of that day, with no sign of the stranger. Dusk fanned alive a fear within him and he ran to his horse and went up into the saddle and by noon of the next day, coming into Santa Fe, he and the animal were both exhausted. In Santa Fe he caught two hours’ sleep, traded the chestnut for a black gelding, and rode on.

Each evening he’d climb a high place and scan his back trail for a good hour before making camp. After six days his fears gradually left him and he no longer hurried. Yesterday at sundown, crossing a high pass through the Wigwams, he had taken his last long look back across the stretch of country he’d covered that day. The only rider he sighted was a man mounted on a roan leisurely crossing an open pasture in the timber a mile below. The road didn't interest him. Last night he had slept well.

This morning, at sunup, he'd had his far look at Coyote Wells with a feeling of keen relief. Deuce Morgan would still be in Coyote Wells. Deuce always had a thing or two that could be done by a man of Blaze's capabilities.

Now, trotting his black down the town's single dusty street, he took a little satisfaction in the knowledge that in this south country the law wouldn't be anxious to spot a man with graying red hair and a slight droop to the lid of his right eye. Blaze Hefflin was a name, but not a name to travel this far.

He picked out Deuce Morgan's glaring red-painted sign, *Lucky Girl Saloon*, along the length of wooden awning that fronted the stores at the street's center, and he swung the black in at the hitch rail in front of the place. Getting down out of the saddle, he faced the opposite side of the street a moment. Across there bright sunlight was reflected glaringly from a polished bit of metal to catch his eye.

Faintly curious, Blaze looked closer and saw that the reflection came from a five-pointed sheriff's star pinned on the vest of a man leaning idly against an awning post. And, since lawmen always interested him, Blaze looked closely at this one. His eyes narrowed a trifle and he breathed: "Hell, I'm seeing things."

The sheriff had the look of a man crowding fifty,

with a lean, hawkish face and a gray mustache. He wore a faded and soiled gray Stetson and stood with thumbs hooked in the sag of his single shell belt. His stance, his sharp features, and the Bull Durham tag hanging out of his Levi's pocket were signs that sharpened Blaze Hefflin's scrutiny.

"It *is* him," he muttered, half aloud. A slow smile shaped its twisted line on his face. "I wonder if Deuce knows? If he doesn't . . ." He shrugged as his words trailed off.

He turned quickly, ducked under the tie rail, and went in at the saloon doors, walking fast and with a pronounced limp he momentarily forgot to hide.

Sheriff John Branch, across the street, happened to look across toward the Lucky Girl at that moment and catch a last glimpse of Blaze before he disappeared. That one glance was enough to bring the lawman out of his slouch against the awning post. Branch's brown eyes became narrow-lidded. *A brick top and a limp,* he thought. *It couldn't get past me.* As he mused he knew not only that it could be Blaze Hefflin, but that it could be no one else.

He stepped down off the walk and let his hand fall to the weapon at his thigh and made certain that it lifted easily from the holster before he started across the street toward the saloon. Given a little more time he'd have done several things; he'd have gone back to his office and made out his will, for one, since it was a sure bet that Blaze hadn't lost his old skill with a six-gun. Now there was no time.

Stepping up onto the walk in front of the Lucky Girl, Branch heard a light, quick step sound against the planks, and a moment later felt a touch on his arm.

It was Ellen, his daughter, who stood at his elbow, smiling up at him. One look at him and her oval face sobered instantly. "Dad, aren't you feeling well?"

"Not so good," he told her, in momentary confusion. "Butch has a new Chinese cook and I ate a piece of his pie after breakfast. Indigestion."

"You go right on home and take some baking soda," the girl said, a look of relief wiping away her frown and turning her clean-cut face pretty once more. She abruptly held out a hand. "That dress material came in on the stage an hour ago. I need three dollars."

"Why can't you women wear dollar pants like us?" Branch chided her as he reached for his wallet and took out the money. A moment ago, when Ellen's smooth features had shaped that look of concern, she'd had her mother's look. It was a hard memory to have brought up just now.

"Remember the baking soda, Dad." The girl took the money and went on down the street.

Branch stood there a moment, watching his daughter's swinging stride, admiring her tall, graceful figure. Her smooth-combed tawny hair caught the sunlight and took on a golden sheen he knew he'd be remembering when he faced Blaze Hefflin a minute or two from now.

"Sheriff."

Branch swung his glance out to the hitch rail in the direction of the voice. A stranger sat the saddle of a roan horse alongside the black gelding Blaze had ridden in a moment ago. The stranger was tall and his shirt and Levi's were dustpowdered and he had the look of having come a long way. He wore two guns.

"Sheriff, did you see the gent that rode this black in a few minutes ago?"

Branch hadn't seen Blaze come in, didn't know who owned the black. "No."

"Was he a redhead?" the stranger queried insistently.

Branch's glance narrowed. He queried sharply: "What would you be wanting of a man with red hair?"

The stranger smiled, came down out of the saddle and onto the walk. "Stick around and watch the fun," he said as he passed the lawman and pushed open the saloon's swing doors.

"Hold on!" Branch called. But by that time the stranger was out of sight.

Branch let his hand reach for the handle of his six-gun as he followed. He was halfway through the doors when it happened.

At the far end of the bar Blaze Hefflin stood talking with Deuce Morgan, whose outfit this morning was a fawn-colored cutaway coat, trousers to match, expensive-looking polished boots. The sheriff looked back at them just as Blaze glanced quickly up front, pushed out from the bar, and stabbed both hands toward his holsters. Deuce Morgan lunged quickly aside. Branch's glance darted to the far side of the doors. The stranger was standing there, spraddle-legged, his right hand already moving in one swift flow of motion to palm up the weapon at his thigh. Branch was too bewildered to move or cry out.

The stranger's weapon blurred upward, froze in line, and blasted out a foot-long stab of powder flame. Blaze Hefflin's upswinging arm hesitated as his body jerked. Then his weapon rose into line and John Branch saw clearly the frantic motion his thumb made to pull back the weapon's hammer.

Suddenly a second shot from the stranger's Colt thundered across the room. Blaze staggered backward against the bar, his .45 fell, and his hand clawed his chest. Then, slowly, Blaze bent at the waist and fell forward, hitting the sawdust floor with a force that skidded him along the planks a half foot.

When Deuce Morgan's right hand went in under his coat lapel toward his shoulder holster, the sheriff drew his .45 and called sharply: "Easy, Deuce, easy!"

Deuce's hand came down, empty. Three men moved out from a poker table at the rear of the room, two more stepped the length of the bar to look down as Deuce Morgan knelt beside Blaze Hefflin. The sheriff dropped his six-gun back into its holster.

"Dead," the saloon owner said. He glanced across at the stranger, whose smoking gun was still leveled rock-steady in his hand. "Arrest him, Sheriff. This was murder."

"You're forgetting that I saw it, Deuce," Branch said, a wave of relief hitting him. "Your dead friend went for his iron first. It was self-defense."

"And why would this gent make a play against a stranger?" Deuce asked, nodding down at the dead man.

"Ask the stranger," Branch answered.

The stranger spoke for the first time. "Twenty-eight days ago he murdered a man in Cheyenne, Wyoming. I took out after him two days later. He's kicked his dust in my face all the way down here."

Deuce Morgan laughed mirthlessly. "A hell of a likely story. You've cut down a friend of mine, stranger. I'm askin' you to prove he ever committed murder."

John Branch could have proved murder on Blaze Hefflin. But for the last twenty years he'd tried to forget that part of his past. He had no wish to make it public now. With Blaze

Hefflin's death, that past would be buried forever.

"You can prove it by writing the sheriff at Cheyenne," the stranger drawled. "The man this redhead shot in the back was my father. He died in a dark alley, on a Saturday night, carrying home a money bag with less than a hundred dollars in it. It was his day's takings from his harness shop. Your friend took the money."

John Branch had only half listened to these details. He was thinking of something else, and now he asked Morgan: "What was your business with this hardcase, Deuce? I've got an idea I may find his picture on a Reward dodger." The lawman knew he was stating a fact. Blaze Hefflin had been wanted off and on for years, for rustling, murder, arson, robbery.

"Maybe you'd like to know what we were talkin' about when you came in, Sheriff," Morgan said suavely.

John Branch's peace of mind left him in a split second. "Maybe I would," he answered.

"Shall I tell it here or will you come into my back office?"

Branch felt the color rise to his face. "I'll come to your office," he said. Then, in answer to the mildly surprised and questioning stares of the onlookers, he said sharply: "The rest of you carry this jasper across to Harry Lodge's. Have Harry nail up a box and bury him. I'll pay the bill."

He forgot about the stranger until he had closed

the door of Deuce Morgan's office. Morgan took the chair behind his walnut desk, opened a box of cigars, and held them out to the lawman. "Smoke?"

"You know damned well I don't smoke your cigars, Deuce," Branch said, suddenly impatient to get this over with. "Spill what you've got on your mind."

Morgan smiled, his bluntly square countenance deceivingly placid. He bit off the end of a cigar, felt at his vest pockets for a match, and, not finding any, he pulled open a drawer of his desk in a casual gesture. His hand came out holding a pearl-handled Colt .38. His left hand whipped the cigar from his mouth and threw it into the wastebasket. With his weapon lined at the lawman's chest, he drawled: "Blaze had a thing or two to say out there before he cashed in. There wasn't much but it was enough."

John Branch's legs went weak under him. He said lifelessly—"Never mind the gun, Deuce."—and stepped back to let himself down into a leather-covered chair at the wall, facing the saloon owner.

Morgan laid the weapon within easy reach on his desk. "John, you and I haven't been seein' things quite the same way for years. For six years, in fact, ever since I came to this country and set up in business."

"The only thing I ever had against you was the

way you took after Ellen," Branch said. "She's not your kind."

"We'll forget that for the moment," Deuce said, his mirthless grin putting an obvious meaning behind his words. "We'll talk about the gamblin'. You closed up my back room six months ago. I'm losin' money since you put through that ordinance to outlaw card games in this town. I want that ordinance voted down at the next meetin' of the town council."

"You can't get away with that," the lawman flared, leaning forward in his chair.

"Can't I?" Deuce breathed. "What about that two hundred head of Broad Arrow horses you and Blaze sold across the Canadian border twenty years ago?"

There wasn't any argument left in John Branch. His past had caught up with him. Twenty years ago, unjustly accused of having framed a crooked card game by a forked sheriff, Branch had for two nights turned outlaw. With Blaze Hefflin and three other men who hated the Broad Arrow outfit that owned that Montana lawman, John Branch had succeeded in driving away the entire Broad Arrow remuda and selling it to friends of Blaze's across the border. Branch hadn't even taken his share of the money they were paid for the horses. Knowing that Montana law would suspect him, he had come down here into Arizona. For twenty years he'd lived an honest life, made an honest name. For eight years he'd served as Coyote Wells' sheriff.

"What about those stolen horses?" Deuce repeated his question.

"I reckon I could go back and square that."

"And come back here again? With these people knowin' they have a horse thief for a sheriff?"

Branch's face had paled, his brown eyes hard as flint. "Deuce, I'll kill you for that."

Deuce Morgan smiled, picked up his gun once more. "In an hour I'll have written a statement and put it in an envelope in the vault at the bank, Sheriff. In case anything happens to me, I'll tell Rex Holden to open that envelope."

John Branch thought that over for a moment. His look changed, not to that of a beaten man but one held powerless by circumstances. "You win, Deuce. I'll have the gambling ordinance changed at the council meeting tomorrow." He got up out of his chair.

"Play along with me and I'll treat you right," Deuce said genially. "In a few days I'll have a few more ideas."

Branch went out the door, the picture of Deuce Morgan's mocking smile clearly imprinted in his mind. He walked down the street and to his office at the jail. He was closing the door behind him before he saw the two people in the room.

Rex Holden, president of the Cowman's Bank and Trust Company, was in the chair at the lawman's desk. The stranger was seated on the broad ledge of the thick adobe wall at the window. The stranger wore a five-pointed star with *Deputy Sheriff* printed boldly across the center-plate. John Branch wasn't sure that he was seeing right.

Holden laughed, catching the momentary bewildered look on Branch's face.

"Meet your new deputy, John," he said. "Calls himself Ed Sims. Hails all the way from Cheyenne."

Branch finally managed to get out: "Rex, you've gone loco."

Holden shook his head. "No such thing, John. This morning I made Bill Edge the loan on that piece of land he's had his eye on. He was going to come around and hand in his badge right afterward but agreed to wait until we found you a new deputy. I got Charley Riley and Sid Hockens together and we were figuring who'd make you a good man when those two shots cut loose over at the saloon." He turned to the stranger to say: "You tell him the rest, Sims."

Ed Sims looked a little uncomfortable at the expression of sudden anger that had come to the sheriff's grizzled countenance. "I needed a job, Sheriff. They offered me one."

"John, he'll make the finest deputy Coyote Wells ever had," Rex Holden said. "They say he's the fastest thing with a gun ever to hit the town. He's honest or my eyesight's going back on me.

With Bill Edge quitting you this afternoon, you'll need a new man. Can you think of a better one?"

The involuntary thought that crossed John Branch's mind was to wonder whether or not Deuce Morgan could have thought of a better man, perhaps one of his friends. But he put down that thought along with the anger he'd felt at Rex Holden's officious way of choosing a deputy for him. If he were to have the gambling ordinance revoked, he'd have to humor Rex Holden along with the rest of the council members.

"Suits me," he said finally. An inner thought shaped a smile on his thin face as he looked at his new deputy. "Your luck must run high, Sims. You missed getting arrested a half hour ago by no more than the thickness of a straightedge razor. Now you turn up wearing a law badge. Maybe you'll be a good man to have around."

The council meeting was set for 4:00 the next afternoon. Fifteen minutes short of the hour John Branch came back to his office to give Ed Sims a few last instructions about meeting the stage that would arrive at 4:30, and guarding the mail while it was being carried down to the post office.

The office door was standing open. The lawman was about to enter when he heard his daughter's voice from inside. "But there's no excuse for killing a man in cold blood!" Ellen was angry. Branch could tell that by her low-toned, evenly spaced words. "Regardless of what he'd done, it was no place for you to take the law in your hands. That's the way killers get their start."

"I'd do it again," came Ed Sims's drawling words in answer. "You're wrong about this, Miss Ellen. Blaze Hefflin could have hired a lawyer and saved his neck. He was a friend of this Deuce Morgan's. Morgan would have bought him."

"Don't tell me the law can be bought around Coyote Wells!" Ellen flared. "My father's honest. For eight years he's . . ."

John Branch stepped in through the door, growling: "Here, you two. What's all the talk?"

Ellen, standing at the back window, turned to face her father, brown eyes flashing in anger. "Dad, you wouldn't have chosen this man for deputy yourself. You've never hired a killer."

Branch looked across at Ed Sims, who was seated on a corner of the desk. Ed's tanned face was darkened with a flush of embarrassment. It was obvious that an inner courtesy was the only thing that checked the words that would have matched the hardness of his gray eyes. Branch recognized this gentlemanly quality immediately and liked the man for it.

"Ellen, you're meddling," he said. "Ed did the same as any red-blooded man would have done.

Let someone murder me and nine chances in ten you'd take out after him with a gun. Now you get on out of here and be thanking your stars we're lucky enough to get Ed to wear a badge. With the pay he's drawing, it's a wonder he'd take the job."

The girl's glance changed to one of bewilderment. Time and again she and her father had discussed this thing—the needlessness of relying on guns when the law could be depended on—and now to realize that her father was against her hit her as hard as a blow in the face.

Branch caught her look and hastily put in: "There's times when nothing but a gun will answer to a wrong, Sis."

Pride, and the wish not to be humbled before this comparative stranger, took its hold on Ellen Branch. She came across to the door with a firm step, head held high, saying: "Dad, if I didn't know you better, I'd say you'd been drinking."

When the sounds of her steps had faded out down the walk, Branch chuckled a little nervously, eyeing his deputy. "She must like you," he said. "It isn't often anyone gets her riled that way."

But Ed Sims was strangely sober. "What she said about you choosing your own deputy, Sheriff . . . I hadn't thought of that. Maybe I'd better look for another job."

John Branch, for reasons of his own, felt more than a slender obligation toward this man. "Given the chance, I'd have asked you to wear the badge myself, Ed. Hell, we need a man like you here." A sudden impulse made him add: "The council meets in ten minutes. Supposing you come along and listen. There're times when you'll have to go in my place and you might as well get to know the ropes."

This show of confidence partly erased the feeling Ellen Branch's words had brought up in Ed Sims. At the bank, ten minutes later, Rex Holden and Sid Hockens and Charley Riley welcomed the new deputy in the way John Branch had thought they would; they were old-timers and it was their instinct to respect a willful man who was fast with a gun and knew when to use one.

Branch had spent a good part of the day thinking about the gambling ordinance, and how he would bring the discussion around to it. But in less than five minutes Rex Holden said abruptly: "I should have called this thing off. That bid of Freemont's on digging the new well is the only thing I wanted to see you about, and Freemont hasn't sent it in yet. So the meeting's adjourned."

"Hold on a minute," Branch said hurriedly. It was a poor way to work around to the business he had in mind, but he was thinking of Blaze Hefflin and the things Blaze had told Deuce, and of what the saloon owner might do if he had to wait two more weeks to open his roulette, faro, crap, and chuck-a-luck layouts. He cleared his throat as the others hesitated. "Rex, I've been thinking about that gambling ordinance we put through last spring. It's costing this town money."

Rex Holden frowned. "I don't get it, John."

"We're losing business," Branch said. "Pinnacle is only twenty miles away and every Saturday night there's at least fifty Coyote Wells men over there, spending their pay in those saloons. That's money that ought to stay in our town."

"But we decided it was better to lose a little than to have open gambling bring in the undesirables, John. I thought that was your idea."

"It was. But a man has a right to change his mind. Now that I've got my new deputy, I think the two of us can keep order if we open the town to gambling. I'm willing to give it a try."

Sid Hockens smiled and said: "I'd like to see it. Hell, in the old days the bunch of us had more fun in a saloon Saturday nights than we do now sitting at home. The Ladies Aid's getting too strong a hold on us."

Holden leaned forward in his chair. "John, you're serious about this? You want to see us throw this town wide open?"

"Why not?" The lawman shrugged. "Deuce Morgan will make a good citizen if we treat him right. He spends what money he makes here. He'll spend more if he makes more. It's good business."

"In another month all the big outfits will be laying off their crews after roundup," Holden aid. “I’ll agree it might bring us business but there’ll be trouble, too.”

Ed Sims spoke for the first time. “It’s none of my affair,” he said mildly. “But I’ve seen it work both ways in the town where I was raised. Gambing finally went out for good when a banker up there married a percentage girl.” Hockens and Riley looked at Holden and had a good laugh. “Well, it isn’t my place to say, but that’s how it was.”

John Branch had gone a little red in the face. Those brief words of Ed Sims’s had turned this from seriousness to a joke.

Holden said: “It may not be me that marries the percentage girl. But Sims has given us a fair idea of what happens when the lid’s off. Let’s forget gambling and let Pinnacle have all that business it wants.”

That broke up the meeting. No one took the things the sheriff had said too seriously; no one lost any of the respect they held for him. But Ed Sims’s timely words had clinched the decision and for the time being it would make the sheriff appear ridiculous to press his point.

Branch left the room shortly afterward, when Sid Hockens started talking to Ed Sims, asking after two or three friends he had in Cheyenne. The sheriff went down the street directly to the Lucky Girl. He wanted to be the first to tell Deuce Morgan of his temporary failure.

Ed Sims was wishing he hadn't opened his mouth, thinking that he'd shown his gratitude for getting his job in a poor way. He left Sid Hockens as soon as he could, wanting to see the sheriff and explain that he had meant what he said but not the way it sounded. He came out onto the street in time to see Branch turn in at the Lucky Girl. Evidently the sheriff was feeling the need of a drink. Sims abruptly decided to go into the saloon after the lawman.

The barroom was nearly empty. Poker hadn't been outlawed along with other gambling games, and now a lone man occupied one of the four tables, playing out a hand of solitaire. Two others stood at the bar and eyed Ed Sims respectfully as he came across the room. They, and every other man in town, had heard of the fight in there yesterday.

"Anyone seen the sheriff?" Ed asked.

The bartender nodded toward a door at the rear of the room. "He's back with the boss."

Ed decided to wait. He asked for whiskey and took it to the back end of the bar and sat on a stool there, not wishing to have to answer the questions he knew the pair up front would be asking him. He had barely let his weight down onto the stool when he heard John Branch's voice sound in Morgan's office. "Deuce, I did my best. It wasn't good enough. You'll have to wait until the next meeting."

Ed turned and looked toward the door. It stood slightly ajar. Then he heard Deuce Morgan say: "You're runnin' a sandy on me, Branch. All right, you asked for it. By tomorrow every man in town will know what Blaze Heflin told me."

Branch's voice came hard and strained: "It'll be your word against mine, Deuce. You can't make it stick even if it is the truth."

"Can't I?" Morgan said. "Wait until you see how I'll make it stick." There was a tense, long-drawn silence, then Morgan said: "Read this, Branch."

A shorter silence this time. At length, the sheriff's words sounded hard and clear: "Deuce, I said once before I'd kill you. That still goes."

"And this mornin' I took that envelope over to Rex Holden. It's in his office safe. Go ahead, friend Branch. If you want a charge of murder along with this other, it suits me." There was the scrape of a chair inside the office. "I'm sendin' this wire off right now."

Ed Sims moved down from the end of the bar as quickly as he could without attracting the attention of the trio farther along the counter. They were busy talking and obviously hadn't heard what was going on in Morgan's office. Ed put his elbows on the bar midway its length and turned in time to see the door to the back room open. Deuce Morgan's square frame stood outlined in it. His glance traveled the length of the room, finally came back to settle on Ed Sims.

A tight smile came to the saloon owner's blunt visage. He spoke back over his shoulder. "Your deputy's out front, Branch. He'd be a good man to run this errand." Then, more loudly, he called: "Sims, I'd like to see you a minute!"

Ed sauntered on back until he stood within arm's reach of Deuce Morgan. He tried to mask the feeling of loathing that came up within him at sight of Morgan's calm arrogance.

Morgan stepped aside and jerked a thumb toward the inside of his office. "Branch is in there. He wants you to take this telegram down to the stage and have the driver leave it at the way station beyond Pinnacle." Morgan held an envelope in his other hand, and now he turned and said to the sheriff: "Isn't that right, John?"

Ed took half a step farther toward the door, so that he could look into the office and see John Branch standing in front of the desk. The lawman's face was pale, unhealthy-looking beneath its tan. But his words were firm as he said: "That's right, Ed."

Morgan reached into a trouser pocket and handed Ed a silver dollar along with the envelope. "You'll have to hurry," he said, his face holding that same mirthless smile. "I heard the stage come in five minutes ago."

"I'm to give this to the driver and tell him to leave it at the way station beyond Pinnacle," Ed said. Getting Morgan's answering nod, he turned and walked out the swing doors up front as casually as he could.

On the way up the street his thoughts were a disordered jumble as he groped helplessly for an explanation for the things he'd overheard. John Branch had the look of being an honest man; back there in the office he'd had the look of being a condemned man. Strangely enough, Ed Sims's thoughts turned to Ellen Branch, to the deep-rooted instincts within her that had made her protest the hiring of a man who had yesterday killed another. No father of a girl with such principles could be anything but honest.

Convinced of this, Ed Sims walked up the street to the stage station, spent two minutes talking with the driver on the chance that Deuce Morgan would be watching from the saloon doorway. Then, the envelope thrust in his hip pocket, Ed headed for the feed stable.

Inside the shelter of the barn's doorway he took out the envelope and ripped it open. Inside was a sheet of paper half covered with Deuce Morgan's unruly scrawl. It read:

> SHERIFF, BLAINE COUNTY, CHINOOK, MONTANA. HAVE YOU INFORMATION ON A JOHN BRANCH AND A BLAZE HEFFLIN WANTED FOR THEFT OF BROAD ARROW REMUDA TWENTY YEARS AGO? IS REWARD BEING

OFFERED? WIRE COLLECT FULL PARTICULARS TO A.L. MORGAN, COYOTE WELLS, ARIZONA.

Ed read the message twice, gradually piecing together occurrences over the last two days that explained many things. He halfway understood Blaze Hefflin's part in this, and it occurred to him that Sheriff John Branch might possibly have been on his way into the saloon yesterday to meet Blaze when he himself arrived. He saw clearly the sheriff's reasons for trying to get the gambling ordinance revoked at the council meeting this afternoon. And he saw, too, that no one but an honest man could have the name John Branch had made in this country.

Before he burned Morgan's message and its envelope he made particular note of the address. Then, grinding the heel of his boot into the curling black ash of the charred paper on the floor of the feed barn, he stepped out onto the street again and went to Branch's office.

The lawman was seated in the chair behind his desk, staring vacantly at the opposite wall when Ed stepped into the room. The lawman brought his attention back to the present with obvious effort, saw who it was, and queried lifelessly: "Did you see the driver before he left?"

Ed nodded.

Branch let a gusty sigh escape him, then laughed

harshly. "Sims, don't ever run from a thing. Don't ever smear your name with something that'll come down on your back trail later on."

Ed tried to look surprised. "That's a hard order for a man to fill. Things happen the wrong way sometimes."

Branch may have heard but gave no sign of it, for the next remark was along a different line. "I've never shot a man in cold blood up unti now. What would you do if you knew you had to murder a man?"

"You know what I did do," Ed answered. "But in your place I might work it out differently. If you've got something on your mind, maybe it'd help to talk about it. To me, I mean."

The lawman smiled, an expression that lacked any hint of amusement. "Ed, you have a way of coming at things squarely from the front. I'd give a lot to be in your boots, thirty years younger, no strings tied to anyone, helling for a good scrap. Maybe I'd buy into a good scrap tonight." Abruptly some inner thought made him clench his lips tightly together. He got up out of his chair and said—"Stick around until I've had supper."—and went out the door.

Ed Sims didn't eat until late, after dark that night. He ate a light meal for a hungry man, mainly because he was in too much of a hurry to take the time over a lot of food. Ten minutes after he'd left Butch's lunch counter, he was in the saddle, headed out the west trail that would take him to Pinnacle.

Shortly after midnight he was pounding at the door of the railroad way station shack five miles above Pinnacle. When the racket his fist set up on the thin pine panel of the door didn't bring results, he drew one of his six-guns and used it. In another ten seconds the window alongside the door was raised and the blunt double-barreled snout of a shotgun was thrust out at him as a man's irritated sleepy voice growled: "Get the hell away from here!"

"Here's a telegram that has to go off tonight," Ed said, not moving off the doorstep even when the shotgun swung around to cover him.

"It'll go off at seven in the mornin'," the agent said. "I'm paid for a twelve hour day and damned . . ."

Ed suddenly stepped in close to hug the front wall, lunging down off the step and streaking a hand out toward the window. The gun swung its arc as tight as it could against the edge of the frame and blasted its double explosion to rip away the night's stillness. The fanning hail of lead chopped to tatters the edge of Ed's right sleeve before his hands closed on the hot gun barrels. He threw all his weight into the abrupt wrench he gave the gun. He stumbled awkwardly and lost his balance as the agent suddenly let go his hold on the weapon. And in the brief interval it took

Ed to get his legs under him the man inside stepped through the window, his short chunky shape a little ridiculous-looking for the bulge of his nightshirt above the trousers he'd pulled on.

He moved fast, coming in at Ed in a practiced fighter's crouch. He ignored the six-gun in Ed's hand and swung in a short choppy blow that Ed dodged and caught on his shoulder. Ed swung around with that blow, and the turn of his body put more weight behind the long swing of his left fist. It hit the agent's chin with such force that the man's jaw moved sideways a good two inches; it brought a rigidity to his legs so that they couldn't move to take up the slack of his body. He fell forward, in the way of a man hit hard and with senses shocked to paralysis.

Five minutes later, when the agent opened his eyes and stared up with a cold, hard anger brightening his glance, Ed showed his deputy's badge. "If you hadn't been so proddy, you could have seen this and saved yourself a couple of teeth. I'm here on official business."

The agent sat up, wiping the blood from the back of his hand, running his tongue gingerly along his loosened teeth. Ed Sims was right; two of those front teeth were nearly falling out. The agent, a surly-tempered but nevertheless shrewd man, muttered: "I thought you was one of those Pinnacle drunks." He got stiffly to his feet and started toward the hut sitting alongside the twin ribbons of steel of the railroad, reaching to his back pocket for his keys.

Inside, ten minutes later, he was tapping out the message Ed Sims handed him. It read:

> SHERIFF, BLAINE COUNTY, CHINOOK, MONTANA. IS A JOHN BRANCH WANTED FOR HORSE STEALING FROM CHINOOK LIVERY STABLE LAST APRIL? ANSWER BRIEFLY COLLECT. A.L. MORGAN, COYOTE WELLS, ARIZONA.

Finished, the agent looked up at Ed, a hint of belligerence still in his glance. "You Morgan?"

"Albert Linlee Morgan," Ed said, giving the first names he could think of to fit the initials. His hand went into his pocket and he took out a $5 gold piece. "Here's pay for your trouble of stopping the stage tomorrow morning and handing the driver the answer to this wire."

The agent pocketed the money, managed a twisted smile. "No hard feelin's are there, Morgan?"

Ed grinned. "I should be asking you that."

The agent sat there at his key until the sound of Ed's roan's earth-striking hoofs had died out in the still night air. He knew Deuce Morgan well, well enough to remember his initials. And he knew, too, that Bill Edge was the only deputy

John Branch had had for the last five years. The thing that brought him out of his chair and sent him back to his shack was the memory of more than one time when Deuce Morgan's money had lined his pockets in payment for the knowledge of just such a thing as had happened tonight. A telegraph operator is the holder of many confidences. Morgan's money had many times loosened this agent's tongue.

He dressed, put on his coat, and went back to the lean-to to saddle his one horse. As he took the Coyote Wells trail, he muttered half aloud: "Maybe Deuce can pay for havin' these teeth fixed." The teeth were hurting now, and he was in an ugly temper. Each time he thought of the deputy who'd taken Deuce Morgan's name his scowl deepened. He wasn't a man who forgot easily.

Deuce Morgan was at the stage station at 9:00 the next morning when the stage pulled in, a quarter hour late. The saloon owner's black eyes were puffy from what a casual observer might have assumed was the morning-after effect of too much whiskey. It wasn't that; Morgan was no heavy drinker; last night he'd had only two hours' sleep.

He sauntered to the edge of the walk as the

stage driver booted tight the brake. "'Mornin', Henry. Anything for me?" Morgan glanced casually around, satisfied in seeing that half a dozen people had heard him. Sid Hockens was one of the half dozen.

"Telegram, Mister Morgan," the driver called down. He leaned down to open the box under the seat and tossed down a yellow envelope containing the telegram. "Scudder flagged me with it at the way station above Pinnacle. Said it was urgent."

Morgan frowned, turned to Sid Hockens who stood just behind him, and said: "Sid, hang around a minute. This may be something that'll interest you."

He opened the telegram, read:

> A.L. MORGAN, COYOTE WELLS, ARIZONA. JOHN BRANCH WANTED FOR THEFT OF BROAD ARROW REMUDA TWENTY YEARS AGO. HOLD HIM FOR DELIVERY TO MY DEPUTY LEAVING THIS MORNING BY TRAIN. REWARD OF ONE THOUSAND DOLLARS WILL BE PAID DIRECT UPON DELIVERY OF PRISONER. BERT WATERS, SHERIFF, BLAINE COUNTY, CHINOOK, MONTANA.

"Read this, Sid," Morgan said, handing across the telegram. But as Sid Hockens reached out a hand to take it, Morgan pulled it back again. "On second thought you'd better come along with me to Rex Holden's office. We'll all read it together."

Hockens, following Morgan up the walk, queried: "Something wrong?"

"Wait and see."

Holden was alone in his office. He wasn't overly glad to see Deuce Morgan, but his tone was civil enough as he said: "Howdy, Sid, Deuce. What's on your minds?"

In answer, Morgan stepped up to the desk and laid the opened telegram on it. Sid Hockens went around the desk to stand behind Holden and read over the banker's shoulder.

Rex Holden's face lost color as his eyes scanned the lines. He read the telegram twice, then looked up at Morgan and said: "This'll bear some explaining."

"I hate it as badly as you do," Morgan said. "But yesterday when this new deputy, Sims, killed that man in my place, I got suspicious."

"Why?"

"Because Blaze Hefflin was just telling me what he knew about John Branch. Tellin' me part of what that telegram tells. Hefflin had recognized Branch out on the street. It seems that Hefflin was in on that horse stealin' twenty years ago. He unloaded what was on his mind to me when he saw Branch. Said he didn't know this Sims, either, who was on his back trail all the way from Cheyenne."

Sid Hockens's long face had gone cold sober. "Morgan, this is a tall story to make stick. I'd as soon believe this of Rex as I would of John Branch."

"That's what I thought until yesterday," Morgan said suavely. "Until John Branch came to me with a proposition."

"What kind of a proposition?" Holden queried.

"To have the gamblin' ordinance revoked. Branch said he could swing it if I'd cut him in for a quarter of my takin's from the gamblin' parlor I'd open up."

Hockens's eyes narrowed in sudden amazement and he breathed softly: "That checks with what we know. Branch tried to get us to rule out that ordinance yesterday at the council meeting. Only it didn't go through."

Morgan smiled crookedly. "It was because it didn't go through that I sent a wire to the Montana sheriff."

Holden said: "Then you'd have played along with Branch if he'd opened this town to gambling?"

"Why not?" Morgan shrugged. "It'd be money in my pocket."

"Why are you double-crossing John Branch," Sid Hockens asked.

Morgan laughed, harshly. "You know I've always hated his guts." He reached up to settle his Stetson on his head more firmly and stepped back to the door, opening it and saying before he stepped out: “Good day, gentlemen. I’ll be waiting for results.”

For a full half minute after the door had closed Hockens and Rex Holden let the ominous silence drag out. Then Hockens said sharply: “Damned if I believe it, Rex.”

“I don’t want to, but there’s no choice here.” Holden pointed to the telegram.

Hockens let a long gusty sigh escape him and queried lifelessly: “What’ll we do?”

“Give John his chance.”

“How?”

“Wait until tonight. You’ll see, Sid. Get Charley and a couple other men you can trust and meet me at the feed barn right after it gets dark.”

“What about Sims?” Hockens asked.

“We’ll deal with him, too,” Holden answered.

IV

It was a bad day for Ed Sims. He had been across the street that morning when the stage arrived. He’d seen Deuce Morgan get his telegram from the driver, seen Morgan go to the bank with Sid Hockens. Morgan’s smile had been that of a satisfied man. Ed didn’t know what to think.

The two times he’d seen Sheriff John Branch that afternoon convinced him that the lawman was held by the same nervousness that possessed him. Branch had read Morgan's telegram yesterday afternoon; he was waiting helplessly for the inevitable, wondering why it didn't come.

A feeling of foreboding made Ed go back to the jail office after eating his meal that night. Something akin to foreboding brought John Branch back to the office, too. The sheriff had only a brief word for his deputy before he took his chair. When it got dark enough to need light, neither man moved to touch a match to the wick of the lamp.

They were sitting there, silently, each mulling over his own thoughts, when they heard the heavy tramp of many boots on the walk outside. Ed Sims's involuntary gesture was to let his right hand fall to the gun at his thigh.

The door opened and Ed could barely make out Rex Holden's form in the opening. He took his hand away from his gun as Holden said: "John, you there?"

"Here, Rex," John Branch answered. The springs of his swivel chair squeaked and he struck a match and lit his lamp. Holden came in, and was followed by Sid Hockens, Charley Riley, and two men Ed Sims hadn't seen before. The last in closed the door.

Holden stepped in close to the sheriff's desk. "Let me have your gun, John."

Branch's glance turned quizzical. "My gun? Why, Rex?"

"It'll make it easier to work this thing out," Holden said. "Morgan brought a telegram around to my office this morning, John."

Those brief words made a subtle change ride through Coyote Wells' sheriff. He reached down, unbuckled his gun belt, and laid it on his desk.

"You, too, Sims," Sid Hockens said.

Ed's hand had strayed toward the handle of the Colt at his right thigh. With a deceptively lazy gesture he now drew the weapon, rising up out of his chair and swinging the blunt-nosed .45 so that it covered every man in the room. "Not me," he said. "You're all making a mistake."

"Give 'em your iron, Ed," John Branch said lifelessly. "I had this coming."

For a moment Ed Sims hesitated. The sheriff's words left him numb, disbelieving this admission of guilt on the part of a man who these two days had taught him to respect personally. Finally, seeing that nothing he could do would change things, he lowered his weapon and handed it across to Hockens, along with his second .45.

"We've got horses out at the edge of town," Rex Holden announced. "We're heading straight for the county line. We're giving you and your partner here a chance, John."

"My friend?" Branch said. "Sims wasn't in this."

"Talking like that won't help things, John."

The sheriff had the look of an old man as he got

out of his chair; his look was resigned. He glanced toward Ed, shrugged as though in apology, and went toward the door. All the way along the street, out past the awnings and the plank walks, he didn't raise his head. It was as though he was watching where he put his feet, afraid to trust them to pick their own ground.

They went out the west trail at a fast trot, taking two hours to bring the lights of Pinnacle into sight. They swung wide of the town, and two miles beyond it Rex Holden, in the lead, reined in on his bay horse and waited for the others to gather around him.

The light of the stars was strong enough so that Ed Sims caught the look Holden fixed on John Branch. There was no loathing in that glance, only a faint hint of a hurt deep inside the man. Holden held out John Branch's gun. "Good luck, John," he said tonelessly. "We'll tell Ellen in the morning, after you've put plenty of miles behind you."

Branch took the proffered gun, belted it on in silence. Then: "Rex, make it as easy for her as you can. Tell her . . ." His words trailed off to leave the sentence unfinished.

"I'll think it over tonight, John. I'll think of something to tell her."

Sid Hockens handed Ed his guns, saying softly: "You're lucky we didn't string you up, brother."

The five of them wheeled their horses and

rode out of sight into the darkness. For a long moment John Branch sat his saddle, staring after them. Then feelingly, softly he cursed. Long checked anger had its way with him. Ed waited until it wore off, then said: "There's a few things I haven't got straight. Let's have it from the beginning, Sheriff."

Branch told his story, told it all, even to guessing what answer the Montana sheriff had telegraphed Deuce Morgan.

"But he couldn't have told Morgan that," Ed said. And then he told John Branch of his ride to the way station beyond Pinnacle last night, of the wire he'd sent in place of Morgan's, of his fight with the station agent.

John Branch laughed at hearing this last. It was a harsh laugh, one with little mirth in it. "So you whipped Bill Scudder?" he said. "I'd have given a lot to see that. Bill once ran a faro layout for Morgan. He's as forked as a coil of rope."

Suddenly Ed Sims halfway understood what had happened. He thought the thing through, saw Deuce Morgan's part in it, and with the cold anger of a man who won't stay long beaten he said to the sheriff bitingly: "You looked at first like a man with guts."

John Branch's eyes took on a hardness Ed could catch even in this half light. "Careful, Sims. They tramped on me because I let them, because every man that rode out here with us tonight has been my friend for the last twenty years. You're a stranger. I don't take talk like this from a stranger."

Ed reined his horse a little away from the lawman. "Get going, then. I'm heading back for Coyote Wells . . . by way of Bill Scudder's place."

John Branch's glance narrowed. His anger of moments ago visibly left him. "Back to the Wells? What for, Sims?"

"To see Morgan. He doesn't throw a big enough shadow to make this stick with me."

Branch was silent a moment, considering. Abruptly his boot heels swung out, then in, ramming his spurs into his horse's flanks. As the animal lunged into a quick run, taking the lawman past his deputy, he said: "You'll have to make tracks if you're sticking with me."

V

Rex Holden and Sid Hockens had stayed to help the stable owner rub down their ponies and were finishing their smokes at the feed barn door. There wasn't much talk, for both of them knew that words were a waste of breath. What had happened tonight would never be talked about between them. John Branch was gone and no one but the five who had seen him to the county line would ever know why he had gone—not even Ellen Branch.

“See you in the morning,” Sid Hockens said as he dropped his cigarette, and ground its glowing red ash beneath his boot heel.

Rex Holden didn’t answer immediately. He was looking up the street at three mounted riders who had swung in at the hitch rail in front of the Lucky Girl. At length, he said sharply: “Take a look up there, Sid. At the saloon!”

Hockens’s glance traveled up the street. What he saw made his plump face settle in rock-like scrutiny. He drawled: “John wouldn’t be damn’ fool enough to pull a trick like this! But it’s him! Come on.” He started up the walk at a run. Rex Holden followed.

They weren’t in time to see how it began. By the time they shouldered their way through the swing doors, Bill Scudder was lying on the floor, his shoulders propped against the bar front. His shirt was torn across his bruised chest. A lump the size of a hen’s egg swelled his right eyebrow, closing the eye beneath. His lips were swollen and dried blood etched two thin streaks of red from the corners of his mouth to the curve of his chin. Ed Sims was standing alongside him, back to the doors. John Branch stood on the far side of the plate-glass window to the left of the doors, his hand on his holstered six-gun. At the rear end of the bar stood Deuce Morgan, flanked by his bartender and a tall, thick-set individual known as Spike, the Lucky Girl’s bouncer.

Ed Sims was saying: "Scudder talked, Morgan, told us how he rode over here last night. It's a federal offense for a telegraph operator to forge a message."

"That's Scudder's business," Deuce Morgan drawled. His look took in the abrupt appearance of Rex Holden and Sid Hockens through the doors and his jaw snapped shut.

"Make your play, Morgan," Ed Sims taunted. His hands hung at his sides loosely, his eyes fixed on the bulge of the shoulder holster at Morgan's left armpit. "Make it fast, Morgan."

From the front, John Branch's level voice intoned: "Stay out of this, Ed. It's my turn now."

Deuce Morgan's left elbow crooked to prod his bartender. The aproned man suddenly whirled and stepped behind the bar, his hand reaching under it for the shotgun that always hung there in its rack. Spike, at the other side of the saloon owner, stabbed his right hand for his holstered weapon as Morgan's hand streaked upward.

Deuce Morgan was fast, so fast that no man could have studied the move of his hand and told afterward how it was that it snaked in so surely under his coat and palmed out the heavy weapon from its holster. As Morgan moved, Bill Scudder gathered his legs under him and suddenly dived at Ed Sims. Ed's .45 was blurring upward with a swiftness that left no doubt as to his beating Morgan's draw. But as the gun settled into line,

Scudder's frame caught Ed at the knees and knocked him sideways. His Colt swung out of line and, as it thundered, a foot-long chip flew from the bar at Morgan's elbow.

Deuce Morgan hesitated a fraction of a second, not wanting to hit Scudder. That instant's pause gave John Branch the time he needed. He took sure aim with his six-gun and squeezed the trigger. The bullet caught Deuce Morgan as he swung his hand through the two-inch arc that would have lined his weapon at the sheriff. His body jerked backward, slammed into the wall, and he slid to the floor and sat there, his head sagging inhumanly onto his chest where a splotch of red centered his white shirt front.

From the floor, Ed Sims whipped his gun down in a tight fanning blow that caught Bill Scudder squarely on the temple and loosened his burly frame in the limpness of unconsciousness. Ed's .45 completed that half circle swing and lined at the bartender as he swung up the sawed-off shotgun from behind his counter. Ed's second shot prolonged the blast of John Branch's gun, punctuated the instant the bartender's shotgun was wrenched from his grasp by an unseen blow. The bartender shook his numb, broken right hand and clenched it with his left.

Spike threw a snap shot at the deputy. Ed's high-built frame shuddered as the bullet caught him squarely in the right shoulder. He moved his wrist a scant two inches as his arm went numb, and his gun jumped across to his left hand to settle immediately into line and stab out an explosion that seemed to beat Spike back into the wall. The man's gun dropped to the sawdust floor, and, as he fell, his face was set rigidly in its last living grimace. Ed's bullet had taken him cleanly through the throat.

Seconds later, Rex Holden helped Ed to his feet, ripped his shirt away, and took a look at his shoulder, calling to one of the crowd that was forming at the doors: "Someone get the doctor!"

John Branch looked at Sid Hockens as though waking from a dream. Some inner thought made his grizzled face take on a slow smile. He handed his gun across to Sid, saying: "I won't need this any more."

Later, in Deuce Morgan's office, Rex Holden faced Coyote Wells' sheriff. "John, this was a fool's play, coming back here the way you did. Now we won't be able to keep this quiet."

Ed Sims jerked upright in his chair, wrenching a bandage from the doctor's hand so that it fell to the floor. He looked coldly at Rex Holden and drawled: "You're a fine bunch of sidewinders. Why don't you ask Branch for the whole story?"

"Well?" Holden said, glancing across at Branch who sat in a chair against the far wall.

The sheriff shrugged. “You know all there is. I’m wanted for horse stealing.”

“Tell him the rest,” Ed said insistently, angered by the lawman’s meekness. He waited a moment; Branch had the look of a beaten man, shoulders sagging heavily, glance directed downward at the floor. “Branch did what you or any man with guts would have done,” he said. “Twenty years ago the Broad Arrow had northern Montana by the tail. It made its own law, put its sticky loop on more rustled critters than any ten outfits north of the Canadian. They pushed every small rancher off free range. Ask Branch about it.”

Rex Holden said: “Let’s have it, John.”

Branch’s head came up. Something in Ed Sims’s words had fanned alive a flame of stubbornness within him. He nodded his head solemnly. “I hadn’t thought of it that way for years,” he said. “A man forgets, looking back at a wrong. But it’s like Sims says. Any man with guts would have bridled under the kind of hand they dealt me. First Broad Arrow broke me by stealing my one small herd, then hired me to ride at starvation wages. There was nothing I could do . . . until their hired lawman tried to arrest me for rigging a forked stud game one night. I beat him to the draw and somehow kept from pulling the trigger. I got out of town. Two nights later Blaze Hefflin and three more of us ran off two hundred head of Broad Arrow broncos, drove ’em across the border, and sold 'em to a Canadian outfit. I never saw a cent of the money we got for those jugheads. But it made up a little for what they'd done to me."

There was a tense, long-drawn silence following Branch's words. In that interval Ellen Branch stepped quietly into the doorway. Ed Sims saw her, knew by the look in her tear-filled brown eyes that she had heard her father's words. That look had its touch of pride.

Rex Holden, his back to the door, suddenly blurted out: "John, you addle-headed old fool. Why didn't you tell us this sooner? We wouldn't have let Morgan run his bluff."

John Branch hadn't seen his daughter, and now he said: "There was more than me to think of. If it hadn't been for . . ."

"Dad!" Ellen came into the room. She started to say something but, instead of saying it, she leaned down and tenderly kissed her father on the forehead.

When she straightened, she saw Ed Sims for the first time. His shoulder bandage was already splotched with blood that had soaked through it. He was hurt, badly. Out on the street not two minutes ago the man Rex Holden had put at the saloon doors to keep the crowd back had let her through, nodding to the two bodies along the far wall, then to the office door, saying: "Your father's in there, miss. If it hadn't been for that new deputy, he'd be out here with these other two." Remembering that, remembering her heated words of yesterday when she'd called Ed Sims a killer, she felt suddenly humbled.

"Ed," she said, haltingly, hardly knowing how to begin. "Can I say I'm sorry?"

Her words brought a flush of obvious embarrassment to Ed Sims's pain-drawn face. "No reason for that," he said. "We all make mistakes."

"You're staying, aren't you?" she queried. "You're staying to help Dad?"

He nodded, and the slight tension of his neck muscles set up a pain in his shoulder that deepened the lines on his lean face. Ellen saw that, turned to the doctor, and said: "He's coming up to stay with us until that shoulder gets well." She looked once more at Ed Sims before she went out with her father, and that one look made Ed think, strangely enough, that he wouldn't be riding north tomorrow morning as he'd planned. That he might never be riding out of there.

Additional Copyright Information

“Back-Trail Bondage” first appeared as “Hellion, Fan That Hammer” in *Best Western Magazine* (2/40). Copyright © 1940 by Western Fiction Publishing Co., Inc. Copyright © renewed 1968 by Dorothy S. Ewing. Copyright © 2012 by David S. Glidden for restored material.

“Death Rides Out of Yuma” first appeared as “Owlhoot Reckoning” in *Western Story Magazine* (8/20/38). Copyright © 1938 by Street and Smith Publications, Inc. Copyright © renewed 1966 by Dorothy S. Ewing. Copyright © 2012 by David S. Glidden for restored material.

“A Badge for a Tinhorn” first appeared as “Ghost-Badge for a Tinhorn” in *Complete Western Book Magazine* (6/38). Copyright © 1938 by Newsstand Publications, Inc. Copyright © renewed 1966 by Dorothy S. Ewing. Copyright © 2012 by David S. Glidden for restored material.

“Even Money He Dies at Noon!” first appeared in *Star Western* (5/40). Copyright © 1940 by Popular Publications, Inc. Copyright © renewed 1968 by

About the Author

Peter Dawson is the *nom de plume* used by Jonathan Hurff Glidden. He was born in Kewanee, Illinois, and was graduated from the University of Illinois with a degree in English literature. In his career as a Western writer he published sixteen Western novels and wrote over 120 Western short novels and short stories for the magazine market. From the beginning he was a dedicated craftsman who revised and polished his fiction until it shone as a fine gem. His Peter Dawson novels are noted for their adept plotting, interesting and well-developed characters, their authentically researched historical backgrounds, and his stylistic flair. During the Second World War, Glidden served with the U.S. Strategic and Tactical Air Force in the United Kingdom. Later in 1950 he served for a time as Assistant to Chief of Station in Germany. After the war, his novels were frequently serialized in *The Saturday Evening Post*. Peter Dawson titles such as *Royal Gorge* and *Ruler of the Range* are generally conceded to be among his best titles, although he was an extremely consistent writer, and virtually all his fiction has retained its classic stature among readers of all generations. One of Jon Glidden's finest techniques was his ability, after the fashion of Dickens and Tolstoy, to tell his stories via a series of dramatic vignettes which focus on a wide assortment of different characters, all tending to develop their own lives, situations, and predicaments, while at the same time propelling the general plot of the story toward a suspenseful conclusion. He was no less gifted as a master of the short novel and short story. *Dark Riders of Doom* (Five Star Westerns, 1996) was the first collection of his Western short novels and stories to be published.

Center Point Large Print
600 Brooks Road / PO Box 1
Thorndike, ME 04986-0001 USA

(207) 568-3717

US & Canada:
1 800 929-9108
www.centerpointlargeprint.com